THE Redemption of ADI

KRISTEN ZURAY

K Zuray
Jeremiah 31:3

www.kristenzuray.com

Kristen Zuray

ISBN: 978-1495363047

DEDICATION

To my children, Anna, Abigail, Lydia, and David. May this book serve as a reminder that you are of great value to God. Don't ever allow anyone to make you feel worthless. He has redeemed you because He loves you with an everlasting love that can never be broken no matter what you may face in this life. Thank you for your faithfulness and encouragement throughout this process. I love you very much.

ACKNOWLEDGMENTS

Special thanks to Norm and Kathy Fuller for their careful editing and to my husband, Josh Zuray, for his tireless efforts in making this book a reality.

List of Characters and Places

King Penuel: Hebrew name for "face of God". He represents God the Father

Joshua: Hebrew name for Jesus. He represents Jesus, God's Son

Matthew: Hebrew name meaning "gift from God". He represents the Holy Ghost, the promised Comforter

Gabriel: Acts as an angelic messenger in the Bible and will continue to be the messenger in the story

Michael: In the Bible, he is the angelic warrior fighting against the opposition, and so does his character in the story.

Thomas: He portrays Thomas, the doubting disciple in the Bible, always questioning.

Adi: Hebrew name meaning "jewel". She represents the individual human, male or female. Malachi 3:17

Rasha: Hebrew name meaning "wicked". He represents Satan.

Ze'ev: Hebrew name meaning "wolf". The "wolf" as referenced in the Bible refers to deceivers.

Miskana: Hebrew for "dwelling place of God". Represents heaven.

Soteria: Greek word for "salvation". Represents our world.

Kristen Zuray

ONE

In the far distance a trail of black smoke rose into the polluted skies. The four observers watched silently from the palace balcony, each absorbed in his own thoughts. With an abrupt shake of his head, the smaller observer sighed.

"Your Royal Highness, I just don't understand why this must be," he said. A weight of confusion and uneasiness settled over the young man's heart as he stared up at the king of Miskana. In the prime of life and despite the stress of ruling a country, the king still posed a force to be reckoned with. His six foot 3 inches with muscles of steel would intimidate most people, but for those who knew him, he resembled a fortress of safety, protection, and care.

"Thomas, I appreciate your concern," the king replied, "but look out there and tell me what you see." Laying a gentle hand on the young man's shoulder, King Penuel pointed to the curling black smoke coming from the distant country. "I see a filthy country that's filled with unspeakable crime and corruption. They have no respect for life, they steal from one another, everything that is considered good they call evil. Despite the death and decay, they parade around in arrogance as if they are most powerful. And even more disturbing of all, they hate you, King Penuel." Thomas stated in disgust.

The king smiled at the protectiveness of his young subject, but as he turned to stare at the distant city, his smile faded into a grim line. Tears pooled in the corner of his dark brown eyes. Some minutes passed before the king could speak, "I see a people crying out for love, someone to soothe away their fears, to guide them with truth. Yes, there are some that seek only power and their own truth. They will do anything in pursuit of it. Look past them, Thomas, and you will see that many are misguided by lies but are yearning to see truth. They react in hate and fear when deep down they desperately want to be loved and forgiven. I hear their cries and I feel their pain. They desperately wish that there was value to their meaningless existence. As king, I cannot sit idly by and watch their destruction from a distance. I must do something to redeem them from the despair they are in."

"But what?"

"Think, Thomas. In times past, what did two kingdoms do to form an alliance with one another?"

"Ah..." Thomas uneasily stared out at the horizon as he searched for the answer. Then suddenly, the solution hit him, and the shock of it caused his back to stiffen. His eyes widened as he stared at the silent prince that had been standing by his father's side.

"Marriage?" he squeaked out. The young prince, who was the spitting image of his father but with lighter colored hair, grinned at the shocked expression on Thomas' face. "Yes, Thomas, marriage!" the king exclaimed.

"You would have your son, a Royal, marry one of them?"

"It's the only way, Thomas. The people of Soteria need love, grace, and hope, not war. Someday, it may come to that, but first I'd rather extend the olive branch to them."

"But . . ."

King Penuel held up his hand for silence, "Enough, Thomas, the plan has been decided." Abruptly turning to the remaining silent observer, the king demanded, "Matthew, are you ready to leave?"

"Yes, sir, I am ready to leave when you give me the command." Matthew gave a slight reverent bow.

Admiration and respect softened the king's features. Faithful Matthew, the king's right-hand man, obediently followed the king's every command. Never in seeking his own glory, rather always seeking to exalt the king and his son. In spite of his soft-spokenness, he was very persuasive in his speech. His humility may be mistaken for weakness, but it was in essence a sign of his great power and strength. As he traveled throughout the kingdom of Miskana, his strong but quiet presence brought comfort and order to the inhabitants. Now he was about to embark on a journey to the country of Soteria as a representative of King Penuel and as matchmaker for Joshua, his son, the Prince. "Do you understand about the girl that we are looking for?"

"Yes, sir. We are looking for—a jewel." A knowing look passed among the King, the Prince, and Matthew. Confused and definitely not apart of this conversation, Thomas stared at the three men as they quietly turned their attention back to the black smoke on the horizon. The expression on their faces sent a chill over Thomas. It was a strange mixture of sorrow, love, pain, and determination. What did all this mean?

With a heavy sigh, King Penuel looked pleadingly at his son. As Prince Joshua stared into his father's tear-filled eyes, love and respect for his father welled up inside, "It's fine, Father. I'm prepared to do this. I love them, too."

Encouraged, King Penuel squared his shoulders and with grim determination faced Matthew. "It's time,

Matthew, go in my name," charged the king. He grabbed Matthew's hand placing his signet ring into his palm.

"Yes, sir, I will return as soon as I can." With a deep bow, Matthew turned and swiftly left the balcony.

"Thomas, I'd like to speak to my father alone," Prince Joshua gently spoke to the bewildered Thomas. Too stunned by the confusing emotions he had just witnessed, Thomas silently nodded and left.

When Thomas was out of sight, the prince turned to his father. Watching him carefully, he asked, "Do you think this will work, Father?"

Deep in thought, the king allowed a few moments to pass before answering, "It will work for some, Son. Those who are yearning for forgiveness, love, and truth will understand what we are doing. Unfortunately, not all will see it or accept it, but we have to give them a chance to hope. Do you trust me, Son?"

The son thoughtfully nodded, "Yes, Father, your plans have always been successful." In an attempt to lighten the mood, the prince smiled and threw his arm around his father's shoulder. Relishing this tender moment with his son, the king quietly stared out at the growing darkness. What kind of heartaches would come their way?

Kristen Zuray

TWO

"You failed to get my money?" the man bellowed in rage. He raised his hand and sent a stinging blow across the cowering girl's face.

Adi threw her hands up in protection, but it was to no avail for her stepfather was no small man. What he lacked in height, he made up for in bulk. He was like a rotund bulldog with a loud demanding bark. He used his mass to intimidate those who ran drugs for him. They all learned rather quickly that if they returned without collecting his money, it would not go well for them. And if they had a moment of stupidity and withheld a portion of his money, he would find out and most likely send them to their graves in a cement block. He was the most feared drug lord in the city. Now the weight of his full wrath was turned upon his stepdaughter, Adi, for not collecting the full amount of money that was owed him. The only reason he allowed her to live was that she had a way of eventually collecting his money especially after putting the fear of God in her. He also had the feeling that someday he would profit greatly from her.

"I ought to kill you right now, you stupid fool!" he screamed as he sent another smack to her head. By now Adi sat crouched in the corner, covering her head with her arms. As he raised his beefy fist again, a man with a snake tattoo on his neck, walked into the room.

"Rasha, there's a problem. The Dragon's leader was just found shot through the head, and they think it's you. They're rallying and might be coming this way." The young bony man nervously shifted from one foot to another, hoping that Rasha wouldn't change the course of the blow his way for daring to interrupt him during his vicious discipline.

With a frustrated growl, Rasha lowered his hand and pointed a finger at Adi, "You better get my money before the week is over, or you'll think that today's beating was a walk in the park." With that final threat, he moved out the door shouting orders to those that were lingering around.

Adi sat there shivering and shaking with fear. Her

head and face were throbbing from the abuse. *Is this all there is to life?* As the cold fingers of fear gripped her heart, she stared at the white powdery mound on the table. *All I would have to do is to overdose and then I could escape this life. But escape to where? Darkness? Nothingness? Or Something else?* She didn't know what she feared more, living life as it was or being absorbed into nothingness, not even a memory. Hopelessness enveloped her, tearing at her, suffocating her as sobs shook her whole body.

Hours past, or maybe it was only minutes, Adi wasn't sure, but as she continued to stare at the tempting white powder, a plan began to form in her mind, a plan that gave her hope.

———

"Where are we going, sir?" Thomas respectfully asked Matthew.

"We are going to a formal dinner. All the elite of Soteria will be there."

"Do they know that we are coming?"

"They should. We've sent them enough letters letting them know that we are coming and what our intentions are. Hopefully, they didn't ignore them." Matthew turned to stare out the small window of the Gulfstream lost in deep thought.

Thomas silently watched Matthew. Something was amiss and it was obvious that Matthew was not going to clue him in. Sensing the unspoken questions, Matthew returned his attention to Thomas and smiled, "I know you have many questions, Thomas, but you are here to observe and learn. All will be revealed in time. The best thing you can do is to sit back and rest. I have a feeling that this will be our last few moments of relaxation for awhile." Without another word, Matthew laid his head back against the seat and closed his eyes. With a sigh of resignation, Thomas followed suit, but his mind would not relax with all the unanswered questions that consumed him.

———————

Adi grimaced with pain as she slowly rose from her crouching position. The room seemed to sway. Leaning heavily against the wall, she waited until everything righted itself, and then slowly picked her way through the filth and garbage that lay around her. Once she reached her bedroom, she quickly shut the door, locking it as a safety precaution. Rushing over to her closet, she reached toward the back where she had safely hidden her one formal dress that she had stolen from an elite boutique. She had never worn a dress before, especially a beautiful gown. Longing to be beautiful, she had broken into the shop during the night and barely escaped with her treasure. Knowing that her stepfather would be outraged that she had risked being arrested for such a trivial item, she had sneaked the dress into the house by way of her backpack. Adi, alone and lost in her fanciful daydreams, tried the dress on and twirled around the room. Now the dress would come in handy as long as she could conceal her bruises.

Tonight was the dinner gala for the society's elite. Once a year, this social event would be televised for the rest of the city to see. As a young girl, Adi would watch in wonder as the rich and famous stepped out onto the red carpeted walkway in their beautiful gowns, sparkling jewels, escorted by handsome young men. She longed to be one of those women. Someday, she had promised herself, maybe she would meet a valiant man who would love her enough to whisk her away from her abusive stepfather. *Love?* Adi gave a half laugh as she tossed the dress onto her bed. *There's really no such thing as love, there's only lust. You give me what I want and I might help you. Isn't love supposed to give of one's self for the sake of another without expecting anything in return?* A tear slipped down Adi's dirty bruised cheek. *Love is lust, Adi,* an unseen voice echoed into her mind, *The only love you will find is the love you have for yourself. Please yourself, Adi. Do whatever makes you happy!*

"Fine. I'll do what will make me happy!" Adi angrily exclaimed out loud, "I am going to disguise myself, attend the dinner, and steal their money. Then I'm going to give my stepfather his money and run away! Or maybe I'll even kill him and take over the business! I'll make people afraid of ME!" With bold determination, Adi grabbed the phone and angrily punched in the all-too-familiar number. Before the man on the other end could answer, Adi rushed right into her request.

"Ze'ev, this is Adi. You are planning on going to the gala tonight aren't you? Because I need you to get me in!"

"What? I can't get you in! It's only for the top socialites, and you are not at the top!" an astonished Ze'ev exclaimed.

"They would never know. I have a beautiful dress and you could lend me some jewels! I just have to get in!" the girl implored.

Ze'ev snickered, "You can't be serious. Besides, I have a date already, Adi."

With a threatening tone, Adi played her trump card, "Need I remind you that you owe me one. If you don't take me, I'll go straight to Rasha and tell him that you stole from him. I don't think he will take too kindly to that no matter who you are. Remember, it was I that covered for you."

It was rumored that Ze'ev, one of the richest and most sought after bachelors, acquired all his wealth by dabbling in the black market, but it could never be proven. With a sigh of frustration, he responded, "Fine. I'll escort you in, but you better look the part. What's this about? You had better not be doing anything that will ruin me."

"Never mind. The less you know the better, and don't worry, I'll be gone before anyone of your precious people notices that I'm with you." Adi replied sarcastically. "I'll meet you in the alley of your townhouse, bring some jewelry." Satisfied, she hung up the phone and smiled, the plan was coming together.

She rushed to the bathroom and climbed into the shower. Taking a few moments to allow the hot water to soothe her sore aching muscles, she pondered her guilty feelings. If it makes me happy then why do I feel guilty? Is there really a right or a wrong? With a shake of her head, she shut the water off. With determination, she vigorously dried herself and began applying the ivory skin-toned concealer to her bruises.

Thirty minutes later, she stood before the full-length mirror to study herself. Other than a slight discoloring on her cheek, all the bruises had been covered. Her dark chestnut hair was swept up and twisted into a French roll. Soft tulle flowers cascaded over one slender shoulder dissolving into a form-fitting bodice, revealing her trim figure. As she turned from side to side, the light pink netting rustled as it rubbed against the white satin underneath. Adi had been transformed from a girl in ripped jeans and stained t-shirt to a beautiful, elegant young woman. No one would know that she was a drug runner. Satisfied, Adi grabbed a long overcoat to hide her dress from those who would report her to her stepfather and slipped out of the house.

Kristen Zuray

THREE

As soon as Thomas stepped out of the plane, he immediately wanted to gag for the stench of Soteria was strong. The acrid smell of sulfur from industrial plants contaminated the air.

"Ugh! How can they breathe this?" Thomas gasped as he attempted to cover his nose and mouth.

Matthew chuckled, "You will get used to it, Thomas, but pull it together, man. Remember, we are on a mission of good will. Any signs of disgust towards them or their city will be offensive."

The gentle rebuke silenced Thomas. Matthew looked

about and sighed, "No one is here to meet us. They must have forgotten. Well, let's get a taxi and head to the motel to change."

As they sped along the freeway, Thomas stared at the filth of the city. Where there once was lush grass and fragrant flowers, there was now a mass of tangled weeds and thorns. The crumbling buildings boasted of pornographic graffiti. Children dressed in rags ran barefoot through sewage-filled streets. Everywhere, people walked aimlessly about, their eyes blank and empty. They were the walking dead. Fights would break out over the most trivial items. Thomas' heart grew heavy. Why would King Penuel want to make an alliance with these people? Does Prince Joshua know what he's getting into?

Noticing the fights on the street, Matthew turned to explain to Thomas, "Even though those items are unimportant, they believe it will bring them happiness. So, whoever gets the object first, will be relieved temporarily of their emptiness. Do you see now why we must give them another alternative to living?"

"I guess so."

"We are about to drive into the better part of the city where the dinner will be held."

Matthew was right. In a few minutes they entered another part of Soteria. Here, the buildings partially glistened in the sunlight. They were at least clean with colorful landscaping. Still, it was a sad sight in comparison to Miskana. Here, children played in trendy clothes as the adults chatted and laughed, showing off their newest technological devices. Strange thing, though, they all held the same beverage in their hand, wore similar clothing, and sported similar accessories. It was as if they were afraid to be unique individuals and instead tried to be clones of one another. Thomas was confused.

"What do you see, Thomas?" Matthew asked his student.

"It definitely looks better than the poorer district of town, and the people definitely are rich. You can tell by their appearance. Still, if they only knew how magnificent the kingdom of Miskana is, they would not think their city nor their garments so beautiful."

"Hmmm. What else do you notice?"

"There's no fighting." Thomas strained to get a closer look, "They look a little happier, but their eyes still look empty."

"Yes, their eyes are still empty. They are good at keeping up appearances. As far as the fighting, it still goes on but behind closed doors. To the rest of their peers, they appear dignified, but when no one is watching, they still cheat others out of their money all in the name of business. They steal one another's spouses with no thought of the confusion they cause to the children. Often, children are seen as an inconvenience or a way to succeed financially by pressuring them to become famous or to go to prestigious schools."

"For what purpose do they struggle so hard?"

"That's just it. In the end, there really is no purpose. They might succeed for a brief time to hold power and wealth, but that's it."

"It seems so pointless."

A sense of urgency spread over Matthew, "Yes, it is. That is why we are here, to give them meaning to their existence."

As they pulled up to a modest looking motel, Thomas was surprised that they were not staying at one of the plusher extravagant hotels that they had passed. He wanted to ask why but thought better of it. Quietly, he fell in step behind Matthew. Matthew paused at the check-in desk to confirm his reservations.

Puzzled, the receptionist searched the reservations on her computer screen, "No, I don't have any reservations for you, sir."

Frowning Matthew replied, "That's odd. I made advanced reservations."

As if in a rush, the lady replied hotly, "Well, it's not here and besides that there is no room. We are booked." Before Matthew could reply she loudly called, "Next!"

Feeling hopeful, Thomas suggested, "We could always try one of the nicer ones."

Deep in thought, Matthew murmured, "No, that would defeat the purpose."

After hailing a taxi, they were on the freeway heading back to the poorer district. Thirty minutes later, they pulled up to what resembled more of a shack than a motel. The bed sagged while the sheets looked as if they hadn't seen a wash in a very long time. Peeling wallpaper donned the cracked walls. As they stood there examining the room, a rat scurried by their feet.

Thomas had enough, "Really," he exploded, "You are an ambassador of the Royal Court of Miskana. This is how they treat you?"

Matthew smiled, "Don't worry so, Thomas, we are not here to be exalted. We have a job to do." Looking at his watch, he frowned, "We are running out of time so dress quickly."

Managing as best they could with the cracked mirror, both rushed to clean up and put on their formal wear. Stepping out into the darkness, they carefully avoided the muddy potholes of the parking lot. As they reached the street corner to hail a taxicab, a figure clothed in a long dark overcoat plowed into Matthew. Instinctively, Matthew grabbed the falling figure to steady her.

With a surprised gasp, the frightened girl looked up, "Oh, I'm sorry. I didn't see you."

Matthew chuckled, "It's no wonder with that streetlamp out. It's hard to see!"

The girl pulled back in fear as if waiting for a sharp rebuke, or worse yet recognition as belonging to Rasha.

Sensing her fear, Matthew gently spoke, "It's alright. No harm has been done. You don't need to be frightened."

Feeling slightly relieved that the stranger didn't recognize her, Adi mumbled her thanks and pushed past him. She had to hurry if she was going to make it in time to meet Ze'ev.

"May we offer you a ride in our taxi? We'll drop you off wherever you need to go!" Matthew called after her.

Adi hesitated, confused by the stranger's kindness. Or was it kindness? Maybe he did know who she was and was planning to harm her, but then again, she had never heard such tenderness before. Her heart stirred within her. Before she could listen to her doubts anymore, she rushed back to Matthew who stood holding the taxi door open for her.

After giving the driver her destination, Adi nervously sat back in the seat and stared out the window. Matthew slid in next to her while Thomas chose to sit in the front by the driver. "I'm Matthew and you are?"

The girl fumbled, obviously scared by the question, "Umm, Catherine." She lied as she went back to staring out the window.

Sensing that the girl did not want to talk, Matthew settled back in the seat. Occasionally, he would steal a glance at her, but in the darkness he could only make out her silhouette. He was troubled by the fear he had sensed in her. His heart ached to help her understand that she could be free from the life she led. But the time was not quite right. Something had to happen before she would understand.

Time passed in silence. At last the driver pulled to the side of the curb. Relieved that the uncomfortable situation was over, Adi jumped out of the car without a word of thanks. Matthew and Thomas both watched her as she disappeared into the darkness.

Thomas gave a frustrated grunt, "She didn't even say thank you! How ungrateful!"

"It's okay, Thomas. Appreciation and love are very minimal here. The common belief is that society owes them for the hardships that have been imposed upon them. They deserve to receive kindness not to give kindness."

Confused, Thomas turned to look at Matthew, "But if everyone has that mentality, then no one gives kindness and so no one receives it, do they?"

Matthew chuckled, "It's rare. Often the kindness of others comes with a price. If you scratch my back I'll scratch yours. Kindness is conditional. People here have a difficult time expressing encouragement, compliments, or appreciation to others."

"Why is it difficult when giving encouragement brings so much joy, both to the giver and to the receiver? It's a win-win situation!"

"Pride for one thing. They seek to exalt themselves not others. Jealousy, bitterness, selfishness to name a few reasons, but when they have never truly experienced real love, how can they possibly give something that they don't have? That is why we are here—to show them the real meaning of Unconditional love."

Shivering in the cold damp night, Adi clutched her torn overcoat about her. As soon as the taxicab pulled out of sight, she stepped from the shadows and hastily walked the block to Ze'ev's place. A mixture of emotion coursed through her, confusing her. She was curious about the kindness that was shown to her by the man named Matthew, but at the same time it irritated her. For years, she had carefully buried deep within her the longing to be loved and cherished. Matthew's gentleness caused those longings to once again resurface and bring with them the depressing emptiness of her life. Before she could dwell on it further, she angrily held the tears back, "I deserve a little kindness for all I go through; besides,he was probably hoping to get something anyways." Adi muttered.

Suddenly, a tall black figure reached out of the shadows and grabbed her arm, yanking her into an alley. With a startled gasp, Adi began punching and kicking trying to break free from the man's hold.

A deep chuckle of amusement escaped from the man, "Still spunky, I see!"

Angrily, Adi attempted one more swing at the man's head, but the man was quicker than she. Grabbing tightly to Adi's wrist, he pulled her against him. "I wouldn't do that if I were you, Adi." Ze'ev growled.

Despite her fear, Adi whispered through clenched teeth, "You're hurting me, Ze'ev. Let me go!"

With a laugh, Ze'ev pushed her away and looked her over with disgust. "I can't take you to the banquet in a dirty, torn overcoat!"

Quickly Adi discarded the pitiful coat to reveal her beautiful pink gown with its cascading flowers. Ze'ev pulled her closer to the glow of a streetlight and let out a low approving whistle causing Adi to blush. "You clean up well, Adi. Here's the jewelry." Ze'ev handed a black velvet bag to her and, with a second thought, snatched his hand back warning her, "You had better give this back to me by the end of the night, or I'll come after you."

"Don't worry, I'll give your precious jewels back to you," Adi stated sarcastically while snatching the velvety bag from his hand. "Now help me put the necklace on."

Kristen Zuray

FOUR

"Well this is embarrassing!" Thomas muttered as he watched the line of limos, Porsches, Lamborghini's, and other such extravagant cars slowly pull up to the red carpet to deposit their elegant passengers. As they gracefully stepped out of the car, cheers erupted from the crowds and cameras flashed creating an electrifying atmosphere.

"What's wrong, Thomas?"

"This is just awful. Look at all these fine vehicles and here you, the representative of the Royal Family of Miskana, are arriving in a run down taxi cab!" Thomas exclaimed.

"Hey! My taxicab is just fine! If you don't like it, you can walk!" The driver bellowed in a huff.

Matthew quickly patted the gruff looking man on the back while giving Thomas a rebuking stare. "No, you're cab is just fine, and we appreciate you taking us all the way here."

Feeling humbled, Thomas mumbled, "Yes, thank you. I apologize for my offensive words."

At last, the dented and scraped yellow cab pulled up at the red carpet. As if to proudly announce its Royal occupant, the car let out a loud backfire and a puff of black smoke. Thomas hung his head wishing that he could just crawl under the seat and be on his way, but Matthew was not fazed by it. Confidently, he stepped out of the car and opened Thomas' door. "Come on, Thomas." He grinned at the mortified expression on his companion's face. Reluctantly, Thomas stepped from the car and turned to face the crowd. All was silent. Matthew graciously smiled at the crowd and continued walking down the red carpet toward the door. As Thomas self-consciously walked next to Matthew, he glanced towards the crowd. A chill went down his spine as he noticed the confused expressions on many faces while others openly showed their hatred and disdain for them. With a sigh of relief, they reached the door at last.

"Just a minute, there. You can't go in." The registrar huffed.

Patiently, Matthew looked at the man. "We should be on the list. We sent advanced notice that we would be attending."

"Names?" the man snapped.

"Matthew, Ambassador for the Kingdom of Miskana and spokesman for King Penuel. This is Thomas, my student."

Pulling himself up to his full five foot five inch height and puffing out his small chest, the registrar flipped through his guest list with an air of authority. After what seemed like hours, the small man finally noticed the names at the very bottom of the list. "Fine. You may enter." He curtly responded.

Once they were safely inside, Thomas pulled Matthew aside. "Why am I getting the feeling that they don't like us?"

Matthew smiled sadly, "They don't, Thomas. You see, their city, Soteria, once belonged to King Penuel. Soteria wasn't always like it is now. It once was beautiful and exotic, a paradise. People lived in harmony and love with one another and with King Penuel. He would come to Soteria quite often to just be with them."

"Really? What happened?"

"A very high ranking official in the King's court became jealous of King Penuel and Prince Joshua. In his pride and arrogance, he sought to take the throne away from King Penuel. He succeeded in deceiving over a third of the King's officials and they sought to divide the kingdom. To make a long story short, they now have temporary control over Soteria. With that control, they have sought to destroy anything that would remind the citizens of King Penuel. Anything that stands for beauty and purity, they destroy in an attempt to create their own kind of beauty."

Shocked by this revealed history, Thomas exclaimed, "And King Penuel does nothing to restore his kingdom?"

Matthew's brow furrowed in disapproval at the accusation, "Nothing? Does that sound like your king? Do you really think King Penuel would sit by and watch this destruction from a distance? You should know him better than that, Thomas."

"I'm sorry...I-I-I didn't mean..." Thomas stammered.

Matthew hastily cut him off, "King Penuel has done something. For many years, he has sent representatives to this city in an attempt to persuade them to return Soteria back to him, but no one would listen. In fact, they killed the representatives!"

Thomas gasped. Nervously his fingers tried to loosen his bow tie as he glanced about to see if there were any eavesdroppers. "Then why are we here?" He whispered.

Before Matthew could respond, a man in a black tuxedo with a white towel draped over his arm stepped out into the lobby and announced, "Dinner is served. Please take your seats."

———————

Adi nervously fidgeted in her seat as she watched the elegant cars pull up to the red carpet. The moment that she had dreamed of for so long was about to come true. Ze'ev's laugh broke through her thoughts.

"Don't worry, Adi, just hold onto my arm and I'll escort you up the red carpet."

Adi sheepishly smiled at him. Worry overcame her joy as a thought came to her.

"Ze'ev, I don't think you should call me Adi, just in case."

"Hmm. Good idea. I would hate to be thrown out and humiliated if someone were to recognize you." Then he let out a sneering laugh, "I don't think we have to worry about you being recognized. You look like a princess instead of a tramp tonight. Well, let's call you Julia, just in case."

Shame washed over her as Ze'ev's cutting words pierced her heart. Just then the car pulled up and her moment for making a grand entrance was here. Ze'ev stepped out of the car, opened her door, and graciously extended his hand to her. As she started out, the crowd cheered wildly.

"Hey, Ze'ev, whose your lady?" someone from the crowd hollered.

Ze'ev pompously waved to the crowd as he escorted a very shy Adi up the red carpet. Once they were inside, Adi breathed a sigh of relief. Still clutching onto Ze'ev's arm, she looked about in wonder at the colorful gowns all around her.

"Now what?" Ze'ev's demanding voice startled her.

"Wh-what?" Adi stammered.

"I got you in here. Now what?" Ze'ev pressed on.

"Oh, after dinner there's a dance right?"

"Yes."

Adi revealed her plan. "During the dance, I'll slip away. There's a safe in the hotel manager's office in which the hotel guest's store their money and jewels for safekeeping. Once I clean it out, I'll come back and explain that I'm not feeling well."

"That's your plan? Sounds ridiculous!" Ze'ev snorted in disdain.

Before Adi could respond, a man in a black tuxedo with a white towel draped over his arm loudly proclaimed that dinner was served and that they were to be seated. Ze'ev once again offered Adi his arm and escorted her into the hotel's luxurious dining area. Sparkling crystal chandeliers hung from high vaulted ceilings that were framed in by glossy white crown molding. In the far corner of the room, an orchestra played lively tunes as the guests casually sought out their table number. As if in a dream, Adi walked wide- eyed beside Ze'ev, her heels making a soft clicking sound against the marble floor.

———

"Here we are." Ze'ev motioned to the table that corresponded with their reservation number. Acting as a gallant gentleman, Ze'ev pulled Adi's chair out with a flourish and seated her. Once they were seated, both of them glanced about to see who they would be sharing their meal with. Adi's heart thumped excitedly as she recognized the stylish young woman from television. Loretta Van Hilt was a famous actress and the most sought after bachelorette of Soteria. It was rumored that she was dating her producer, Michael Sorenson, a much older man who now sat next to Adi. To the right of Loretta was a distinguished man in his fifties with salt and pepper hair. It took a moment before Adi was able to place him and his wife. Aiden Bristol was a highly acclaimed lawyer who defended the televised murder trial of William Bennett. William Bennett, an affluent banker and politician, had been accused of brutally murdering his wife. Everyone knew he was guilty, but due to his wealthy status, it was rumored that through Aiden Bristol's negotiations, they were able to buy off the jury and obtain a not guilty verdict. Sitting to the right of Aiden's wife was William Bennett himself and his new, much younger girlfriend. Adi didn't know what Bennett saw in the woman other than her looks. Any ability to think or reason seemed to totally escape her. All she could do was giggle and bat her eyes at him. Between Bennett's girlfriend and Ze'ev sat two unrecognizable gentlemen. It seemed as if they were from a different country, but oddly familiar.

Ze'ev's voice broke through Adi's thoughts, "I am Ze'ev and this is my, uh, date, Julia." He finished lamely. Heat rose up Adi's neck as she realized all eyes were on her.

"Hello. Nice to meet you all." She stammered.

The man sitting next to Bennett's girlfriend quickly broke in, "My name is Matthew. I am the ambassador to the kingdom of Miskana and the spokesman for King Penuel. This is Thomas, my student."

Adi let out a small gasp. The gentleness and deepness of the man's voice was the same as the Matthew in the taxicab. Her heart began to pound. Would he recognize her? She stole a glance at him. Sure enough, he was looking at her with a small grin and an eyebrow raised in an unspoken question. He recognized her! Just then Ze'ev broke through the uncomfortable silence.

"Ambassador to Miskana? I've heard of it, but mostly in fairytales. Does it really exist?"

"Yes, sir, it does." Matthew responded matter of factly. "As a matter of fact, Soteria used to belong to King Penuel."

The mood of the table changed instantly to hostility. "Ah, yes, King Penuel. I've heard his name. He is spoken of in hushed tones by people who are unable to handle the pressures of life and need to create a "dream king". Those people are weak and useless." Ze'ev scoffed while the others echoed his mockery.

"I've not heard of him. Is he really real?" Adi quietly asked in spite of the angry look Ze'ev gave her.

Nonplussed by the scoffing, Matthew gently responded, "Yes, Julia, King Penuel is very real."

Aiden Bristol shook his head in disgust, "If he exists, then why would he have abandoned his people? He makes a terrible king!"

Matthew sat silently contemplating his words carefully. "King Penuel has not abandoned his people. They chose to walk away from him."

"What?" The guests exploded in unison.

Matthew held up his hand, "Let me finish. The people of Soteria were given a choice as to whom they would follow. They chose to follow the King's highest official. When the decision had been made, there was a breach in the two kingdoms. Since that time, the rulers of Soteria have sought to remove anything that would remind people of King Penuel and the former paradise that they once lived in. His name and the kingdom of Miskana have been reduced to fairytales, if that. That is mostly likely why you have never heard of him, Julia, he's been replaced."

"How sad." Adi murmured.

"Oh, good grief!" Ze'ev's fork dropped with a clatter on his plate.

Matthew continued his story, "In spite of the rejection, King Penuel still desired to repair the breech before..." Matthew paused, thinking, then continued, "Anyways, he sent many representatives to Soteria as a gesture of good will and forgiveness and to warn them, but the people would not listen. Instead, they killed the representatives."

"And with good reason!" bellowed William Bennett. "They were scaring everyone by saying that Soteria will be destroyed. The only one that could save Soteria would be King Penuel, naturally." he added sarcastically.

"They were rather frightening!" Loretta dramatically fanned herself as if the conversation was getting to be too much for her.

Matthew calmly took a sip of his lemon water and then placed the glass down with deliberation, "If the people of Soteria do not make a treaty with King Penuel, he will not be able to protect them from what is coming. That is why I am here, to form a bridge between our two kingdoms by the marriage of Prince Joshua to a woman from Soteria."

———

A shocked gasp went around the table. Eyes widened in astonishment as jaws dropped in horror. "I don't think so!" exploded Aiden.

"Marry a Prince, you say?" Lorretta sat up straighter in her chair with sudden interest. Her boyfriend, Michael, shot her a cold stare, but Loretta seemed not to notice. "Now that sounds delightful! Have you found a woman yet?" she asked, batting her eyes at Matthew.

Matthew hesitated. "We're looking for the right one."

Loretta blushed, placing her delicate hand over her

heart. "Oh my," she gushed.

William Bennett angrily stared at the flirty actress, "Calm down, Loretta. It's not going to happen. I can get a law passed that anyone accepting this Prince's marriage proposal will be considered a traitor!"

"Oh, William, don't be so dramatic. That's a bit overdone, don't you think?" Loretta's silky voice did nothing to calm the man down as they broke into a heated discussion. Growing uncomfortable with the talk, Adi became nervous, anxious to get on with her plan. Noticing that other couples from other tables were getting up and moving to the dance floor, she leaned over and whispered into Ze'ev's ear, "Let's dance."

Ze'ev hesitated not wanting to miss out on the argument, but when he noticed that Matthew and Thomas just quietly sat there listening to the others, he decided the conversation would soon get boring. "Excuse me, gentlemen, I promised a dance to Julia." No one took notice of his leaving. Irritated, Ze'ev roughly grabbed Adi's arm and hastily led her to the floor. Both of them remained silent as they twirled and spun. Adi tried not to think too much about Ze'ev's arm around her waist and how handsome he was. For this brief moment, she knew that she was the envy of many girls in the room. If things were different, maybe Ze'ev would have been the gallant man in her childhood dreams. The desire to belong and to be loved tore through her heart so suddenly that she stumbled.

Ze'ev tightened his grip to steady her. For a brief moment, their eyes locked. "You are beautiful, Adi." Ze'ev murmured as if seeing her for the first time.

With heart pounding, Adi quickly stepped back. "I had better go. I'll meet you back here in a few moments." Before she could give in to her desire to remain in the safety of Ze'ev's arms, she turned and rushed out of the banquet hall. With a chuckle, Ze'ev returned to the table.

As predicted, the conversation had quieted down to money and politics, the strangers completely forgotten or mostly forgotten. Loretta was still trying to capture the Ambassador's attention. Eventually Matthew and Thomas stood to excuse themselves with Loretta in quick pursuit of them.

Loretta sidled up to Matthew as he stood watching the colorful display of dancers. "Beautiful sight isn't it?" she asked provocatively.

"Not anywhere close to the beauty of Miskana!" Thomas proudly defended.

Loretta shot him an impatient look. "Ambassador, are you really looking for a woman to marry the Prince?"

Amused Matthew politely responded, "Yes, ma'am, I am."

A sly smile spread across her face. "Did you know that I am the richest and most sought after woman in Soteria? I could contribute much to the Princes' cause."

"I see. In exchange for your riches, he can give you a

title and a secure position as well as possibly acquiring more wealth."

"Well, you needn't make it sound so unpleasant. I'm not a ninny, you know. Usually, when a kingdom is trying to unite with another, it's usually because they are low in funds or are in need of protection themselves. Maybe it is Miskana that is in danger of destruction and that is why King Penuel is seeking an alliance with Soteria." Loretta huffed at the Ambassador.

Matthew stood there, hands clasped behind his back, watching the dancers. His six foot 3 inch well built frame stood in stark contrast to Loretta's slim elegant figure. Chuckling, he turned to her, "I can assure you, Miss Van Hilt, that King Penuel is in no need of your funds nor does He need the protection of Soteria." Matthew sobered as he changed the course of the conversation, "Let me ask you, do you see yourself as hopeless? Do you see the destructive path that you are on and are in need of someone to rescue you from it?"

With a harsh laugh, Loretta exclaimed, "Are you out of your mind? I am rich! I am beautiful! I have built my life into something that every man and woman envies! Do I need to be rescued? People come to me to be rescued, Ambassador! I am not hopeless!"

"I hope you will reconsider, Miss Van Hilt, before it's too late." Matthew said sadly.

"Well, some gratitude, Ambassador! I withdraw my

offer to help! I think I'll even send word to King Penuel and let him know how rude his Ambassador was! You should start looking for another job!" Before Matthew could respond, Loretta whirled around and stomped off.

"Wow! I guess you're not going to make a match with her!" Thomas stated dryly while watching Loretta huff off.

Matthew's shoulders slumped as grief etched his face. "She doesn't know what is in store for her. I hope that once Prince Joshua comes, she'll change her mind."

They stood there in silence for a few moments listening to the music and watching the empty laughter of the dancers. Thomas broke the silence, "Do you think any of those women would make a good bride for the Prince? They all are from high society!"

Matthew sighed shaking his head, "No, the King wants the Prince to marry someone who understands they have no hope, who needs Him, and who will return his love."

"I guess that wouldn't be them, would it? They don't see they have a need for protection." Thomas stated flatly.

"It will be harder, but not impossible, for them to see their need. They are self-sufficient." Turning from the colorful scene, Matthew said, "Let's go, Thomas, we have an appointment to keep."

FIVE

With feigned confidence, Adi walked resolutely across the lobby and down a darkened hallway. Earlier on in her life, she learned that if she appeared to know what she was doing, then few people paid little attention to her actions. This lesson proved her well on this night. The merry partiers never looked her way as she quietly picked the lock to the manager's darkened office. As soon as she heard the soft click of the lock sliding from its hold, she slipped into the room. She stood a few moments allowing her eyes to adjust to the dark. Glancing about, she could not find the safe. Disappointment and fear filled her. What was she going to do if she could not bring the money home to Rasha? Frantically Adi began rummaging through the shelves, behind picture frames, and in shadowed corners. Nothing! She slumped down in the manager's chair. *Think, Adi. Where else would they place a large safe?*

In an attempt to work out a sudden leg cramp, Adi flexed her foot, bumping into something hard on the floor. She dropped to her knees and pulled out a brown leather bag from underneath the skirts of her dress. Quickly pulling out a tiny flashlight, she flicked it on illuminating the small box before her. Letting out a surprise gasp, she whispered to herself, "I can't believe they would use such a small safe, and a digital one, too!" She quietly laughed, "This is going to be like taking candy from a baby!"

Just then the door of the manager's office opened and the light turned on. Adi scooted as far back as she could under the desk. Two men walked in.

"The paperwork is on my desk, sir. Just one moment as I find it." The manager stood just mere inches away from Adi. Shuffling through a pile of papers, the nervous man let out a relieved sigh, "Here it is."

The other man grumbled a response.

"Are you enjoying this marvelous party, sir?" the manager continued to prattle on as he and the other man exited the room.

As the lights flicked off, Adi continued to wait as she listened to the voices grow dim. Not ever hearing the door shut, she cautiously moved from the safety of the desk and peeked around the corner. No one remained in the room, but the door stood ajar. The manager neglected to lock the office. Adi realized that she had better hurry before anyone noticed. Turning on her flashlight and tucking it between her teeth, she wiggled the knob on the safe. She then hit the top of the safe several times and wiggled the knob again. Repeating this process a few more times, the safe finally opened to reveal a bundle of cash. Adi quickly counted it out, twenty thousand dollars! Knowing that she was running out of time and hearing several voices approaching in the distance, she shoved the bills into her bag and fastened it under the skirts of her dress. Hoping to make it out of the office before anyone saw her, she quietly ran to the door. Before she could grab the doorknob, the door swung open. There stood two men. Adi froze.

"Miss Julia! What are you doing in the office?"

Nervously, Adi looked into the man's face. It was Matthew, the Ambassador of Miskana. "Oh, I was looking for the women's restroom and went in the wrong door." Her body trembled with fear.

Matthew and Thomas stood there watching her. Guilt and fear pierced her soul. From their expressions, she knew that they did not believe her. At last Matthew spoke, "Just be careful, Julia or Catherine or whatever your name is, every poor decision has a consequence." With that, both men turned and walked away. *How could they know what*

I have done?

———

Adi tried to calm her pounding heart as she slipped back into the banquet hall. Quickly she looked about to see if anyone took notice of her reappearance, but everyone was lost in their own conversations to pay any attention. As she walked towards the dinner table, she could feel the now filled pouch rubbing against her leg. Amazingly her simple plan of breaking into a safe went quite smoothly. Much to her surprise, the safe was flimsy and very similar to the other safes she had broken into before. There were no jewels as she had hoped for since they were all being worn, but there was enough money to pay back Rasha and to set aside for herself.

Ze'ev looked up as Adi slid into the seat next to him. Noticing her flushed appearance, he frowned feigning concern, "My dear, you're flushed. Are you feeling alright?"

"I am feeling ill, but I don't want to ruin your evening, Ze'ev." Adi gushed.

"Nonsense, Julia, I'll take you home. If you'll excuse us, gentlemen." The men politely nodded and returned to their conversations.

"Where's the Ambassador and his student?" Adi quietly asked as they walked away from the table.

"Who cares." Ze'ev snapped.

Adi stood nervously fidgeting waiting for the valet to bring Ze'ev's sleek red Porche around. Ze'ev reached over and silently grasped Adi's hand in his to calm her. At last they were speeding down the road into the protected cover of darkness. Neither of them spoke until Ze'ev pulled up to his place.

Turning to face her, he held out his hand, "So where's my cut?"

"What?"

"Hey, I got you in. You didn't think I'd help out of good will do you?" he coarsely laughed. "You are so naive, Adi."

"I have to pay Rasha, Ze'ev!" Adi pleaded.

"Alright, alright. How much do you owe Rasha?"

"Ten thousand was owed to him, and I couldn't get it from the customer. He doesn't care how he gets the money just as long as he gets it." Adi struggled to hold back the tears.

"How much did you steal?"

"Ten thousand." She lied.

Ze'ev laughed. "You're a horrible liar, Adi. How much?"

Angrily Adi replied, "Fine. I got twenty thousand."

Ze'ev let out a low whistle. "Not bad. Do you really think that you could keep the other ten grand a secret from Rasha? You're a dead man if you do that." Ze'ev looked thoughtfully at her, "I'll tell you what I'll do. You pay Rasha his ten and you give me 9. That gives you at least a grand to stow away."

"What???" Adi exploded. "That's not fair, Ze'ev!"

Ze'ev shrugged, "Who says life is fair? Now, if you want to wake up alive tomorrow, you'll pay me the nine grand and give me back my jewelry!"

Adi knew that it would be impossible to fight Ze'ev. Angrily, she flipped up the bottom of her dress to unpin the bag. Ze'ev raised his eyebrows in amusement. "Here's your nine thousand." Adi shoved the bills into his hand. "And here's your jewelry."

"Thanks. Nice doing business with you!" he laughed.

"Can't you at least drive me closer to my home?"

Ze'ev threw his head back and laughed harder, "Drive you home? I can't be seen driving in your neighborhood, Adi. I have an image to uphold."

Without another word, Adi reached down to the floorboard where she had crumpled up her overcoat and jumped out of the car. Quickly, she threw on her coat and ran to escape the sound of Ze'ev's mocking laughter.

Once she was out of sight, she slowed down to a walk. Her thoughts were whirling. *For a moment I thought Ze'ev cared. Rasha should be home by now. I wonder if he'll be angry that I was gone. How am I going to explain this dress? Well, the money should make him happy. I thought Ze'ev cared. He held my hand and said I was beautiful!* Tears streamed unchecked down the sorrowful girl's face washing away the concealer once again revealing the dark bruises. A car drove by sending a splash of muddy water over her, but she no longer cared, she was once again empty.

————————

Thomas and Matthew sat in silence as the taxi cab passed
into the rough neighborhoods of Soteria. Having the
cabbie wait throughout the evening was the only thing that
went right, but of course, the cabbie wouldn't have missed
being apart of this prestigious event no matter who his
occupants were.

"Uh, sir, we just passed our motel." Thomas pointed
at the motel's sign.

"We're not going to our motel just yet." Matthew
quietly stated.

"Is this another 'just wait and see, Thomas'?"

Matthew laughed. "Yes, Thomas, it is."

Thomas sighed as he returned to his musings. A few
minutes later, the cabbie pulled up to what appeared to be
an abandoned house. Blankets and old newspapers covered
the cracked windows. Steps up to the front porch were
missing. Cardboard boxes, soda cans, cigarette butts, and
other trash covered the floor of the sagging porch.
Matthew and Thomas carefully picked their way through
the overgrown grass and the trash finally arriving at the
front door. After several persistent knocks, a deep voice
bellowed, "Snake, get the door before I crack you one!"

Thomas looked apprehensively at Matthew, "Sir..."

Before he could express his complaint, the door slowly
opened. All that could be seen through the small opening

was a pair of vacant dark eyes. "What do ya want?"

"My name is Matthew and I am an ambassador from the kingdom of Miskana. I would like to speak with your boss, Rasha."

The eyes continued to stare as in a daze. Thomas began to wonder if the man had heard Matthew hoping that the man would turn them away. With a delayed reaction, the man's eyes widened and then disappeared from the doorway.

"Hey, Rasha, there's two guys saying they're ambassadors from...from...someplace. They want to talk to you." Snake slurred.

"Ambassadors? Gimme a break! Can't you do anything right, you worthless slime!" Rasha angrily stomped across the room to the door.

Another set of hostile eyes peered out the crack of the door. Thomas shifted uncomfortably in his dress shoes. At last the door was flung open revealing a short bulky man with a deep scar across his right cheek. Noticing the sharply dressed men that stood before him, the hostility in his eyes only deepened.

"Come in," Rasha grunted.

As Thomas followed Matthew through the front door, he tried not to gag at the stench of urine and the sickly sweet smell of drugs. He tried to remain expressionless, but he had a difficult time not staring at the squalor that surrounded him. Men and young women layed about the room half dressed in a drug induced stupor. He struggled to fight the nausea that threatened to overwhelm him. Seeing the tenderness in Matthew's eyes, gave him a new perspective on the pain that these people endured. The door slammed behind him causing him to jump. Snake was leaning on the wall next to the door trying to look alert.

Rasha eyed Matthew with disdain, "So, how's King Penuel, Ambassador?" bitter sarcasm laced his tone as he broke into a mocking chuckle.

Matthew ignored the mockery. "I'll just state my business, Rasha."

Annoyed, Rasha was about to make a retort but thought decided against it. Thomas was confused about the familiar exchange between the two men. How would they know eachother? Matthew's voice cut into Thomas' musings,

"The King would like to make a match between the Prince and your daughter." Matthew stated diplomatically.

This proclamation silenced Rasha. He stood there speechless, eyes wide with unbelief. At that moment the front door flew open, startling him. He stared at his wet shivering stepdaughter. "Where've you been, girl?" He roared.

"Rasha, I got your money and..." Adi cut off short as she recognized the men in tuxedos standing next to her stepfather. Self-consciously she touched the bruise on her cheek hoping that it was still concealed. Matthew frowned in concern as he noticed the gesture.

Immediately, Rasha calmed down. "Show me." He commanded.

Embarrassed, Adi slowly reached under the bottom of her skirts and unpinned the brown leather pouch. Fearfully, she handed her stepfather the bag forgetting about stowing away some money for herself. Rasha greedily grabbed the bag and emptied its contents.

"Eleven thousand! Well, girl, you saved yourself from a beating." Then turning to Matthew he proudly announced, "Your Prince can't marry my step-daughter. She's too valuable to me. Who else would collect my money as well as her?"

Adi nervously fidgeted as she shyly looked up to Matthew, "Marry?"

Matthew kindly looked at her, "Yes, Rasha, your daughter is valuable, she's a precious jewel."

Rasha threw his head back and let out a cruel laugh, "Adi? A jewel? Ha! Your Prince would be in for quite a surprise! She's no jewel, but if you really want her..."

"Yes, with..Adi is it?" Matthew looked inquiringly at the shaking girl. Without looking up, the girl nodded. Matthew continued, "With Adi's consent the Prince would like to make her his bride."

As in a daze, Adi stared at Thomas and then at Matthew, "Prince Joshua wants to marry me? But why?"

Before Matthew could answer, Rasha grabbed Adi's arm and pulled her roughly to him. "NO! Adi will not marry your silly Prince Joshua!" He exploded.

"It's Adi's choice," Matthew stated firmly staring at Rasha.

With a trembling voice, Adi began to respond, "I'd like..."

Just then the front door flew open with a bang as a dozen police officers invaded the house. It turned to chaos as the shouts of the officers overpowered the startled screams and groans of the drugged residents. Within a few minutes the house was cleared with the exception of a terrified girl in a torn overcoat, a young red-headed young man with his mouth hanging open, and a dignified strong built man with a cool, calm demeanor.

"Who are you?" an officer snarled at Thomas.

"I-I-," Thomas stuttered.

Matthew quickly interjected, "This is Thomas, my student."

"Ya, and who are you?" he barked.

"I'm Matthew, the Ambassador of Miskana."

The officer humphed, "I heard ya was here."

"Watcha doin with Rasha?" The question seemed to remind the police officer that they had not apprehended the leader of this drug ring. Before waiting for an answer from Matthew, he shouted to his men, "Hey, anybody seen Rasha?"

"He ran out the back door," Adi quietly pointed to where he ran.

The stout officer motioned for two of his men to check the back and then turned narrowed eyes towards Adi. "We finally got ya this time, Adi. Your numbers up!"

"What did I do?" Adi protested.

"Does breakin' into a hotel safe and stealin' twenty grand sound familiar?"

"What? I don't know what you're talking about." Adi made sure she looked insulted.

"We've got it on the security cameras, Adi. It was a girl your age, height, and in a pink gown with her hair up." The officer looked her over carefully.

Adi self-consciously touched her hair that was still up but with damp wisps hanging about her face and neck. "What would I be doing in a gown? You know I wouldn't own a dress!" Adi said haughtily as she hugged her coat closer to her.

"Uh, huh, sure. Take off your coat then if you don't got anything to hide," The officer smugly said.

"I'm cold."

Matthew, who had been standing quietly observing, broke into the conversation, "Adi, it would be best to just do as the officer has requested."

Knowing that she couldn't fight it any longer, she shrugged off her coat to reveal the pink gown. With head down Adi stood there in defeat shaking from the cold and fear.

As the police officer slapped the handcuffs on her, he chuckled, "Well, Adi, this is the best I've seen ya even in spite of your hair bein' wet and mud on your dress." He leaned in closer to her face and humphed, "I see Rasha's beatin' on you again. Well, at least you'll get a break from him while you're in prison!" He let out a laugh as though he had made a joke.

Shame overwhelmed Adi as the police officer grabbed her arm to usher her out to the car. She didn't have to look, she knew Matthew's eyes were on her. *Why should I care what he thinks anyway?* A longing stirred deep within her as she realized that she did care about what Matthew thought of her. Without knowing it, she had thrown away her opportunity to escape her hopeless existence. She would never marry Prince Joshua. She would never become a princess. Her needs would never be met, but worse of all she may never experience the love that she so craved. Loneliness shrouded her heart as a tear slipped down her face. As she passed by, she felt a gentle hand on her arm. Looking up, she saw that Matthew's eyes were moist.

"Adi, don't despair. This changes nothing, and the offer still stands. Prince Joshua loves you, and we love you, Adi. Don't lose hope!" Matthew's pleading tone sent Adi into confusion, but she had no time to question as the officer shoved her out the door.

The slam of the car door brought finality to her present life. Life was about to change but not for the better. *Every poor decision has a consequence.* The memory of Matthew's warning broke into her thoughts. *Was this worth it, Adi?* she chided herself. *I thought this was going to make me happy.* Then a flicker of hope sprang to life as she remembered Matthew's parting words. *What did he mean that the offer still stood and that Prince Joshua still loves me?* Another question immediately interrupted her thoughts, *How could anyone love you after all the things you've done? You're unloveable.* Adi hung her head giving into the sobs. She wasn't crying in fear for the future, but for what she thought she had lost.

"Quit your bellyachin', girl! Your lyin' and thievery and whatever else has caught up to you and now you have to pay the consequences. Should 've thought of that afore!" The police officer grumbled at her as the squad car raced down the darkened highway towards a future that would be worse than her past.

SIX

Cockroaches scurried towards their hiding places when Thomas flicked the light on in the motel room. He grimaced at the sight, but remained silent about it. Matthew hadn't spoken a word since they left Rasha's house. Sensing Matthew's troubled mood, Thomas wasn't sure if he should try to break the silence.

"Thomas, I know you probably have many questions, but it's been a long night. Let's get to bed. We'll have more time to talk on our way to Miskana tomorrow." Matthew wearily took off his bow tie and threw it down on the bed.

Thomas' mood instantly brightened, "We're going home tomorrow?"

"Yes, but we won't stay for long. We need to notify Prince Joshua and King Penuel immediately about what happened tonight. Time is running out for Adi." With that, Matthew flipped open his phone indicating that he wasn't going to explain any further. After talking with his pilot who had been waiting nearby, Matthew quickly changed and crawled into the filthy bed. He was immediately asleep, but Thomas, on the other hand, tossed and turned, replaying the events of the night trying to figure out what it all meant.

As they settled in for the flight the next morning, Thomas couldn't contain his curiosity any longer. "Sir, I really don't understand ANYTHING!" He blurted.

Matthew smiled, "You may not understand everything now, Thomas, but someday you will."

Thomas sighed with impatience, "Okay, I'll just have to trust you on that, but can you answer one question?"

Matthew chuckled, "Okay. What is your one question, Thomas?"

"It seemed like Rasha knew King Penuel on a personal level. Did he?"

Matthew hesitated. "Yes, Thomas, he does know King Penuel, very well as a matter of fact. He was the King's highest official."

Thomas' mouth dropped open as past conversations came to mind. "Wait a minute. I thought the official split the kingdom, and. .and. . ." He couldn't finish as he struggled to comprehend the full meaning.

"Yes, Rasha was King Penuel's official that split the kingdom. He desired to be just like King Penuel. But when King Penuel cast him out of Miskana, he sought to destroy everything that King Penuel worked so hard for, including turning His own people against him."

"Then why isn't Rasha mingling with the high society crowd? Why live in a dump?"

"Trust me. He controls the leaders of Soteria. He just works behind the scene because it's easier to deceive and manipulate when people can't see who really is giving the orders. Someday, Rasha will reveal himself and will ultimately destroy everyone! Life as they know it will become unbearable under his tyranny if he reigns openly. Through drugs, poverty, and the promise of wealth and power, he is subtly grooming people to blindly follow him. That's why King Penuel and Prince Joshua want to give the citizens of Soteria a chance of escaping from Rasha's ultimate destruction."

"But how is marrying Adi going to achieve that?"

"Would people really feel that they could be given hope if Prince Joshua married a self-sufficient woman? No, they would just feel more resentful that she gets all the 'luck' so to speak. But, if a Prince married a woman such as Adi and offered her a change of life, then they will be more inclined to believe that Prince Joshua and King Penuel really do care about them and their offer is sincere."

"It seems as if Adi is just a symbol of diplomacy, but does Prince Joshua really love her?"

Matthew smiled wistfully, "More than you can ever imagine, Thomas. You will soon discover how much he loves her." Again, Thomas noticed the strange mixture of pain, sorrow, and love on the Ambassador's face. Chilled, Thomas stared out the plane window with a heavy sense of foreboding.

————

"Did you find Adi?" A pair of expressive chocolate brown eyes looked anxiously at Matthew.

"Yes, sir, we did." Matthew hesitated.

"And?" the Prince prompted.

"Adi was arrested for stealing twenty thousand dollars."

The three men who looked so similar silently stared at one another as if reading each other's thoughts. With a sigh, King Penuel stepped out onto the balcony. For a long moment he stood staring at the black smoke rising in the distant Soteria. He turned when he felt a gentle hand on his broad shoulder.

"Father, it's time isn't it?" Prince Joshua quietly questioned knowing the answer already. "We knew this day would come. She needs us, they need us."

"Yes, my Son, it is. You must go; it's the only way." King Penuel stated heavily.

"Then I will go immediately, Father." Prince Joshua

looked lovingly at the man whom he spent endless time with. As he turned to go, the King quickly reached out and grasped his son's arm.

"Joshua, what I'm asking you to do will be – difficult." The King choked on the last word.

"I know, Father, but I love them, too, and am willing to do whatever it takes to show them our love."

Tears formed pools in the King's dark eyes. "We've never been separated before."

"We will be reunited again when it's all over." The Prince gave his father's hand an encouraging squeeze.

As King Penuel hugged the Prince, he sobbed, "I love you, son!"

Tears streamed down Prince Joshua's face as he returned his father's embrace. "I love you, too, Father. I won't disappoint you."

"You never disappoint me. You have always pleased me."

Matthew and Thomas stood in respectful silence as they waited for father and son to say goodbye. Thomas never felt so confused as he did now, but he knew better than to interrupt the tender moment.

At last, King Penuel pushed Joshua away. "Go," he said simply.

Prince Joshua turned on his heels and left the balcony, motioning to Matthew and Thomas to follow. King Penuel leaned against the rail. An unbidden tear slid down his cheek as he stared at the distant dark horizon. Horrific scenes flashed before his mind's eye, scenes of pain, rejection, and betrayal. "Joshua! Adi!" He cried, as sobs shook his body.

————

Adi shuffled towards the table where her lawyer sat, her shackles chaffing her ankles. This was the first time she had a visitor since being arrested. The lawyer coldly stared at her through his round spectacles. He did nothing to hide his disdain for her.

"You don't look like much," he grunted looking at her dirty orange jumpsuit, tangled hair, and faded bruises.

Adi ignored the remark, "Who are you?"

"I'm your state appointed lawyer, although I don't know why they bother. It's quite obvious you're guilty," he smirked.

Adi angrily stared at him. He continued, "Anyways, I just dropped by to tell you that your court date is in two days."

Adi sat up straight in her chair exclaiming, "Two days? How can that be?"

The lawyer shrugged, "Hey, you're the daughter of a well known drug lord and..."

"Step-daughter," Adi interrupted.

The lawyer impatiently waved aside the comment, "Whatever. Like I said, you're guilty. Everyone knows it, so why prolong the inevitable. They mean to use you as an example. This has become a high profile case, and people are anxious to get on with it. Good publicity. Well, that's about it. See you in two days!" The lawyer quickly stood, picking up his briefcase.

"Aren't you going to ask me questions? Set up a defense for me?" Adi pleaded.

"No need to. I don't get paid enough to deal with the likes of you. I've got other appointments that are more in need of my services." With that, the snobbish lawyer rushed out of the interrogation room.

Stunned, Adi sat staring at the cuffs on her hands and feet. All hope fled with the lawyer as an emptiness settled over her. A guard stepped up roughly, grasping her arm as he ushered her back to her lonely cell.

Thomas stood once more watching the cockroaches scurry across the motel room floor. He didn't even get a chance to sleep in his own soft, comfortable bed. *Surely Prince Joshua will insist upon staying somewhere nicer! He* thought hopefully.

"This will do." The Prince stated as he glanced around the filthy room. Noticing Thomas's disappointed look, he laughed. "Poor Thomas, you must be very tired and very confused."

Thomas sighed, "I'm getting used to being confused, sir."

Joshua and Matthew both laughed. "You're a good

sport, Thomas." Joshua patted the weary young man on the back. Growing serious, Joshua turned back to Matthew, "Tomorrow I want you to find any information you can about Adi, and I will find Rasha."

"Rasha?" Thomas squeaked out.

"Don't worry, Thomas."

"Should I go with you?" Thomas puffed his slender chest out as if he thought he could protect the Prince.

Coughing in his hand, Joshua tried to conceal his laughter, "No, Thomas. I need to do this alone. You go with Matthew."

"Well," Matthew interrupted, "I think we had best get some rest."

Joshua nodded, "I agree."

The next morning, the men departed, agreeing to meet back at the motel for dinner. Prince Joshua roamed through the alleys, asking the loiterers for information on the whereabouts of Rasha. All the answers were the same, no one knew, or pretended not to know. After several hours of searching, a skinny man with a snake tatoo on his neck approached the Prince.

"Word is, you're lookin' for Rasha. What do ya want with him?" He slurred.

"My business is with Rasha. Tell him Joshua wants to speak with him. He knows me." Joshua calmly stated.

The man snickered and sauntered off. Joshua waited in the alley for another hour wondering if the man would

return. Just as he was about to leave for the motel, the man
appeared.

"Follow me," he said simply.

The man led Joshua through a maze of cluttered back
streets. The stench of garbage was overwhelming. After
twenty minutes of wandering, the tattooed man finally
stopped at the back of a brick apartment building. He gave
three raps on the peeling door and then pushed the door
open. Joshua had to dip his head upon entering so as not to
hit the doorframe. Rasha sat in a dirty white tank top,
stomach bulging against a small kitchen table. He eyed
Joshua with hatred as he took another drag on his
cigarette. Blowing out the smoke towards Joshua, he
motioned for him to sit.

Joshua stared evenly at Rasha. "I prefer to stand."

Rage coursed through Rasha as he jumped up
clenching his fist. "What's your business, Prince?" he
demanded.

"You've turned the people of Soteria against my father
and me. You've killed our representatives. You may
succeed in your plot of tyranny, but let me tell you, it will
be short-lived. My father will win in the end!" Joshua
stated emphatically.

"Ha! If that's true, which I doubt, let me assure you
that I will bring down as many people as I can, including
Adi!" Rasha bellowed, the veins in his neck protruding.

"Adi will have to choose, but I am going to do

everything in my power to make sure she sees the truth." A flicker of righteous anger burned in the Prince's eyes.

"You will never have her. She is mine!" Rasha growled. "Now get out!"

"You're not to hurt her, Rasha! She will have to choose, and if she chooses to follow you, then so be it, but if she chooses me, hands off!"

"What difference does it make? She's going to rot in prison for a long time," Rasha laughed.

"Because she did your dirty work. You've used her and abused her and now you won't even help her. Typical of you!" Joshua said disgusted.

Rasha's eyes widened in alarm, "If you try to help her, I have the power to destroy you." He pointed his finger in Joshua's face.

"No, Rasha, you have no power over me. You may be able to hurt me for a time, but only because my father and I have chosen to do this. In the end, I will have the victory, not you!"

With a shout of rage, Rasha lunged toward Prince Joshua, but the Prince sidestepped him and quickly slipped out the door and out of sight.

———

Joshua hurried through the filthy streets as darkness made its descent. Little children dressed in rags ran towards him with hands outstretched. "Money, mister?" Joshua stopped and looked down at them. Compassion swelled up as he stared into their imploring eyes.

"I'll tell you what. You all come here and sit down. I want to tell you a true story. When I'm finished and you've sat very still, I'll give you some money. How does that sound?"

The children looked at him suspiciously and then at one another. In silent agreement, they gathered around to listen to the stranger's story.

"A long long time ago, before you were born, there was this beautiful kingdom called Miskana. Do you know what Miskana means?" Joshua asked the wide-eyed children. In unison, they silently shook their heads. "Miskana means the dwelling place of God." Joshua continued. "This kingdom was paradise! There was gold and jewels everywhere!"

"Ooh!" The children whispered in awe. "Was there lots of food, too?" One emaciated boy spoke up.

"Oh, yes. As a matter of fact there was a big tree by a flowing river. This tree was special like no other tree around. It grew all sorts of fruit all year long!" The children licked their lips and rubbed their empty tummies.

"There was a mighty powerful king that ruled over the kingdom."

"Was he a bad king, mean and cruel?" A boy asked.

Joshua chuckled, "No, he was the exact opposite. He loved his people very much and he loved talking to them and spending time with them, but then one day, the king's highest government official became prideful and jealous. He wanted to be just like the king. So, he began to persuade other lower government workers to follow him."

A little girl gasped, "Did he kill the king?"

"No, he did not kill the king. When the king found out, he threw the official and his followers out of Miskana. He had to protect his kingdom."

"Yay!" The children cheered. After Joshua quieted them, he continued, "The official took over an extended part of the kingdom and over time destroyed everything that was beautiful. Now the people who live there have no hope. They are hungry, sad, and constantly fight."

"Sounds like where we live." A boy chimed in.

"Yes, it is." Joshua stated quietly. The children looked at one another in astonishment.

"Knowing what was happening to the people he loved and knowing the coming destruction of them, he sent representatives to warn the citizens. Instead of listening to the warnings, the leaders killed them."

Another gasp circulated through the group of young listeners. "That didn't stop the King from trying to reach out to his people. He sent his son, the Prince, to help show them the love his father has for them."

"What happened to the Prince?" A girl looked frightened.

"You will have to wait and watch for the rest of the story." Joshua smiled sadly.

A stalky tough boy stood up, "Wait a minute. I thought you said this was a TRUE story!"

"It is. It's a story that's still being written."

"If it's still being written, then does the kingdom of Miskana still exist?" Another child piped up.

"And is the tree with all the fruit still there?" The emaciated boy cut in.

"What about the gold and jewels?"

The Prince held up his hand laughing, "Whoa! The answer is yes to all those questions!"

Still doubtful the stalky boy spoke up, "What's the king's name and is his son here now?"

"The King's name is Penuel, and yes, his son is here now."

The kid's burst into laughter as the boy responded, "That's a good tale, Mister. My dad says Penuel doesn't exist!"

"And my dad said that if we speak of Penuel, we can get in big trouble with the law!" another girl stated emphatically.

"We did what you wanted. Now where's our money?" the boy challenged the Prince.

Joshua nodded as he dug into his pockets and produced money for each of the children. As they grabbed the coins, they ran off without another look at the stranger. As Joshua turned to find his way through the darkened street, he felt a tug on his hand. Looking down, his deep brown eyes locked with brilliant blue ones. It was the little girl who was worried about the Prince.

"I liked your story very much." She whispered.

Joshua's heart melted, "Thank you."

She glanced about, fearful of being overheard, "Are you the Prince?"

Joshua knelt in front of her, "Yes, I am."

Tears filled the cobalt blue eyes. "Can I come to Miskana with you?"

"Yes, someday you can, if you believe that I've come to help you and love you."

"Oh, I do!" The little girl wrapped her arms around Joshua's neck in a quick embrace, and then raced off towards her mother's demanding voice.

"I'll see you soon, little one." Joshua whispered into the night air.

———

"Where is he?" Thomas paced back and forth. "This was a bad idea."

Annoyed, Matthew looked up at Thomas from where he was sitting. "Calm down, Thomas. Have you no faith in Prince Joshua? He's perfectly capable of taking care of himself. He'll be along shortly."

"But what if Rasha..." Matthew set his book down on the little table with a thud. "Thomas, do not think for a moment that Rasha can overtake the Prince. As much as he would like to think that he's more powerful, he is not. He is still completely under the Prince's authority."

"Oh." Thomas sat on the bed humbled and embarrassed by the rebuke.

Just then the motel door opened and Joshua walked in. Both men quickly stood to their feet. "Sorry I was late. I was telling a group of children about Miskana and the King." Turning his full attention to Matthew he asked, "Any word of Adi?"

"Yes, sir, I discovered that she is to be brought to trial the day after tomorrow." Matthew said soberly.

Joshua sighed, "They're not wasting any time are they?" A heaviness settled over the room as the three men stood silently, lost in their own thoughts. Joshua at last broke the silence; "We had best get some dinner and discuss our plans for tomorrow."

———

The next day was spent walking the streets of Soteria giving a helping hand to those who needed it and sharing the story of King Penuel's love for them. By the end of the day the rumors were circulating throughout the city that there was a man claiming to be the Prince of Miskana who wanted to marry the criminal, Adi. Most rolled their eyes and waved the talebearer away. Others were intrigued and curious by the story while the imaginations of the little girls carried them away on dreams of romance.

"Hey, Adi, I hear your Prince is here!" A big hefty woman with short, cropped hair cackled.

Curled up on her bunk, Adi straightened up and looked at the woman in the next cell across from hers. "What did you say?"

"Marta's mother, who visited her today, told her that she had heard from a friend who said there was a man in Soteria claiming to be Prince Joshua from Miskana. Rumor also has it that he wants to marry you!" The inmate burst into hysterical laughter. "Hey everybody, we've got a Princess here! Better be nice to her!" Laughter was heard from other surrounding cells.

Adi glared at the woman and then retreated to the farthest corner of her bed. *Could it be true? If this Joshua is real, why would he want me?* Adi's thoughts tumbled over one another. *What if he's mean and wants to make me even more miserable?* Her eyes widened in fear at the thought. *No. Matthew said he loved me. Oh, that makes it worse! I would never be able to face him, not after all the things I've done!* She paused in her thoughts, *After all the things I've done...* Adi curled her knees up to her chest in an attempt to hide. *He could never love you, Adi!* The all too familiar voice whispered in her mind.

SEVEN

Adi awoke with a start as the guard ran his beat stick across the bars creating a loud clanging sound. "Eat your breakfast, girl. You meet with your lawyer in one hour." He shouted, shoving a covered plate under the bars.

Tiptoeing across the cold cement floor, Adi knelt beside the covered plastic plate and peered inside. She grimaced as she stared at the already cold, tasteless scrambled eggs and rancid fruit. She shoved the plate away and retreated back into the security of her bed. Fear washed over her causing her small frame to tremble, but as she stared at the colorless wall a memory brought a flash of hope. Rasha had bribed and intimidated the witnesses and the jury when Snake had been caught and tried a few years ago. Because the court couldn't get any witnesses to speak up, Snake was set free. Maybe Rasha will do the same for her since she was his best drug dealer. When the guard returned, he found Adi still curled up blankly staring at the wall with a small hopeful smile.

"Get up, girl. It's time to go." He said roughly as he unlocked the cell door.

The next several hours passed quickly. As if in a dream, Adi listened to her lawyer drone on about the proper courtroom etiquettes, changed into the clothes he had brought her, and faced the barrage of cameras and reporters as she stepped into the heavily guarded truck that would transport her to the courtroom.

"Rasha's going to come for me. You'll see." Adi quietly stated to the guard sitting next to her. The officer just stared straight ahead as if Adi weren't even there. Adi hung her head as the feelings of fear fled and in its place a hope took hold.

As the van pulled up to the courthouse, Adi could hear the commotion before seeing it. The back door flew open and several officers reached towards her pulling her out of the vehicle. Reporters were shouting questions while jostling one another in an attempt to get close to Adi.

"Adi, do you think that your father will show up and attempt a rescue?" One reporter had succeeded in breaking through the crowd.

Looking at the microphone that had been shoved close to her face, Adi confidently stated, "He'll help me one way or another."

"But do you think he'll show up?" the reporter insisted, even though the police pushed Adi forward.

Once inside, she was ushered into the crowded courtroom. Angry glares and hushed whispers followed her as she walked down the aisle to the front. Unwilling that any should see her sudden fear, Adi kept her head down. She wished that her hair was a little longer so it would shield her from the stares. Three men looked up from their quiet conversation as Adi passed by.

"Adi, I'm here," Joshua whispered. "Have faith."

Adi turned her head slightly in the direction of the whisper. Did someone actually talk to her? Have faith? She shook her head. She must have imagined it she concluded as she slid into the chair that was waiting for her.

"All rise for the Honorable Judge Wilson!" an authoritative voice called out, silencing the crowd.

Everyone stood as Judge Wilson entered and took her seat behind the great mahogany desk. "Court is now in session. Be seated," the silver haired woman said as if in a rush.

Adi studied the hard, set line of the judge's mouth and the cold icy blue eyes that glared at her. There was definitely no hope to receive any amount of compassion from the judge. Her reputation for showing no mercy matched her physical uptight demeanor. Adi's stomach twisted into a nauseating knot.

The prosecutor strutted back and forth in front of the jury as he eloquently gave his opening statement. "And I will prove that Adi, the daughter of the drug lord, Rasha, is guilty of drug running and theft!" He finished with a flourish, dramatically pointing a finger at Adi, causing her to cringe.

"Step-daughter," Adi mumbled.

"Hmm? You say something?" her attorney looked pointedly at her.

"Nothing," she muttered through gritted teeth.

Time passed painfully slowly, while Adi listened to the mounting evidence that seemed to prove her guilt.

Witnesses appeared confident and almost gleeful in their statements to the court. Why didn't Rasha bribe the witnesses? He's done it before when those who worked for him got caught. Why not for me? A horrifying thought clawed at her mind, What if he's abandoned me?

It was about three in the afternoon when the prosecutor announced that there were no more witnesses. Adi looked expectantly at her lawyer who had hardly said a word the entire time. He slowly stood up, buttoned his suit, and cleared his throat, "How can the defense argue when the proof of her guilt is so clear? All I can do is to plead for the court's mercy to take into consideration that she is just a young woman who has been forced by her father to commit these crimes. Hers was one of survival, not of malicious intent." He sat down and thumbed through his leather folder, unaware that Adi stared at him in horror.

"The court will take a recess until the jury reaches its decision," the black robed judge declared as she pounded her gavel.

"Want to grab a bite to eat?" Adi heard a female's voice behind her.

"No, this won't take long. The jury will be back in no time. It's not hard to see that she's guilty." A male voice snickered in response.

Thirty minutes later, a man stuck his head in the guarded room where Adi anxiously waited with her lawyer. "Jury's back," he informed the courtroom, and then quickly was gone.

Adi's face turned to an ashen color as despair replaced the hope that she once had. Slowly, she stood to her feet, wishing that her legs would give way and she could pass out into nothingness. Then she could avoid what was about to happen, but they didn't, and the lawyer was motioning for her to move.

The atmosphere of the courtroom was filled with morbid anticipation. People were chattering and laughing. Their lives were going to move on while Adi's life was going to miserably change, and no one seemed to care. Adi slumped down into her seat trying to choke back the sobs as she realized that she deserved everything she was now getting.

"All rise for the Honorable Judge Wilson!" The bailiff bellowed, once again bringing order to the courtroom.

The Judge hastily walked in and began speaking before even sitting down, "Has the jury reached a decision?"

The foreman rose from his position in the jurors' box, "Yes, your Honor, we have."

The Judge's eyes narrowed as she stared at Adi, "Will the prisoner please rise?" It was more of a command than a request.

Trembling, Adi stood to her feet with her lawyer next to her. "Proceed," the Judge nodded her head to the juror.

The foreman straightened, cleared his throat, and with all formality pronounced, "The members of the jury find Adi guilty on the charges of drug running and the theft of twenty thousand dollars as well as the theft of a certain pink gown."

The Judge's icy cold stare settled back on Adi, "This court finds you guilty on the charges of drug dealing and theft. I hereby sentence you to seven years of hard labor in Soteria's Women's Prison with no chance of parole!"

A murmur of approval rippled throughout the crowd causing the judge to pound her gavel. Adi's knees buckled causing her to fall back into her chair. Soteria's Women's Prison! Hard labor! She had heard horror stories of the place. Most women sentenced there never came out, and if they did, they were never in their right minds! Stories had circulated about food deprivation, beatings, rats, and diseases. This was a death sentence! Adi closed her eyes as she choked back the hysteria that threatened to overwhelm her.

Just then a deep voice from the audience shouted out, "Wait! Your Honor may I approach?"

Startled and annoyed, the Judge snapped, "And who

are you?"

"I am Joshua, the Prince of Miskana." The simple statement sent a ripple of shocked gasps throughout the crowd. Adi whirled around in her seat, her eyes growing wide with fear. There stood a young man with bronzed skin, six foot three inches in height with broad shoulders, and powerfully built. His deep expressive brown eyes looked with determination at the judge.

The Judge stared at him, weighing the potential impact of this man's presence. At last she sneered, "You may approach, Prince Joshua." Emphasizing the title *Prince* in a mocking way.

"Your Honor, I would like to take the prisoner's place," the Prince stated firmly, ignoring the Judge's sarcasm.

Astonished, the Judge questioned, "Do I understand you correctly? You would like to take this girl's punishment?"

"Yes, your Honor, I will serve the seven years in her place." Joshua didn't waver in his proposal.

"But why? You've done nothing wrong!"

Joshua turned fixing his gaze upon Adi. "Because I love her!"

The gently spoken words hit Adi with such force that before she could think, she cried out, "No! You can't do this!"

In a few strides Joshua was by Adi's side, "Adi, I love

you, and when this is all over, I wish to marry you, if you'll have me."

"But I don't know you!"

"You will. Matthew will tell you all about me."

Adi couldn't bear to look any longer in Joshua's pleading eyes, "I've done all this. This is my fault! I'm not worthy of your love!"

"Adi, " Joshua reached out and cupped her face in his strong hands, "My dear sweet Adi, I love you and will always love you no matter what you have done. I know it's difficult for you to understand this right now, but to show how much I love you, I am willing to take your place."

Adi stood in shocked silence staring into his warm brown eyes. The room seemed to grow very quiet and still, even the judge seemed mesmerized.

"Judge?" Joshua looked up at the stunned woman.

She wiggled uncomfortably in her seat trying to decide what to do. "This is most unusual. The sentence must be fulfilled." She said sternly. In an attempt to dissuade Joshua, she continued, "Adi has broken the law, and punishment must be served; do you understand that?"

"Yes, your Honor, and I would like to take her punishment" Joshua stated resolutely.

The Judge looked at the crowd and then to the jurors with a questioning look. Flustered, she repeated, "This is most unusual."

Someone called out from the crowd, "Go ahead, Judge,

let the Prince take her place! One less nut job on the street!" Everyone laughed, nodding their heads in agreement.

"We'd rather have Adi walking the streets instead of this guy stirring up trouble by saying he's the son of King Penuel!" another jeering voice was heard from the back of the courtroom.

A woman chimed in, "Yes, lock him up! He's been brainwashing our children's minds with such ludicrous stories about a faraway paradise!"

People began shouting in agreement. Growing nervous at the prospect of losing full control, Judge Wilson pounded the gavel until the room quieted. "There must be order in this courtroom!" She admonished the crowd and then, turning back to Joshua said, "I don't think you know what you're in for, but the crowd has spoken, and I will allow you to serve out Adi's sentence. You will be sent to the Men's Correctional facility and serve out seven years. Once you have completed the seven years, Adi will receive full pardon contigent upon her acceptance of your proposal."

Joshua nodded his head in agreement. "Your Honor, I have one request before I leave."

The Judge leaned forward, "Yes?"

Joshua looked longingly at Adi. "Judge, I'd like for a marriage contract to be drawn up. While I am gone, I'd like Adi to know my intent. When the contract has been fulfilled at the end of the seven years, she can decide whether or not to accept my proposal."

Judge Wilson motioned for the court stenographer, "Type this down." Then looking back at the Prince nodded for him to continue.

The Prince reached out and tenderly held Adi's cuffed hands. "In my kingdom, there are several traditions that we follow when a man wishes to marry a woman. First, we send out a matchmaker, which in this case was Matthew. Next, the father of the groom pays a bride price. Let it be known in the contract that my father, King Penuel has sent me here today to take Adi's place. Once the seven years have been fulfilled, the bride price will have been paid."

A sob escaped from Adi's lips while tears coarsed down her cheeks. Prince Joshua tenderly wiped away the tears, his touch bringing comfort and strength to her. He smiled and continued, "I also want the rights of the bride to be included in the contract. Adi, if you should accept my proposal, then you will also be adopted into King Penuel's family. You will have all the rights of a daughter of a King. You will be an heir to the kingdom."

"How can this be?" Adi whispered wishing that she could believe him.

Joshua leaned towards her, "My father loves you, Adi." he said in a voice filled with emotion.

The Prince straightened and looked back at the stenographer, "One last item to be included in the contract is my promise as Adi's groom." He turned back to Adi, his gaze intent upon her face, "Adi, I promise to never abandon you. I promise that you will always be provided for, and I will protect you from all harm. I will watch over you for all time. I shall be yours, and you will be mine. I will love you with an everlasting love. This I promise."

Confusion rattled through Adi's dulled senses. Everything was happening too fast for her to be able to comprehend. She stood there trying to form her thoughts. Before she could reply, Joshua looked at the crowd and said loudly, "My father, King Penuel and I care and love each of you very much. He wishes to extend forgiveness and restoration through me. It is our hope that you will come to understand this and accept that the only way to be saved from the coming destruction is to turn to me. I can help you!"

A roar of outrage erupted from the crowd. "Cuff him!" the crowd shouted. "Get him out of here!" The courtroom went into chaos. Several men rushed forward tackling the Prince to the ground. Adi screamed as the men smashed their fists into Joshua's face and stomach. The judge's gavel could hardly be heard above the mayhem as she attempted to restore order.

Thomas jumped up from his seat, hands clenched ready to defend. Matthew stood quickly blocking his path. "Thomas, let it be."

"What? Matthew, we have to help!" Thomas struggled

to get past Matthew, but his small frame was no match against Matthew's strength.

"No, Thomas. This is a part of the plan; let it be." Matthew said firmly. Thomas stepped back in stunned silence and watched as the guards pulled the men off the Prince and roughly helped him to his feet. The bailiff rushed over to Adi, unlocking the cuffs from her wrists and turning to slap them onto Prince Joshua. Their eyes met, and time seemed to stand still for a brief moment. Adi stared in fright at the blood streaming from a gash on the Prince's face. His right eye and bottom lip were quickly swelling. In spite of the obvious pain, Joshua looked at Adi with compassion, "I love you," he mouthed, and then the moment was gone.

The crowd pressed in with anger as the guards propelled Joshua out of the courtroom. As the side door slammed with finality, the hostile crowd rushed out the back hoping to get one last glimpse of the Prince before the prison van drove away. Adi slumped down into the chair and sobbed. *Why am I crying? Shouldn't I be relieved that I'm free?* Adi thought. *But the Prince was innocent! Why did he do that for me? No one has ever shown me kindness before.* Another unwelcoming voice broke into her thoughts, *Don't think you're free yet, Adi. Seven years is a long time, especially in prison. He'll soon change his mind and realize that you're not worth it.* Adi cried harder.

EIGHT

A gentle hand squeezed her shoulder. Startled, Adi whirled around and looked up to see a man that bore an uncanny resemblance to the Prince. Confused, Adi began to say the Prince's name but caught herself as she realized that it was Matthew who stood before her. Matthew, a man of quiet authority, now had tears in his eyes. His lip trembled slightly as he struggled to conceal the pain he felt for the loss of the Prince. Shame and guilt washed over her causing her to tremble. She couldn't bear to look at Matthew.

Seeing Adi shaking, Matthew quickly took off his sports coat and wrapped it around her thin shoulders.

Squatting down before her, he gently lifted her chin forcing eye contact. "Adi, you can stay with us. We'll take care of you."

Adi stubbornly shook her head.

"You don't have anywhere to go, Adi. Prince Joshua wants me to watch out for you while he's gone." Adi didn't move.

Sighing, Matthew stood to his feet. "We need to talk, Adi, so let's get you something to eat." He reached down pulling her to her feet. Her emotions were in turmoil. A part of her wanted to desperately bolt and put as much distance between her and Matthew as she possibly could. Another part wanted answers to just who Joshua was. Sensing her indecision, Matthew gripped her arm, propelling her forward, out the courtroom and into the taxi.

———————

Across the street and hidden in the shadows, a short bulky man intently watched the angry crowd pouring out of the courtroom. A sly smile slowly spread across his face as he spotted the reason for the jeering crowd. The police was escorting Prince Joshua, suit torn and blood running down his face, to the waiting prison van. A small chuckle escaped from the thick lips of the hidden observer. Sensing the man's presence, Joshua looked up and for a brief moment both men stared at one another. Joshua's gaze resolute while the other was one of victory. Rasha watched as the officers roughly pushed Joshua inside and slammed the doors closed. Excitement coursed through Rasha's veins as he relished this long awaited moment. With Joshua out of the picture, he could get Adi back. *Wouldn't that be the ultimate victory to persuade Adi to refuse the Prince's proposal?* He thought. *Better yet, to find his bride- to- be married to another man! And I know just the man!* Rasha burst into laughter as he pictured the anguish that it would cause the Prince. *Rasha, you are brilliant!* He commended himself.

His laughter came to a sudden stop as he noticed the three walking down the stairs from the courtroom doors. Recognizing Matthew with his arm around a shaken Adi and Thomas, his eyes narrowed in hatred. "You belong to me, Adi!" He growled through clenched teeth. Agitated, he whirled around and stomped off determined to fulfill his plan.

Thomas slipped in on the other side of Adi. There was no way of escaping. She would have to hear Matthew out. An uncomfortable silence settled over them as they drove to a secluded diner. Once they were seated and had placed their orders, Adi looked expectantly at Matthew waiting for him to speak.

Looking at Adi's haggard tortured face, Matthew took a deep breath and began to speak, "Adi, I'm sure you are feeling overwhelmed right now. I understand. I'm here to answer any questions that you might have." Matthew paused, hoping that Adi would respond, and when she didn't, he continued, "I'd like for you to stay with us. You'll be safe, but that is entirely up to you."

"Just who is Prince Joshua?" Adi finally blurted out.

Thomas proudly responded, "He is King Penuel's son, the Prince of Miskana!"

"I get that, but I was told that King Penuel was just a myth, a fanciful story created by weak-minded people, and now today, the Prince is standing before me telling me that he loves me and then he's taken away and I'm free. What if he's some kind of madman? But if he were a madman, he wouldn't exchange places with me, now would he? But then I suppose if he were a madman, maybe he would, because he's not in his right mind, so he wouldn't know what he was doing and...and.." Matthew and Thomas stared wide-eyed at the rambling girl who was teetering on the brinks of hysteria.

Matthew awkwardly reached across the table patting her on the arm. "Slow down, it's going to be okay, Adi."

Bursting into tears Adi cried, "How is it going to be okay? An innocent man just went to prison for me! How is that OKAY?" Her voice was rising into a high pitch that drew several curious glances from customers.

"Calm down, dear one." Matthew continued to talk in a gentle calming manner until Adi had settled down to a few sniffles.

"I'm okay now." She said as she dried her eyes with a napkin. "Please explain to me who is this Prince?"

As Matthew explained the turbulent history of Miskana and the previous relationship of the Soterians with King Penuel and Prince Joshua, Adi sat there dumbfounded. Doubts filled her mind. She had heard this story before from Rasha and others, but with a completely different twist. The villain in Matthew's story was always the hero in Rasha's version. As a child, Adi just assumed that this was a make-believe story to entertain and now Matthew was claiming it to be an actual event! She didn't know whom to believe. When Matthew finished, Adi sat there in silence, contemplating what she had just learned. Finally she asked,

"How do I know that King Penuel and Prince Joshua actually exist? How do I know that the man in the courtroom really is who he claims to be?"

Matthew took a moment to stare out the nearby window. Above the darkening sky, stars sparkled through the breaks in the stormy clouds. Turning to Adi, Matthew pointed up toward the stars, "Look at the stars, Adi. For years Soterians have studied the stars. Each constellation tells the story of King Penuel and the sacrifice that Prince Joshua has made, but the enemy has turned the study of stars into a means of fortunetelling and horoscopes. What the enemy cannot do is to take away the beauty of the stars. They still remain faithful in sharing King Penuel's story to all who are open-minded to search it out. Take for instance the constellation Virgo. Virgo is the Latin name for virgin. Prince Joshua was born of a virgin. Each constellation speaks of the sacrifice that the Prince will be making for all of Soteria and of the promises to deliver all those who believe. The story comes full circle with Leo, the Latin for lion. The lion represents kingship. Someday when the battle is over, the Prince and King Penuel will once more reign over a new Soteria." Awed by this new information, Adi stared at the stars with deeper appreciation.

"I never knew that," Adi whispered.

Matthew looked down at his dinner and sighed, "No, I suppose not."

———

"How else can I know that what you say is true about King Penuel?"

"Consider the complexity of creation. In an effort to rid themselves of the memory of King Penuel, the people of Soteria allowed their city to decay. However, you can still see his handiwork, especially when you leave the crowded city. Look at the rugged mountains that resolutely stand as a reminder that King Penuel is a fortress to anyone seeking refuge. Have you ever seen a magnificent waterfall cascading down the face of a mountain, Adi?" Matthew's eyes sparkled with dreamy enthusiasm, "It looks like a woman's bridal veil. It anticipates the hope for a new way of life in union with King Penuel and Prince Joshua. Have you thought about the inticracies of trees, rocks, flowers, animals, and even your own physical body?" Matthew paused for a moment in thought. "Have you heard of Charles Darwin, the evolutionist?"

Adi shrugged, "Everyone has."

Matthew continued excited to make his point, "Even he had a hard time explaining how the eye evolved. He once said, 'To suppose that the eye with all its inimitable contrivances for adjusting the focus to different distances, for admitting different amounts of light, and for the correction of spherical and chromatic aberration, could have been formed by natural selection, seems, I confess, absurd in the highest degree...The difficulty of believing that a perfect and complex eye could be formed by natural selection , though insuperable by our imagination, should not be considered subversive of the theory.' Adi, even your eye is a sign that King Penuel does exist!"

Adi looked at him confused. Matthew rushed on in his explanation, "Today, you experienced Soteria's justice system. Even though it might not always be fair in its decisions, the bottom line is that there is a moral code that Soterians follow. Where did that moral code come from, Adi? Who set the standard?"

Adi shrugged, "Law makers who want power?"

"Who told the law makers that murder was wrong?"

"I don't know."

"The moral code was given to every Soterian from King

Penuel. The enemy is laboring to destroy that moral code, and someday the people of Soteria will be given over to their immoral desires, but it will be to their ruin." Matthew paused considering his next statement. "Adi, you mentioned that the story of King Penuel and Prince Joshua was just that –a story. If it is just a fictional story, then why is it so controversial? Why is there a movement to get rid of the story and why do some still whisper the story to their children? The reason is that in every Soterian there is a longing for the story to be true. Sadly, many have put their own twists on the events and have fabricated other kings to replace the true King."

Adi nodded in agreement, "Yes, I've heard this story before not just from Rasha, but others. Many have called the King by different names, and they have their own ideas as to his character. That's why I just assumed that this was a figment of people's imaginations or that it didn't matter what people believed just as long as it made them feel good."

Thomas who had been sitting silently interjected, "Isn't that just what the enemy wants, to take people's eyes off the true source of help?"

Matthew nodded, his face becoming taut with the heavy burden he felt. "Yes, it is. We are in a battle, Thomas, a battle of lies, deceit, and will. When destruction comes, the Soterians will discover that they had put their hope in something false, and by that time it will be too late."

Adi shuddered at the gravity of the two men. "You keep talking about a coming destruction. What is it?"

"Right now, King Penuel and Prince Joshua are extending peace, love, and opportunities for restoration, but someday, someone will come to power in Soteria that will make grand promises of peace and restoration. He will appear as if he is the 'hero' of the story, but the reality of it is that he will lead them into battle against King Penuel and Prince Joshua."

Adi gasped in horror. "Will he win?" She whispered nervously glancing around for any eavesdroppers. The thought had crossed her mind to ask who the enemy was, but the less she knew, the better it would be for her, or so she assumed.

Matthew looked gravely at her, "No. All of the Soterians who choose not to follow Prince Joshua will be destroyed and punished for all time. Today, the Prince stood before a judge and allowed himself to take on your punishment, but someday, the Prince will be the judge."

Adi held her breath in shock at this revelation. Is this an ugly joke? Anger coursed through her. Prince Joshua a judge? How can he marry me, a criminal? Feeling the sting of disappointment, Adi blurted out in mid-thought, "What kind of a marriage would that make?"

Startled by the outburst, Thomas asked bewildered, "What are you talking about?"

Understanding Adi's turmoil, Matthew took Adi's hand in his and looked deep into her eyes. "Adi, you are a jewel to Prince Joshua. You must understand that he desperately loves you. You must also understand that you are in danger of all that we have discussed. If you choose to reject the Prince's proposal, someday you will stand before him not as a bride stands before her groom, but as a prisoner stands before her judge. He does not wish to judge you, he wishes to marry you and protect you from further punishment."

Adi snatched her hand away indignantly, "That's a contradiction! How can Prince Joshua love me and then condemn me? That doesn't make sense!"

"Does a father withhold correction from a child when the child has done something wrong? No, he doesn't, no matter how much he loves the child. In this case, Adi, the Prince will not be at fault. You have to admit that he has gone through great lengths to convince you of his love and his desire to protect you. If you deliberately choose to ignore his attempts and in so doing, choose to stand with the enemy, then what choice does he have but to judge you?" Matthew looked at her pleadingly.

A cold dread crept through every ounce of Adi's body, causing her to shiver. This was too much information. The confusing turn of events of the day and this dreadful story from Matthew completely overwhelmed her.

Seeing her exhaustion, Matthew gently touched her hand again, "This has been a trying day, Adi. Maybe after a good night's sleep, things will make sense in the morning. I'd like for you to stay with us at the motel. I've rented another room for you." He stood, stretching to his full height. Quickly, he stepped next to Adi, offering a hand to help her up. Adi placed her small delicate hand in his much larger, stronger one. Adi wanted to refuse, but Matthew's presence was so commanding and so compelling that she couldn't voice her rejection.

———————

In spite of the disguise, Ze'ev instantly recognized the overweight man who was sitting on the park bench staring at the water. Nervously, he pulled his hat lower to shade his face so as not to be recognized. Ze'ev smoothly slid onto the bench and flipped open a newspaper. Without looking at the man, he questioned in a low voice, hoping that his voice wouldn't reveal the fear he felt.

"Why the meeting, Rasha? I don't owe you anything."

Keeping his eyes fixed on the water, Rasha softly chuckled, "Afraid Ze'ev?"

Ze'ev gave no response.

"As it should be," Rasha sneered. "I have a job for you to do."

"I'm not a drug runner!" Ze'ev squirmed.

"It's nothing to do with drugs, you Imbecile! I want you to win a woman over!" Snapped Rasha.

Surprised, Ze'ev glanced quickly at Rasha." You want me to do what?"

"Shut up and get back to your newspaper," Rasha reprimanded.

Not wanting to cross this brute of a man, Ze'ev silently obeyed and waited for this cruel being to continue.

"You heard about Adi gaining her freedom because of that man who claims to be Prince Joshua?"

Ze'ev nodded.

"Well, he promised to marry her when he gets out, even had a contract drawn up."

Ze'ev shook his head in amazement, "Did she sign it?"

Rasha laughed, "No, she's too stupid to do that. She has until the Prince is released to make her decision."

Ze'ev hesitated, "So. this woman you want me to win over is Adi?"

"Absolutely! The Prince and I have been long time enemies. It brings me great joy to know that he is going to suffer immeasurably in prison. I'll make sure of that." Rasha rubbed his hands together in eager anticipation. A shudder passed through Ze'ev. This man was pure evil. Rasha continued, "Torturing this Prince will not be enough for me. What better way to get the ultimate revenge than to take away the woman he loves." A wicked laughter erupted from the vindictive drug lord.

At first, the confused Ze'ev chuckled, and then, stopped abruptly. "That's a great plan, but when you say that you want me to win her over, do you mean to marry her?"

"Of course, you have to marry her!" Rasha growled.

Ze'ev sat silently soaking in the news. He grimaced as he thought about his reputation. "I don't know, Rasha, I'm not the marrying kind, and what about my reputation? I can't marry a street urchin, a thief!"

Rasha turned glaring at the young man. "A street urchin? A thief? And what are you, Ze'ev? You're a thief, a con. The only difference between you and her is that you dress up and live in a nice place. If you don't do what I tell you, I'll destroy you. I'll make sure you lose everything."

Ze'ev swallowed hard, "Alright, alright, I'll do it. What am I to tell her?"

"Tell her that I sent that man to take her place. I couldn't allow my daughter to suffer in prison, now could I?" answered Rasha sarcastically. "Tell her that I used the whole 'Prince Joshua' thing as a cover for her. Win her trust, Ze'ev. Convince her that if she marries you, she will be rich beyond imagination and that all of Soteria will bow before her!"

Perking up at this unexpected twist Ze'ev asked hopefully, "That means I'll be rich and powerful? You'll make that happen?"

"If you do as I say, Ze'ev! You'll be the most powerful man in all of Soteria!"

Ze'ev feeling exhilarated about the prospect of riches and power, enthusiastically exclaimed, "I'll do it!"

"Good. Now go find her," Rasha ordered.

Without hesitation, Ze'ev jumped up from the bench and quickly set out to accomplish his mission. An evil smile spread across Rasha's scarred face. "Sucker!" he muttered, and then threw his head back in a fit of hoarse laughter.

———

Adi thrashed and groaned upon the bed. Terrified shrieks and wails coming from a deep dark endless abyss engulfed her as she was being dragged to the pit by a monstrous shadowed form. "I've got you now, Adi, you're mine!" The monster let out a deep guttural laugh that sent a cold chill throughout Adi.

"Someone please help me!" She screamed out as she kicked and punched at her assailant, but he was too strong for her.

"It's too late for you!" The massive form ground out. "You chose this!" He yanked her harder towards the pit.

"I didn't choose this!" Adi cried as she dug her heels into the ground.

The monster grabbed her by the arm dangling her over the fiery abyss. Adi could feel the extreme heat engulfing her back. "Oh, but you did, Adi. Joshua gave you a chance and you didn't accept it and now you have to pay for your crimes!" Throwing his head back the shadowed form let out a roar of giddy laughter.

"Please," she begged, "don't drop me!"

"I've worked hard to pull you away from Joshua and I must say I was quite successful!" With that he let go of her arm sending her spiraling down into the flames.

Adi screamed out, "Joshua save me!"

Just before her body reached the flames, a strong and mighty hand reached out grabbing her arm. Looking up, Adi stared at the face of her rescuer. Blood was flowing down his cheeks from a long gash that circled his forehead much like a bloody crown. His beautiful brown eyes and perfectly shaped lips were swollen and bruised. In spite of the pain he was suffering, Joshua pulled her up until she was settled onto solid ground. An angry evil voice shouted in rage from the edge of the pit, "NO! She's mine! You can't have her!"

Adi woke up with a start, sweat pouring down her back. She lay there in the darkness trembling. Unable to get the torturous scenes of her nightmare out of her head, she threw back the covers and turned the light on. Feeling somewhat relieved to see the normalcy of her room, she began to pace, but the more she paced, the more the walls seem to close in on her. *I've got to get out of here!* Adi thought. I can't think with Matthew so close in the other room. Even in spite of Matthew's kindness, Adi felt uncomfortable around him. His presence made her painfully aware of her failures. Dressing quickly, Adi quietly unlocked her motel door and slipped out into the night.

For several hours Adi wandered the streets, carefully avoiding the nightlife spots. Growing weary, she searched for a corner to curl up in. Just as she found one, she heard a squeak of a shoe behind her. Adrenaline coursed through her as she whirled around ready to fight off a possible attacker, but to her surprise no one was there except for a distant shadow retreating behind a building. Adi carefully watched the spot until her eyes blurred. Must be my imagination, she decided. After finding a few cardboard boxes and ripping them apart to form a somewhat cushioned bed, Adi curled up and fell fast asleep.

NINE

"Adi! Adi wake up!"

Adi groaned. Her whole body ached from the hard, cold ground. Squinting against the mid-morning sun, she noticed a black form leaning over her. Frightened, she sat up and began to swing at the man.

"Whoa!" The man laughed, grabbing her arms. "When are you going to learn that you can't fight me?"

Adi's eyes widened, "Ze'ev! What are you doing here?"

"I could ask you the same question!" he said, eyeing her ragged appearance and her strange choice of accommodation.

"I—I didn't have any place to go," she lied.

Ze'ev's eyes narrowed, "I thought you would be staying with that Matthew fellow and his side-kick."

"Well, they offered, but I didn't feel comfortable."

"Why you ungrateful girl, you, after all what Prince Joshua did for you?" Ze'ev feigned mocked horror.

Adi defensively pulled her arms away from his grasp. "I don't know this Prince Joshua. Besides, I needed time to think." Angrily, she stood up as she tried to smooth out her shirt.

Ze'ev followed suit, towering over her. With an unexpected gesture, he gently laid his hand on her shoulder. "You don't have to get defensive." Concern replaced his sarcasm. "As a matter of fact, I'm glad you left that guy. I was on my way to find you."

Amazed, Adi asked, "You were? Why?"

Pretending embarrassment, Ze'ev looked down and kicked at a pebble. "I was worried that the Ambassador might mess with your mind or something."

Hope sprang into Adi's eyes, "You cared?" she timidly asked.

Ze'ev laughed pulling her into a warm embrace, "Of course, I care!"

Adi snuggled in close relishing the scent of his cologne. After a brief moment, Ze'ev pushed her away from him so he could better examine her. "Hey, you don't look so good. I insist on taking you to my place so you can clean up and then I'll take you to any restaurant you like, my dear!"

"Really?" For the first time, the fear and torment of her life began to subside.

"Absolutely!" Ze'ev said with a flourish. "After you, Madame!"

Adi laughed and stepped out from her hiding place.

"This is going to be easier than I thought!" Ze'ev mumbled under his breath.

———

Adi let out a contented sigh as the hot water soothed her sore muscles. Ze'ev had prepared a lilac-scented bubble bath for her and then immediately left, telling her to take as long as she needed. Closing her eyes, she replayed Ze'ev's unusual concern for her. A small smile played on her lips and quickly disappeared as the thought of Rasha erased any hope of romance. If all of Soteria knew about yesterday's events, then so did Rasha. He would be looking for her. What if Ze'ev turns me in to him? Adi shuddered. No, that's impossible. Ze'ev tries to stay as far away from Rasha as possible; but then again, he knows better than to hide me from Rasha. If Rasha found out, he would have Ze'ev killed. Fear twisted her insides as doubts began to form about Ze'ev's sudden interest in her. I should have stayed with Matthew! Deciding to talk to Ze'ev about this matter over lunch, Adi reluctantly climbed out of the tub and dressed.

Seated across from Ze'ev, who looked amazing in his tan three- buttoned suit with his periwinkle shirt unbuttoned at the collar, Adi wondered if she really did have anything to worry about.

Noticing Adi staring at him, Ze'ev smiled, "Something on your mind, Adi?"

"Are you going to turn me over to Rasha?" She blurted.

Ze'ev looked surprised, "Turn you over to Rasha? Of course not!" Ze'ev grew pensive as he swirled his water in his glass. Finally, he looked longingly at Adi. "Adi, I have a confession to make." He halted as if suddenly unsure of himself.

"Yes?" Adi prompted.

"Since that night we were together at the dinner gala, I've not been able to get you out of my mind. It was then I realized how beautiful you are!" Seeing that his words were making an impact, he quickly continued, "I was so scared when I heard that you had been arrested. You've got to believe me when I tell you that I pulled every possible string I could to get you released, but obviously nothing worked."

Adi was amazed at this revelation, "You did?"

"Of course! A man doesn't let the woman he loves go to prison without trying to stop it now would he?" Ze'ev lied.

Startled, Adi gasped, "Love?"

Just then a deep voice interrupted, "I've been worried about you, Adi."

Adi froze as she recognized the voice. Looking up into Matthew's disapproving face, she attempted an air of indifference, "Oh, hello, Matthew. I didn't want to wake you and Thomas."

"It wouldn't have been a bother." Looking at Ze'ev, Matthew motioned to the two empty chairs at the table, "May we join you?"

Heat rose up into Ze'ev's face, "No, you may not! We are having a private conversation!"

Non-pulsed, Matthew nodded, "Very well then." Turning to the empty table right next to them, he motioned to Thomas to take a seat.

Ze'ev grew angry, "You can't sit there!"

Looking amused, Matthew responded, "Why not? It's empty isn't it?"

Ze'ev grumbled, searching for an excuse but was unable to find one. Glaring at Matthew, he scooted his seat closer to Adi so that his back would shield her from Matthew. Protectively, he grasped Adi's hand whispering, "Just focus on me. Don't worry about him."

But it was too difficult for her to focus with Matthew being so near. Visions of Joshua standing so boldly and courageously before the judge danced before her mind's eye. As his tender words of love for her whispered in her thoughts, she found it difficult to hear what Ze'ev was saying. Guilt tore at her. Part of her wanted to run to

Matthew and another part wanted to just run out of the restaurant.

Unable to stand the inner turmoil any longer, she shoved her plate aside urgently whispering, "Please, Ze'ev let's go. I've got to get out of here."

A look of triumph brought a grin to Ze'ev, "Of, course, my dearest Adi, we will go." He said loudly enough for the men at the next table to hear.

Embarrassed, Adi quickly rose from her seat and turned to leave. Matthew instinctively reached out and touched her arm, "Adi!" Reluctantly, she turned to stare down into his eyes. They were like warm chocolate pools ready to engulf her. "Adi, you know where we are. Don't hesitate to come to us for help . We're here for you! As a matter of fact, here's my phone number that you can call anytime." Matthew shoved a card into her hand.

Ze'ev angrily snatched the card away from her. "She doesn't need this! If she needs anything, it'll come from me, not you!"

Matthew sent Ze'ev a threatening look that shut Ze'ev up. Reclaiming the card, Matthew placed it back into Adi's hand. "If you need anything, Adi..." his soft words trailed off. Confused by what she had just witnessed, Adi whirled and made a hasty escape with a humbled Ze'ev close behind.

Frustrated, Ze'ev yanked the door of his red Porsche open and waited for Adi to slip in and then, forgetting himself, slammed the door. Without a word, he slipped behind the wheel and squealed out of the parking lot, unaware of the two creatures in pursuit.

After taking a few moments to calm down, he remembered Adi. Looking over at her, he noticed that she had scooted very close to the door with her hand gripping the door as if ready to jump. "Adi, you don't have to be afraid of me." Ze'ev said. "Something about that Ambassador makes me so angry! I'm sorry."

Adi nodded silently.

In an attempt to lighten the mood, Ze'ev reached over and squeezed her left hand. "Hey, why don't I take you to the Boulevard and you can shop for clothes, and we can get some ice cream! Would you like that?"

Adi hesitated, "I don't have any money to buy clothes, especially clothes from the Boulevard!"

Ze'ev laughed, "This is my treat, Adi. I can't have you looking like a shaggy dog if you're going to be my girl!"

Adi's head jerked up, "Your girl? I don't know, Ze'ev."

Hiding his agitation, Ze'ev just smiled, "Don't worry about it. Guess I'll have to prove my feelings for you. So in order to do that, I'm taking you shopping! The way to a girl's heart is through shopping, right?" he laughed.

Adi laughed as the tension subsided. She shoved the rest of her doubts away. She was going to enjoy this moment! Wasn't this every girl's dream to shop on the Boulevard? She was determined that nothing would

dampen this time with Ze'ev. It was the happiest day that
Adi could ever remember having. Ze'ev took her to every
shop on the Boulevard and insisted that she buy something
in every store. It became a type of game to find something,
even if it was a small trinket. They laughed and joked the
entire time, taking silly pictures everywhere. This was a
side of Ze'ev that she had never seen. Ze'ev wasn't so scary
after all rather he was playful and loving!

———————

A sharp rap sounded on the motel's door startling Thomas.
Jumping up from where he sat, he moved cautiously
toward the door. Opening it slightly, he was able to make
out a man in the moonlight. "Yes?" he questioned
suspiciously eyeing the man dressed in a navy blue polo
shirt and khaki pants.

"I must speak with the Ambassador," the man stated
crisply. Everything about his manner and posture spoke of
being a military man. `

Thomas stared at the muscular man with suspicion,
"Who's asking?"

"Gabriel."

Thomas waited for more information, but seeing that
the man was not going to offer any explanation, he
humphed and closed the door. A few seconds passed when
the door reopened.

"Gabriel, come in, quickly!" Matthew urgently waved

Gabriel in.

Once Gabriel passed through the doorway, Matthew made a quick glance about the dark parking lot making sure that no one was lurking in the shadows. Satisfied, he shut the door and turned to face the messenger.

"Sir." Gabriel gave a respectful bow to Matthew.

"You must have orders from the King," Matthew stated.

"Yes, sir. Michael has been sent specifically to watch over Adi."

Matthew nodded, "Good, good. Tell Michael that he needs to stay close to her, but not to interfere. She needs to make the choice, he is to just keep her safe."

"Yes, sir. Michael wishes me to inform you that she has spent the day with that man, Ze'ev. He has offered for her to spend the night."

"Yes, I knew he would." Sighing, Matthew paced back and forth in deep thought. Gabriel stood attentively watching his commander.

Thomas looked at both men, confused. He desperately wanted to be a part of the conversation. Before he could think, he blurted, "Well, that could be a good thing! At least Rasha hasn't found Adi!"

Matthew stopped in his pacing and looked squarely at Thomas, "A good thing? Do you have any idea who Ze'ev is?"

Thomas shrank regretting his outburst, "No, sir."

"Ze'ev is a con man, a deceiver. He's a master at manipulating people. Everything he does is to benefit himself. So, how is it a GOOD thing for Adi to be with Ze'ev, Thomas?"

Completely embarrassed, Thomas mumbled, "It's not."

"No, it's not. Adi is in a vulnerable position to be deceived by Ze'ev."

Gabriel cleared his throat, "If I may interject, sir, a meeting between Rasha and Ze'ev was observed the day before Ze'ev met up with Adi."

Anger fickered in Matthew's eyes, "I'm aware of the meeting. It's quite clear that Rasha wants Ze'ev to lure Adi into marriage."

"Why would a man like Ze'ev want to marry a girl like Adi?" Thomas quietly asked.

"Like I said before, Ze'ev will do anything that will benefit himself. Rasha loves to promise people wealth and power. He tells them that they can be creators of their own destinies; they are responsible to no one. I'm sure that he gave quite a compelling speech to Ze'ev, promising him all these things if he would marry Adi!" Matthew shook his head in disgust.

Thomas' eyes widened with understanding, "Rasha doesn't want Adi to marry the Prince because then he loses control over her. He also knows that this would inflict great pain upon Joshua if Adi rejects him, and also it will ultimately destroy Adi!"

"Precisely, Thomas, now you see why she is in danger. We've got to show her the truth that's the only way she will be set free from Rasha's deception."

Thomas humphed, "Isn't that ironic? Ze'ev is deceiving Adi, and yet, he himself is being deceived!"

Matthew sadly nodded, "We hope that in the process of rescuing Adi, Ze'ev, too, will come to see the truth!"

"Ambassador, Michael says that Ze'ev will be taking Adi to the play *The Goddess of Soteria* tomorrow night at the Emerald Theatre on the boulevard." Gabriel informed. Matthew nodded deep in thought. "Gabriel, tell Michael that I will be there at the play. At the end of the play, it is imperative that I speak to Adi alone. He needs to distract Ze'ev as well as Rasha's horde who have also been following Adi. Understood?"

"Yes, sir." Gabriel hesitated a moment before asking, "Sir, what may I tell the King about the Prince?"

Matthew quietly responded, "The King already knows. It is His plan."

Gabriel hesitated, agony filling his vivid blue eyes, "May we protect the Prince?"

"Absolutely not. Did Joshua summon you? Did the King send you to him? No, they didn't. The contract with Adi must be fulfilled without any interference, do you understand?" Matthew snapped.

"Yes, sir." Gabriel crisply responded.

Softening his tone, Matthew laid a gentle hand on his

messenger's arm, "We are all grieving. It is difficult not to protect the one we love, but we must remember that all things will work together for good."

A tear gathered in Gabriel's eye, "Yes, sir." he whispered, swallowing hard.

Matthew stiffened, once again becoming authoritative, "Now, go. Give the orders to Michael and report to King Penuel."

"Yes, sir!" Gabriel saluted, clicked his heels, and quickly vanished into the night.

TEN

"Thanks for letting me spend the night, Ze'ev." Adi smiled gratefully at the man that stood before her. Glancing about the elegant bedroom that boasted of a queen size bed adorned with a soft, gold duvet and an abundance of colorful, silk pillows. "This is a beautiful room!"

Ze'ev reached out and began to massage Adi's shoulders, "You don't have to stay just one night, Adi. You can live here. Like I said before, you're my girl." He whispered seductively into her ear.

Adi stiffened. "Ze'ev, I need time..."

"Of course you do." Ze'ev snapped quickly dropping his hands to his side.

"I don't mean to hurt you! These past few days have been so overwhelming, and I just need time to sort it all out." Pleaded Adi.

Not wanting to push Adi away, Ze'ev softened his tone, "I really do understand, Adi, take all the time you need, but while you are recovering from your traumatic experiences, I want you to know you can stay here for as long as you need to."

"Thank you. That's very kind." Adi blushed.

"Hey, that's what friends are for, Adi!" Reaching into the drawer of the Queen Anne style nightstand, Ze'ev pulled out a CD entitled, *Delta Spirit*. Handing it to Adi he explained, "You look like you could use a deep relaxing sleep, this music will help."

Mystified, Adi took the CD and studied the picture of a beautiful cascading waterfall gracefully flowing over the majestic mountainside into a tranquil pool at its base. "How does this help me relax?"

"According to research, the brain responds to different noise frequencies. It's called binaural beats, and it helps the body heal itself. This CD primarily has the delta binaural beat which creates a rejuvenating, dreamless sleep. Just close your eyes and envision yourself floating away on the water! It really helps!"

Scrunching up her nose, Adi looked up, "What?" Ze'ev laughed, "Never mind. It's all the rage in Soteria. An acquaintance of mine gave it to me when I was under tremendous stress. I must say, it has worked for me. I feel much more peaceful and at ease. I guarantee you will feel much better tomorrow!" Leaning down, he gave her a quick playful peck on the cheek and walked to the door. Remembering one last final instruction, he turned and said, "Oh, it works best with headphones which are in the drawer of the nightstand. Goodnight, Adi." Winking, he closed the door.

Adi slowly undressed as she replayed the day's events in her mind. In the beginning, she had a hard time accepting that Ze'ev's concern for her was genuine, but now after he had gone out of his way to meet all her needs, she began to reconsider what she had first thought of him. She once had considered him to be conceited, arrogant, and completely self-centered, but the events of today had shown a different side to this man. He was gentle, thoughtful, and caring. He had even called her "his girl", if only that could be true, if only she could belong to someone such as he. What had held her back from giving herself over to him?

The memory of Prince Joshua looking deep into her eyes and declaring his love for her came back in answer to her private musings. She realized that it was the Prince that was holding her back from getting too comfortable with Ze'ev. *I must discover the truth about these two men first*, Adi decided. Feeling overwhelmed with fatigue, Adi slipped into the luxurious silk, purple sheets, giving a contented sigh as the mattress conformed to the contours of her body. Remembering her nightmare from the night before, she reached over to feel for the headphones in the drawer and then pressed play to listen to the relaxing music that Ze'ev had given her. A dreamless sleep is just what she needed tonight.

The ethereal sounds of synthesized strings and voices mixed with the melodic, rhythmic sounds of a waterfall floated through the headphones. Adi closed her eyes savoring the soothing sensations that calmed her mind and emotions. Visualizing herself floating lazily on the tranquil, blue lake, she began to sense every muscle as it released the tension and relaxed. She was one with nature, she was one with herself.

––––––––––

Unseen by Soterian eyes, a tall well built man with chestnut brown hair stood near Adi's bed. White feathery wings unfolded from his muscled back. He wore a snowwhite tunic with a glimmering silver sword at his side. Michael, who was sent to protect Adi by King Penuel, patiently waited. Satisfied that she was asleep, he quietly stopped the music and replaced the CD with soft piano solos. Leaning over, he gently pulled one headphone slightly away from her ear and whispered, "Prince Joshua loves you."

––––––––––

The gentle currents pulled her slowly along to the far side

of the lake away from the waterfall. Rolling onto her side on a flotation device, she stared in wonder as the mist from the waterfall swirled and danced in the air. As if in a synchronized fashion, each vapor came together to form a luxurious cascading bridal veil. Adi's dream followed the veil upward towards the mountain as it took the shape of a bride!

"Have you ever seen a magnificent waterfall cascading down the face of a mountain, Adi?" A voice broke into her dreams, "It looks like a woman's bridal veil. It anticipates the hope for a new way of life in union with King Penuel and Prince Joshua."

The voice sounded so familiar, Matthew, Joshua? Before she could look for them, the bride began to turn to face her. Adi strained to see who the bride was under the veil. Gently lifting the veil from her face, the bride smiled radiantly at someone unseen. Shock rippled through Adi at the same moment she heard the familiar voice call her name, "Adi, my love!"

The bride was her, however a beautiful clean pure version of her! Who was she smiling at with such love in her eyes? Who had called her by name? Ze'ev? With arms outstretched a man rushed toward the bride picking her up and twirling her. Their joyous laughter echoed throughout the mountainside. As the man slowly released his bride, he turned toward the watchful Adi. Adi's eyes widened at the sight of him. Joshua! There he stood in regal attire beckoning to her, "Come, Adi, I love you! I can make you pure and beautiful like her!" He said pointing to the Bride Adi.

"Joshua, I want to..."

"Adi, wake up!" Ze'ev's persistent voice broke into her dream.

"Joshua," she mumbled not wanting to leave this tranquil place.

Shaking her, Ze'ev demanded, "Wake up, Adi, you're having a nightmare!"

"I am?" Adi felt confused. Reluctantly, she opened her eyes and stared up at a worried Ze'ev. "What's going on?" She asked groggily.

"I came in here to check on you and found you crying out in your sleep. You sounded so terrified!" Ze'ev lied. "Oh." Adi's mind felt muddled. "Thanks. Sorry to have disturbed you."

Ze'ev shrugged, "You didn't disturb me. I was just checking to see if you were okay. I thought I had heard something." Noticing that the CD player had stopped, he pressed play again. "Maybe you need to listen to this again and just focus on relaxing, Adi. It will help." Reaching down, he playfully tousled her hair, "Goodnight!"

Bewildered, Adi sighed trying to remember her dream until the music caught her attention. She lay still listening. This wasn't the music that she had started off with when she had first fallen asleep! Curious, she flicked on the light and opened the lid of the CD player. Unable to read the turning CD, she turned it off and carefully read the title, "*Redeemed*, Piano Music of the King" she whispered. "Ze'ev must have taken the other one." Feeling a little unsettled, Adi flicked off the light and buried herself under the silky covers.

―――――――

Adi awoke the next morning feeling happier than she could remember. *Ze'ev's music must have worked!* She thought, but then remembered that it was a different CD than what he had put in. "Oh, well! It doesn't really matter. I'm going to have a great day today!" She exclaimed out loud as she jumped out of bed.

Quickly dressing into one of her new outfits and brushing through her tangled hair, she raced down the hallway with anticipation. Disappointment filled her. She didn't see Ze'ev anywhere. "Ze'ev, are you here?" She called.

"I'm in here! Just open the door!" A muffled voice responded.

Following the sound of his voice, she noticed a closed door just off the kitchen. Feeling hopeful again, she bounded across the kitchen and opened the door. Peering in, she saw Ze'ev sitting cross-legged on a mat, his back completely straight; hands turned palms up resting on his knees. The room was void of any furniture or wall hangings. Soft music was playing similar to the one he had loaned Adi last night.

"What are you doing?" Adi asked curiously.

"Meditating. It's a great way to start the day." Ze'ev opened his eyes and smiled. "Come sit with me, Adi." Adi looked apprehensively, "Oh, I don't know. I've never meditated before, seems kind of strange to me."

"Come on. I'll teach you." He patted to another mat next to him.

Shyly, Adi crossed over and sat on the mat in the same manner as Ze'ev.

Ze'ev laughed at Adi's obvious embarrassment. "You'll get used to it. Meditating has the power to change your life."

"How?"

"This world is full of negatives and our subconscious picks up on the negativity around us. When we constantly hear negative statements about ourselves we begin to believe them. Who do you think you are, Adi?"

Feeling uncomfortable, Adi looked down ashamed, "A thief. Trash. Poor." Tears rose to the surface. This was not a conversation she wanted to have.

Ze'ev gently laid a hand on her shoulder, "It's okay, Adi. I used to have a negative view of myself, too. It was shaped by other's opinions. Now that I have used this meditation, my view of myself and of my life has changed tremendously." He paused waiting for a reaction, when none came, he continued, "How would you like to see yourself, Adi?"

A tear slipped down her pale face, "Beautiful. Clean. Valuable. Wanted."

In an attempt to lighten the mood, Ze'ev joked, "Your wish is my command! I have the perfect meditation CD just for that." Ze'ev got up and left the room. A few moments later, he returned with another disc. "This one is for building self-esteem, which you are in desperate need of, my dear."

"I don't understand how that is going to help me."

"It's pure science and spiritual at the same time. We need to reprogram our minds, cleanse our thoughts from all negativity. You believe that you are ugly and a piece of unwanted garbage because you have been told that. Now, you need to embrace a new way of thinking. Science has discovered that our subconscious can retain information that is given on the binaural waves such as alpha, theta, and delta frequencies. Our conscious mind does not hear it, but our subconscious does. Listen to it enough times and our thoughts and beliefs about our world and ourselves will change. It's called subliminal messaging."

Mystified, Adi asked, "What does the message say?"

"For this CD, it affirms that you are beautiful, you are valuable, you are creative, you are divine, you are light. When you are relaxed and your mind is opened to these affirmations, you will begin to believe it and incorporate these positive things into your life. It's known as the law of attraction. If you think negatively, you will attract the negative. If you think positively, you will attract the positive. You have the power to change your life, your destiny. You are in control, you are the master painter!"

Adi slowly nodded, trying to absorb all the information. "It makes some sense, but I want to think about it first."

Annoyed, Ze'ev shrugged, "It's your canvas, Adi, not mine. The longer you delay, the more negative situations you will inherit. I would think that you'd be tired of that by now. Anyone who is anyone in Soteria is involved in this. It is our great destiny to bring Soteria into a new enlightened age. Mankind will take the next step in the evolution process and will possess all knowledge and power as we allow the divine spark to flow through us. You can either be a part of it or be left out to wallow in your pitiful self."

Adi's eyes widened with surprise as the meaning of the words made a painful impact. With a cry, she jumped up and fled to her room. Frustrated, Ze'ev ran a hand through his hair while letting out a stream of curses. After giving himself a few moments to calm down, he approached Adi's room.

"Adi, I'm so sorry for being rude. I was out of line." He waited by the door listening for a response. When none came, he pleaded, "Please, Adi, let me in so I can explain." Still no answer came. "I just said those things because I care. I want you to be all that you want to be and have all that you desire. I know it didn't sound like it, but I do really care."

The door opened to reveal a tear- streaked face. "You were really harsh, Ze'ev. What happened to positive thoughts? I would think that would cause a person to be positive with their words too." She spat out.

Ze'ev feigned humility, "You are so right, Adi, I'm sorry. Let's try this for something positive - I'm going to take you to a play tonight!"

Adi's face brightened, "Really? What's the name?" Ze'ev wiggled his eyebrows flirtatiously, *The Goddess of Soteria!*

"Ooh, sounds mysterious!" Adi gave a soft chuckle.

"Very. And today I will take you shopping for an evening gown! Those clothes we bought yesterday were for everyday wear, but not for a night at the theatre! Now let me see you smile so that I know you're still not angry with me."

Adi managed to give a small smile that satisfied Ze'ev. "Good. Now dry those tears and get ready. We need to leave in fifteen minutes for a lunch reservation!"

———

"Michael, I need a few moments alone with Adi tonight. At the end of the play, you need to get Ze'ev away from her." Matthew slowly paced deep in thought.

"Yes, sir. What of Rasha's horde who are also

following her? Do I engage them?"

"If need be. Do whatever is necessary for me to talk with her alone."

"Yes, sir!" Michael reached into his coat pocket and pulled out a CD case. "Here's the music that I retrieved from Adi's room."

Matthew read the CD, disgust showing on his face, "Delta Spirit." What will Rasha think of next?" He angrily threw the CD into the trash.

Thomas peered over the lip of the trashcan at the CD. "How is that dangerous?"

Matthew responded in a clipped tone, "Basically it's a form of brainwashing. Inside of everyone King Penuel has written a moral law and has given everyone a knowledge of himself. In an attempt to make himself complete ruler over Soteria, Rasha has gone to great lengths to erase all that King Penuel has done. Using subliminal messaging in music is an attempt to rewrite or reprogram Soterians. If successful, it will change their belief system and erase thoughts of King Penuel. Without their knowledge, he's preparing people to accept him when he takes control of Soteria."

"Do they know that there are subliminal messages in this music?"

"Some do but are fine with it because the message appeals to their desires. If someone wants to lose weight, their subconscious can listen to affirmations about losing weight. If they want great wealth, they can listen to statements such as 'The more money I obtain, the more good I can do.' or 'I attract prosperity'. They choose the meditation that they think will meet the need in their life. Follow?"

"But they don't actually hear the message?"

"No, but their subconscious does."

Looking troubled, Thomas inquired, "Then if they don't hear it consciously, then how do they know that what's being said is actually what they wanted and not something else? Just because the cover says these are the affirmations in the music doesn't mean that it is! Their subconscious could be absorbing something entirely different and be made to do things they would never have dreamed of doing!"

"Absolutely, Thomas. Only people with the proper equipment can strip it apart, but most don't have that equipment. This is a great deception by Rasha! That's why Michael took this CD from Adi and replaced it with the King's music." Turning to the silent Michael, Matthew commended him, "Good job on that, Michael, but continue intercepting the music. They are trying to brainwash Adi." To lighten the somber mood, Matthew looked at Michael with a playful smile, "Michael, I have another job for you to do."

Michael noticed Matthew's mischievous grin, "Sir?"

"Thomas, here, has been mystified ever since he first

met Gabriel. I explained to him that King Penuel has an invisible powerful army entrenched in Soteria, but since he's human he has a hard time comprehending what this means. Poor fellow." Matthew laughed, clapping Thomas on the back.

Turning red, Thomas defended, "Well, Michael looks human to me. . ." Before Thomas could utter another word, Michael had transformed himself into a glowing irridescent creature. In his hands, he held a flaming sword. When he moved, a powerful breeze swirled all around Thomas, who stood with lips parted, eyes wide, transfixed by the sight.

Laughing, Michael looked at Matthew, "I don't think Thomas is going to be speaking for awhile. He looks as if he might faint."

Amused, Matthew chuckled. "You're quite right, Michael. You had best be on your way, and I'll help poor Thomas."

"Yes, sir!" With a crisp salute, Michael disappeared from the room.

Matthew stood facing Thomas, "Thomas, snap out of it! We've got work to do!" He commanded.

ELEVEN

Adi turned from side to side looking in the mirror at the
evening gown she wore. She noticed the low-neck line and
grimaced. She didn't care for it, but Ze'ev said it made her
look more attractive and beautiful. Watching the purplish
black sequins sparkle in the light, she sighed frustrated
that she wasn't enjoying the moment. The day with Ze'ev
had been nice. He had gone to great lengths to smooth
things over with her, even taking her to a salon to get her
hair done and a manicure. Despite his kind efforts, Adi
still hesitated in trusting him. He had never cared before,
why now?

"Adi! We've got to leave now if we're going to make the play!" Ze'ev's voice broke into her thoughts.

"Coming!" She called out quickly draping a matching sequined shawl over her bare shoulders.

As she gracefully walked down the hallway toward Ze'ev, he let out a low whistle. "I'm going to be the envy of every man there!" He exclaimed.

Blushing, Adi brushed past him, "You don't look bad yourself," she teased.

"Why, thank you, love. I guess I'll take that as a compliment." He chuckled.

Adi just smiled, not responding. Hearing Ze'ev refer to her as his love grated on her, although she didn't understand why. Just then she heard a soft whisper near her ear, "Joshua loves you." Startled Adi gasped, turning to see who was standing behind her, but no one was there.

"Is something wrong, Adi?"

"Uh, no, I just thought I heard something. I guess it's nothing."

"Well, let's go. We can't be late." Ze'ev held the door open, waiting for her to pass so he could lock it.

As Ze'ev shut the door, a figure of a man emerged from the shadows. It was Michael.

Adi sat spell bound as she watched the play. It was her first time ever in a theatre, but that wasn't what held her attention. It was the tragic romance between a powerful king and a poor innkeeper. According to the ancient legend, Nimrod, the first king of Babylon, met and fell in love with the most beautiful innkeeper named Semiramus during one of his great military conquests. After the two married, he brought her back to his kingdom, making her his queen. Because of their kindness, love, and generosity, people began to worship them as a god and goddess. One day, Nimrod was forced to do battle against an opposing evil kingdom and during the fierce battle, Nimrod was killed, his body being ripped apart. In tribute to his memory, Semiramus deified him as Osiris or the sun-god. Shortly after, she gave birth to a son who she claimed was Nimrod reincarnated. From that time on, their story spread throughout the world. From culture to culture Nimrod's name changed to Baal, Orion, Apollo, Ra, Tammuz, and Osiris, as well as many others. Legends called his wife Fortuna, Aphrodite, Isis, Diana, Madonna, or Queen of Heaven. Adi found herself longing to be beautiful and adored like Semiramus. Oh, if everyone could love her like they did the queen.

As the play ended and the curtain did its final descent, Adi continued to sit there lost in reverie. Ze'ev smiled at her dream like expression.

Leaning closer to her, he whipsered, "From the expression on your face, I can tell you liked the play?" Embarrassed, Adi grinned sheepishly, "Oh, yes. It was a wonderful play!"

Noticing that her mood changed to one of sadness,

Ze'ev questioned, "What is it, Adi? What are you thinking?"

Adi shrugged, "I wish that I could be like her, beautiful and loved by everyone!"

Ze'ev looked at her thoughtfully before responding, "You can be. If you stay with me, I will make you a goddess and all of society will worship you. You'll never want for anything ever again, Adi."

Adi nodded quickly while standing up. Ze'ev followed suit, stepping out into the aisle.

Unknown by all, the theatre had been occupied by more than just Soterians. Lurking about were Rasha's horde— hideous, vile spirit-like creatures that could attach themselves to Soterians for the purpose of mind manipulation. A group of them had surrounded Ze'ev and Adi when they first walked into the theatre. During the play, they had whispered words of deception into Adi's ear, awakening the desires of power and lust. Now as the couple walked down the staircase, the group of grotesque spirits surrounded them.

To stand in opposition to Rasha's horde, King Penuel's able-bodied warriors stood poised and ready for Michael's command.

"As soon as we see Adi, convince Ze'ev to talk with you for a few minutes about a business proposal," instructed Michael. The tall, blonde haired man standing next to him nodded as he pulled at his bow tie. "I don't see why men have to wear bow ties. These things choke!" he mumbled. Michael chuckled, "At least you don't have to wear high-heeled shoes like women do! These are good reasons to be thankful that we are not Soterians!"

The man laughed but quickly sobered as he noticed movement along the coffee bar area. "Rasha's horde is here. If there's a fight, do I leave Ze'ev and join you?" "No. I'll handle it. Ze'ev must not know that you are a part of this. Keep him distracted."

Glancing up at the broad, red-carpeted staircase, the two defenders watched as the flow of people descended. Sensing Matthew's presence, Michael spotted him standing to the left of the stairs nearest the restrooms. Matthew was signaling with a slight nod of his head that he had spotted Adi and Ze'ev.

"Here they come," Michael whispered.

As the couple came into view, the blonde watched with disgust the trio of deceptive spirits that were twittering back and forth between Adi and Ze'ev. "Will they let me near Ze'ev?" The man asked.

"They won't recognize you as long as you stay in human form, but I'll still have to engage them to get them away from Adi or they'll never let Matthew near her." The two stood silently watching as the couple neared the bottom of the stairs. "Are you ready?" The man nodded. Brandishing his gleaming sword, Michael instantly transformed into an invisible light force. In unison, the man and Michael advanced upon the startled grotesque creatures. With a shrill cry, the demons attempted to raise their swords in defense, but it was too late. With one swoop of his sword, Michael sent the three deceivers into the invisible cavernous abyss that had opened up in the foyer floor.

As soon as the demons went tumbling into the abyss, three of King Penuel's defenders surrounded Adi, their swords raised in readiness for other attackers. Seeing that Adi was protected and Ze'ev free, the man calmly stepped up to him. "Ze'ev?"

Unaware of the intangible forces that had surrounded him, Ze'ev looked up in surprise at the sound of his name. A blonde man was extending his hand, "My name is Jordan. A friend of mine said that he saw you here and that you would be the perfect one to help me in my dilemma." Turning to Adi, Jordan shot her a pleading look, "Would you mind terribly if I snatch him away? I promise this won't take long."

Adi looked at the bewildered Ze'ev. "Of course, I'll just slip into the ladies' room a few moments." Excusing herself, she slipped away into the crowd while the blonde man pulled a reluctant Ze'ev toward the coffee bar chatting at full speed.

The flash of brilliant lights from King Penuel's forces instantly caught the attention of Rasha's hideous gang that was lurking about the coffee bar. With a mighty guttural roar, they charged toward the oblivious Adi. Michael intersected the first one, a small bat-like creature with green foam around his twisted mouth. Impaling the thing on his sword, Michael quickly flicked it into the abyss as if he were flicking a mosquito. Two more rushed towards the defender while a third skirted around the trio and headed for Adi. Gripping his sword tightly, a blinding bolt of light radiated from his hands bursting through the sword causing the disoriented demons to fall back. Holding the sword horizontally, Michael swung whipping them into the dark cavern. Quickly turning, he saw the angels who surrounded Adi were in full battle against a horde of sulfur-smelling, red-eyed beings. Just as he was about to strike at the mass, a powerful blow on his back sent him crashing into the stairs.

"Michael, you're fighting a losing battle. Adi belongs to my master!" A dark, snarling form loomed over the stunned Michael.

Gathering up his strength, Michael shouted back, "We'll let Adi decide that, Dagon!" Both looked in Adi's direction and watched as a warrior sent the last demon sailing into the abyss. Matthew stepped from a protected alcove, quickly pulling Adi into its shadows while the King's warriors formed a wall of flaming swords protecting Matthew and Adi. At the sight of Matthew, Dagon lunged with an angry roar across the foyer toward the

Ambassador.

A tall man began pulling her into the corner. Adi punched at the man's chest, but the grasp on her arms was too strong.

"Adi, quiet down, it's me, Matthew!"

Outraged, Adi hollered, "What are you doing?" Quickly covering her mouth, Matthew shushed her. "Adi, I have to talk to you! Just give me ten minutes and you're free to go! Will you be quiet?" Matthew looked away from her and out towards the foyer. Seeing Dagon thundering towards the wall of warriors and towards him, he knew he didn't have much time. Looking back at Adi he asked, "Well?"

Wide-eyed, Adi nodded her consent. Once satisfied that Adi wasn't going to shout again, Matthew released her. Staring at her intently, Adi could see the urgency in his eyes. "Adi, I've come to warn you about Ze'ev. He's not who you think he is."

"How do you know?" Adi retorted.

"He's a wolf in sheep's clothing who will say and do anything for wealth and power. Don't trust him."

Adi crinkled her nose in confusion, "He's a what?"
"A wolf in sheep's clothing. In other words, he's a con. Don't believe his flattery."

Angrily, Adi pushed Matthew back, "His feelings for me are real! He's given me a roof over my head, food, clothes, and love. He's promised me that I can be a goddess just like Semiramis!"

"Semiramis?" Matthew asked incredulously. "I know that the play made her and Nimrod out to be wonderful admirable people, but the truth is they were evil! Another legend has it that Semiramis' lust for power drove her to sacrifice her own husband. She had him ripped to pieces! In order to keep her power, she made her infant son king, and, of course, she ruled in his stead while he was too young. She led people to believe that Nimrod was a god and even suggested that her son, Damu, was Nimrod reincarnated. She deified her son and she herself became the Queen of Heaven, brainwashing everyone into thinking that the constellations told the story of King Penuel cruelly overtaking the rightful king's kingdom and that someday a son would be born of a divine woman. The son would grow up to be a god and reclaim the kingdom and give it back to the original king. The truth is that King Penuel is the rightful king and his kingdom was snatched away by evil." Matthew paused allowing this to sink in and then asked, "Do you know that when Damu grew up and could fulfill his role as king, Semiramis planned to have him killed?"

Adi slowly shook her head, eyes wide at the story. "What happened?" She whispered.

"Damu learned of the plot and killed her himself." Matthew's voice grew urgent, "Is this the woman you want to be, Adi? Ze'ev made promises of food, shelter, riches, and love. The Prince will do all those things for you and so much more, Adi. With Ze'ev you will never be satisfied, but with the Prince you'll never want for anything." Matthew shook his head despondent, "Don't be placated by temporal things."

"The Prince? Where is he now?" Adi grew indignant and embarrassed as Matthew pointed out her shallowness. "Sacrificing for you, Adi." Matthew responded quietly. A brilliant flash of light visible only to Matthew captured his attention. Michael had intercepted Dagon temporarily blinding him. Dagon wildly swung his sword in an attempt to slash Michael who stepped back raising his sword in a circling motion bringing it down onto Dagon's shoulder.

Seeing Matthew's concern and attributing it to her outburst, tears formed in Adi's brown eyes, "I'm sorry." Swallowing back a sob, she continued, "It's just so hard and so confusing. I need time to think."

Returning his attention to her, Matthew slowly nodded, "While you're thinking, Adi, ask yourself this question: would Ze'ev have taken your place in prison like the Prince has done?" Matthew glanced behind him staring intently at the battle. Dagon was retreating spewing sulfuric green slime and obscenities, "We will meet again, Michael. Don't think you've won!" With that threat, he disappeared. Breathing heavily from the exertion, Michael looked towards Matthew. Adi noticed Matthew give a nod at someone that she couldn't see. Confused, Adi looked in the direction of Matthew's gaze but saw only people milling around. Matthew turned back to her, giving a small smile, "You know where I am, Adi. I'll be waiting." Then he was gone.

Unseen by Soterian eyes, Matthew stood next to Michael. "Good job, Michael. Close up the abyss and keep Adi in your sights."

"Yes, sir. Any progress with her?"

Matthew tenderly watched Adi slip away from the alcove, "She's sensitive to what I tell her, but she does not trust easily. At least I've cast doubt in her mind about Ze'ev." Clapping the King's officer on the back, Matthew again complimented Michael, "Good job tonight. I had better get back to Thomas. He's a little put out that he could not come along."

The blonde- haired man looked past Ze'ev and into another world. Seeing that Michael was motioning for him to come, he turned his attention back to Ze'ev, "Thank you so much for giving me your time."

Ze'ev looked at him quizzically, "I don't understand. You said you wanted to discuss a business proposal."

"Oh, another time, another time." The man waved away Ze'ev's concern. Stopping suddenly, he turned with a word of warning, "Ze'ev, I wouldn't believe everything Rasha says."

"Rasha? How do you. . ." Ze'ev stood there dumbfounded looking at the milling crowd. The man was nowhere in sight.

"Ze'ev!"

He turned toward the voice calling him and saw Adi coming toward him. Noticing his perplexed expression she asked, "Is everything alright?"

Shrugging, Ze'ev mumbled, "Weird. The man just disappeared."

"Did he say what he wanted?"

"No, he just rambled on and on about the weather, who's playing in the championships, and stuff like that."

"But I thought he had to talk business?"

"That's what he said, and when I asked him, he just rushed off!" Ze'ev gave an exasperated sigh. "What a weirdo!"

Feeling a little unsettled about the strange encounters, Adi suggested that they return home. She wanted to escape to the privacy of her room to think about what Matthew had told her. Whom to believe, Matthew or Ze'ev?

Later that night, Adi sat curled up in her bed listening to the King's music CD she had found in the player. Without her knowledge, a dark formless shape cowered in the far corner of the room. Alternating between angry hisses and fearful whimpers, he looked furtively towards the nightstand. Michael stood attentively with arms crossed blocking the music player. A half hour earlier, Michael had discovered the hideous creature planting another CD called, *Discovering the Beauty of Self.*

Surprised by Michael's sudden appearance, the creature dropped the CD and fled to the corner, hissing his disapproval over the destruction of the music. Now they both were engaged in a standoff while Adi sat oblivious in her own thoughts.

Matthew had said not to trust Ze'ev, but how am I to trust Matthew whom I just recently met? Adi pounded a pillow in frustration. She thought back to the time when Ze'ev had approached Adi for drugs. He had promised her a cut in the profit if she added a little extra in each brick which normally would be about 5,000 mg, give or take. Ze'ev's plan was for Adi to add extra when measuring the heroin and then sell the drug at a lower cost, undercutting Rasha. The plan worked for a while until Rasha noticed that he was losing customers to an unknown dealer. Flying into a fit of rage, Rasha had threatened a torturous death to the dealer as well as to anyone who was helping him.

Terrified, Adi had gone to Ze'ev to collect the money owed Rasha before he could discover that it was his black tar that was being sold, but Ze'ev had just laughed and refused to pay leaving her frantic to find a way to pay back her stepfather. The only quick way to earn the money was to prostitute herself. Rasha never found out and was rather giddy about the extra money Adi had brought to him. Shame and guilt tore through Adi as she remembered these things.

"Matthew's right, Ze'ev can't be trusted! I'm such a

fool!" She exclaimed out loud. Michael smiled at the small victory, while the blob let out a sulfuric hiss. Angrily, Adi punched the pillow and crawled deep into the covers. *Tomorrow, I'm telling Ze'ev that I'm leaving. I can make it on my own.* She thought with determination.

The next morning, Adi dressed feeling a little apprehensive about Ze'ev's response to her decision to leave. A twinge of guilt hit her as she donned on a new pair of snug jeans and a lightweight silk sleeveless floral top. *How can you think of leaving when Ze'ev just bought you this outfit and many more?* The grotesque blob had ventured out from his corner during the night and now hovered near Adi, planting doubts into her mind. *You're wrong about Ze'ev, he's changed.* Michael glowered at the demon, but kept his distance. His orders were not to engage, Adi had to make the choice.

Before Adi could give into her thoughts, she quickly undressed replacing her new outfit for her old torn clothes. "I am not going to owe anyone anything!" She declared out loud. With resolve, she yanked her bedroom door open and marched down the hallway.

She found Ze'ev sitting in the lotus position in his meditation room. "Ze'ev, I need to talk to you."

Without opening his eyes, he calmly stated, "I'll be with you in a moment, Adi."

Impatience gnawed at Adi. She wanted to make this quick before she changed her mind. "I need to talk to you now, Ze'ev!" Adi demanded.

Ze'ev let out a frustrated sigh. Standing up to face Adi, he placed his hands on his hips to show that he did not appreciate the interruption. "Fine. What's so important that it can't wait?"

Suddenly unsure of herself, Adi fumbled, "Uh, I've been doing a lot of thinking, and I've decided that it would be best if I moved out." Seeing alarm on Ze'ev's face, she rushed on, "I appreciate all that you have done for me, Ze'ev, but I really want to try making it on my own. I need to discover who I am!"

Ze'ev ran a hand through his hair, frustrated, "Adi, don't you get it? That's what I'm trying to do for you! I'm helping you see who you are and what you can be! The problem is that you won't try anything that I tell you!"

Adi wavered. *Don't trust him,* Michael whispered into her thoughts. "I just have to do this on my own. I've always been under Rasha's control, and now I'm free! I need to have time to think my own thoughts, discover what I want to do. Can't you understand that?"

Ze'ev threw his hands up in the air in exasperation. "Again, that's what I'm trying to help you with! Remember last night you wanted to be like Semiramis, a goddess? You already are one. Everyone has the divine spark inside of them; they just have to tap into its energy. I can show you how to reach your full potential to be a goddess and accumulate wealth and power. You really think you can do that on your own?"

"If everyone's a god, then why is there poverty and sickness everywhere?" Adi shot back.

"Because people are still stuck in their old brainwashed ways of thinking that there is a higher power even though they can't agree on who the higher power is. With this weak-minded thinking, they are crippling society. Until they accept that *they* are the higher power and begin to evolve into their powers, we will still have poverty and sickness." A spark of anger flickered in Ze'ev's eyes. Adi fidgeted. She didn't feel like a powerful goddess, on the contrary, she felt weak and worthless. Picking up on her hesitation, Ze'ev crossed over to her and held her hands, "Adi, don't you want to be a part of this New Soteria? You don't want to miss out!"

Warning bells went off in her head, "Miss out? If Soteria changes, why would I miss out? What will happen to those who believe differently?"

Ze'ev replied in a low husky voice, "They'll believe."

"But what if some don't?"

Ze'ev's face hardened as he dropped her hands. "Go, Adi. I see that you don't trust me, nor will you listen to me. Go find out for yourself."

Confused by Ze'ev's sudden change in demeanor, Adi turned to leave. "Adi," Ze'ev's voice softened, "I understand. If you need me, I'm here. I'll be waiting for you."

Without another word, Adi rushed out of the room leaving Ze'ev watching after her. A scowl of contempt spread across his face. What was Rasha going to say when he found out that he was unsuccessful in gaining Adi's heart? He knew Rasha would somehow find out, he always did. It would be better if he heard it from him first, Ze'ev decided, reaching for the phone. A slithering voice answered at the other end. Ze'ev cleared his throat in hopes to feign confidence, "Tell Rasha, we need to meet asap," a slight pause, "same place." Ze'ev hung up. His hands were shaking. He went back into his meditation room in an attempt to detach himself from his troubles.

Kristen Zuray

TWELVE

As the front door closed with finality behind Adi, the full impact of her decision overwhelmed her. Maybe she had just made a mistake and ought to turn around and beg Ze'ev to overlook her lapse in judgment. Or maybe she should give Matthew a call. Taking a deep breath to calm her pounding heart, she squared her shoulders with determination. No, she was going to make it on her own without anyone's help. She will not live indebted to anyone.

Adi slowly made her way to her favorite park. Whenever Rasha sent her on a mission to the upside of

Soteria, she would treat herself to a few moments of relaxation in the park. It was fun watching the children ride their bikes and scooters or begging their moms for ice cream when the ice cream truck came by. As she watched from her favorite bench, she saw a mother kneel down next to her four year old daughter. Adi wondered for the hundredth time what it would have been like to have a mother. Rumor had it that Adi's father and mother had been killed by a drive-by shooting while taking an evening stroll. At five years of age, Adi had been left standing in shock while watching her parent's life's blood flow from their twisted bodies. One of Rasha's men who was hiding in the shadows took pity on the small girl and took her to Rasha for protection. From that point on Rasha trained her in stealing and drug dealing. No one would suspect a little girl with an angelic face! A commotion of quacking and squawking tore Adi away from her reverie. She watched as the mother and daughter threw pieces of bread towards the ducks swimming in the serene lake. The little girl giggled as the ducks abandoned their swim to swarm around her, quacking and pecking for more bread.

Michael stood nearby keeping a diligent watch over Adi.

Unbeknownst to Adi, across the lake a sinister meeting was taking place.

"I failed," Ze'ev looked as penitent as he could, which really wasn't too difficult. He hated the way his heart pounded when he was in the presence of Rasha.

An uncomfortable silence followed Ze'ev's confession. At last Rasha let out a low hiss, "What do you mean you failed?"

Ze'ev shifted nervously on the park bench. He didn't dare look at the evil man next to him; instead he focused on the ducks swimming on the lake before him. "Adi decided to leave me. She wanted to make it on her own, to discover who she is."

Rasha began to chuckle and then threw his head back in a loud fit of laughter. Ze'ev didn't know whether to be relieved or terrified, but curiosity got the better of him. "What's so funny?" He ventured.

Rasha quickly wiped the tears from his eyes. "That must have been a blow to the ego!" He jabbed Ze'ev hard in the ribs. Ze'ev winced but said nothing. "Here you are, the most sought after man in Soteria, and you got turned down by a street tramp!" Rasha laughed again, but the humor was lost on Ze'ev. When Rasha quieted down he asked, "Didn't you tell her that she could be rich and famous?"

"Yes! I gave her the music to listen to. I invited her to meditate with me. I even took her to the play, *The Goddess of Soteria!* That's what doesn't make sense! She wants to be like the goddess of the play, she wants to be famous, and wealthy! I don't understand why she left."

Rasha was silent. Ze'ev sneaked a peek to gauge the

man's emotion. What he saw sent chills throughout his body. The veins in his neck and temple were popping out, leaving purplish streaks throughout his skin. His crimson face contorted in rage while green ooze dribbled from the corner of his mouth causing a sulfuric odor. Ze'ev quickly looked away and once more stared at the ducks.

"Matthew." Rasha finally growled.

"Matthew?"

"Yes, this is Matthew's doing. He and his dominions." Confused, Ze'ev defended, "But Adi hasn't seen Matthew in awhile. She's been with me! I've made sure of that!"

"You idiot!" Rasha lashed out causing Ze'ev to shrink back in the bench. "Matthew and his warriors were there last night at the play."

"But how? I didn't see ...warriors? What warriors?"

"Of course you didn't see them, they're not of this world. My shedim reported that Matthew with his winged creatures sabotaged last night."

Ze'ev scrunched up his face in confusion, "Winged creatures? Shedim? What are you talking about?" Impatiently Rasha retorted, ""Matthew's winged creatures are his warriors, his dominion that fight against the Shedim which works for me! They, too, are not Soterians, but are helping Soteria move into the New Age! You must learn to listen to them, Ze'ev!"

"How and why?"

"Through meditation. Through your chakra! They will

come to you when you learn to relax and open your mind. I will send you Semyaza, and she will instruct you on how to accomplish our goals and to get in touch with your divinity."

"I would like that!" Ze'ev felt a rush of excitement at the thought of power.

Rasha broke through Ze'ev's daydream. "Don't worry about Adi. I'll have her running back to you and when she does, you had better accept her with open arms." He warned.

"Open arms? More like a slap on the face!" Ze'ev huffed indignantly.

"Put your ego aside, Ze'ev, and show her love, love, love." Sarcasm oozed from the brute's mouth.

"But I showed her that and look where it got me!"

"Ze'ev, the moment you get a ring on her finger, I'll give you half of Soteria to rule over!" Rasha continued quietly wooing Ze'ev with promises of power and wealth. Ze'ev sat there hypnotized by the drone of Rasha's voice. Lust, greed, and pride burned within him. A duck quacked snapping Ze'ev out of his trance. Looking about, he was surprised to see that Rasha had vanished. Ze'ev jumped up and rushed toward home with eager anticipation to invoke Semyaza.

Weeks passed since Adi left Ze'ev. Things were not turning out as she had imagined, and her determination to make it on her own was diminishing. Finding a job was harder than she had expected. Every day Adi went from storefront to storefront asking if they were hiring, but the managers just glared at her and sent her away. "Why would I want a thief working for me?" was a common question. With all the stress of the trial, Adi hadn't realized how publicized and well-known she had become. It was as if someone warned them in advance that she would be asking for a job. Her appearance didn't help matters either. She regretted not bringing some of the new clothes that Ze'ev had bought her.

Adi thrust her hands into her ragged coat as she stared hungrily at a diner's overflowing trashcan. Memories washed over her as she remembered the plentiful food in Ze'ev's cupboards. "Maybe I ought to return to Ze'ev," she thought despondently, but pride welled up inside. "No, I said I'll make it, and I will. I'm not going to grovel back to him!" Adi declared out loud. Just then a movement to the side of her caught her attention. A man with a long unwashed beard and claw-like yellowed nails stared hungrily at the trashcan. Adi crinkled up her nose as the smells of urine and body odor polluted the air around her. Staring at the bedraggled man with disgust, she realized that he was about to plunge into her trashcan! Panic surged through her as his crazed eyes challenged her. As if someone had shot a gun into the air, both lunged toward the garbage in a furry of desperation. With determination she held tightly onto the opposite side of the can and leaned across the opening blocking the man. Bellowing in rage, the man grabbed at her with his claws yanking her off with incredible strength. Adi slowly stood to her feet watching the raving man throwing out crumpled papers and empty bottles. She knew if she didn't claim this trashcan, she may not be able to find another meal for awhile. Gathering her courage and strength, she lowered her head and charged the man like a bull charging a matador. Flinging her full weight into the man, she knocked him to the ground. Surprised that he had gone down so easily and not wanting to waste any time, she dove both arms into the trash frantically sifting through the garbage to find her one meal for the day. Pulling out a half eaten burger, a fistful of greasy french fries, and a mega sized plastic cup half empty with diluted soda, Adi jumped away from the transient's leather hands grasping for her ankles. "Run, Adi!" Her mind screamed. She ran for several blocks until she was out of breath. Slowing down to a walk, Adi found a dark doorway in an empty alley to hide for the night. Staring at her meager sustenance, she wondered how she had arrived to this point in her life. At least with Rasha she knew she would be able to eat. The only fond memory of her life with Rasha was when he would purchase her favorite food or even take her out to a restaurant to reward her when she brought in extra money. Upon consuming her simple meal, Adi pulled her coat closer around her, snuggling down as best she could for the long night ahead.

————————

Michael recognized the bearded man instantly as being one of Rasha's Shedim. Arman was often sent disguised as a Soterian to bring pain to those who crossed Rasha. He was the one responsible for the brutal death of Tim McGyver, a convenience store owner who snitched to the police about a drug deal. When the police raided the old dilapidated barn on the outskirts of the city and arrested some of Rasha's prime sellers, he was fit to be tied vowing to find out the person who had revealed the location. A week later, Tim McGyver was found beaten beyond recognition. His broken body had then been shoved in a portable ice cream freezer. There were no witnesses. Eventually the police dropped the case because the mystery killer had vanished into thin air without a trace, literally.

Now Arman stood near Adi disguised as a smelly, half-starved transient. His mission was to make life as difficult as he could for Adi in order to force her back into the arms of Ze'ev. It was because of him threatening that he would kill anyone who gave Adi a job, that Adi was still wandering the streets. Hatred smoldered in the demon's eyes as he silently challenged Adi to the contents of the trashcan. He failed to see Michael standing in the shadows of an outdoor stairwell watching intently. As soon as Arman grabbed Adi and flung her backwards to the ground, Michael stepped out poised and ready to defend his charge.

"Rush him, Adi." Michael whispered into her thoughts. "NOW, Adi!"

Adi ran, throwing her full weight at the man, but her 110- pound frame was no match for Arman, and Michael knew this. Gripping his sword tightly, a beam of light burst from the sword. The force knocked Arman off his feet, stunning him long enough for Adi to find her food. Michael grabbed a hold of Adi's thin arms, "Run, Adi!" He yelled as he flared out his massive wings to form a wall between her and Arman.

Arman lay sprawled on the concrete, his physical body morphing back into his animal-like form, a goat face with two sharp horns curling up from his forehead. Green slime foamed from his mouth as he struggled to pull his massive frame up. Unfolding his scaly, 3- foot bat-like wings, he hovered, prepared to fight what had to be one of King Penuel's warriors. Looking around, he saw no one. Letting out a stream of curses, he flew away in search of his victim. Michael found Adi curled up in a dark doorway slowly munching on her fries. Compassion welled up inside of him as he stared at the lonely sight. Unfolding his wings, he stood forming a supernatural canopy over Adi, shielding her from Arman.

———

"How is Adi?" Matthew asked in a hushed tone. Gabriel took a sip of his coffee and glanced about the quaint coffee shop for any signs of the Shedim. It was a noisy little place with baristas shouting orders and clanging ceramic plates and cups as they hurriedly filled orders. The espresso machine gave a loud hiss as steam escaped into the air. All was well.

"Michael says she is beginning to doubt her decision to leave Ze'ev, but at the same time is remaining determined to make it on her own." Gabriel responded. "There is a Shedim that has threatened business owners not to hire Adi. She's been unable to procure a job."

Lost in thought, Matthew stared into the rich milky swirls of his latte. At last he looked up and asked, "Arman's been assigned to her hasn't he?"

"Yes, sir."

"What's a Shedim?" Thomas' voice broke into the conversation.

Matthew looked heavily at him. "The Shedim is a group that works for Rasha. They are invisible hideous, vile creatures of the most evil sort that torment people in their minds. They can take on physical forms or they can possess people, making them do horrific acts. Arman is a bloody murderer. He's behind the mass killings that have occurred in the past, and he's the one that is behind the disappearances you hear on the news." Looking back at Gabriel, Matthew stated soberly, "If Arman has been sent to follow Adi, it means that Rasha is planning to..." Matthew stopped, clenching his teeth in anger.

Puzzled, Thomas asked, "Planning to what?"

Ignoring Thomas, Matthew stared at Gabriel, "Tell Michael I'll visit her in a few days. We'll use Rasha's shunning of Adi to our advantage. In the meantime, Michael is to help her just enough to deter her from going back to Ze'ev."

"Yes, sir." Gabriel took his last swallow of the bitter brew and left the table.

Thomas watched Gabriel as he walked out the door and vanished. No one seemed to notice. Turning his attention back to Matthew he inquired, "Why don't we just go get Adi and bring her back?"

"I wish we could, Thomas, but it's not that simple. Adi has a free will to make her own decisions. For now, she's on the fence as to whom to trust, Ze'ev or Prince Joshua?" Thomas gave a small snort, "That seems to be an easy decision to me!"

"To you, maybe, because you know King Penuel, Prince Joshua, and me. Adi doesn't know us yet. It's harder for her to understand what the truth is when she's surrounded by a world filled with lies."

"Then how will she ever know?" Thomas frowned in concern, the first sign of compassion for Adi's predicament. Folding his arms, Matthew leaned back in his chair. "Well, all we can do is to continue to give her truth whenever possible. Rasha's plan is to keep Adi homeless, hungry, and shunned. He knows that when people are at their lowest emotional and physical point, they will turn to anything that will get them out of their predicament whether it's drugs, sex, religion, sports, anything. When life is crushing, Soterians are more open to being seduced into believing lies. On the flip side, I, too, can use the same opportunity to present them with truth about King Penuel and of Prince Joshua and the love they have for them, and to give them the opportunity to choose to be apart of Miskana someday. Everyone has a crushing moment in life, and it is in these times a person can either choose to believe the empty promises of Rasha or the eternal hope of King Penuel."

Thomas nodded, "It makes sense because that is when they are most vulnerable."

"Exactly."

"So, you're not visiting Adi right away because you want to make sure that she is ready to hear the truth?" Thomas ventured.

"That's right."

"Isn't that dangerous, because what if Arman influences her before then?"

"That is why Michael is there watching over her. He is there not to stop Arman from swaying Adi, but to give her an alternative way of thinking. Arman can't choose for Adi anymore than I can force her to accept Prince Joshua. All either side can do is to influence her. In the end, it's her choice."

Thomas furrowed his brow, letting out a big sigh, "This

is going to be hard!"

Matthew slowly nodded in agreement, "Yes, Thomas, it is difficult."

———

With each passing day and no hope for a job, Adi grew more and more despondent. A chill was in the air announcing that fall had arrived, and winter would soon be following. Panic gripped her mind as she stepped out of Birches hamburger restaurant. Once more the manager had laughed at her, "A job? You seriously think that I would give you a job? You're a felon!"

"No, I'm not! I was never convicted! I was pardoned!" Adi retorted.

"Pardoned? That's not what I heard; it was more like a temporary suspended sentence. If the Prince wants out of his promise or you reject his offer, then you're in the slammer paying for your crimes. Why don't you go back to your father?" The manager sneered.

"Step-father," Adi corrected him through clenched teeth. Desperation took hold, "Look, I know I messed up, but doesn't everybody? All I need is a second chance!"

The tall man leaned over the counter and looked her in the eyes, "I don't need a daughter of Rasha's working for me. Now get out of here, you're disturbing the customers!" The manager turned away indicating that the conversation was over.

Angrily, Adi stormed out of the restaurant fully aware

of the people watching her. Tears streaked down her cheeks as the chilled wind whipped through her thin coat. Her stomach cramped, reminding her that she hadn't eaten in two days. The tantalizing smell of hamburgers grilling was more than she could bear. *I've got to go back to Ze'ev.* She thought.

Arman gave Michael a triumphant smile. He had succeeded in convincing Adi to return to Ze'ev. Nonplussed, Michael held out his clenched hand toward Arman. Unclenching his fingers, Arman leaned forward to see what Michael was holding. A fifty- dollar bill materialized in his hand. The two locked eyes in a challenge. A small smile slowly spread across Michael's angelic face as he dropped the bill at Adi's feet. Arman lunged toward it before Adi could notice, but Michael whipped out his sword holding it up in front of the creature's face.

Adi stood there, defeated. As she looked at the bustle of people along the sidewalks, something floated on the air before her. Adi ignored it assuming that it was a leaf. She shuffled out onto the sidewalk oblivious to the help that had just been provided.

Arman chuckled with delight. Spotting a cat skulking near the entry- way of the restaurant, Michael flared his wings. The cat froze. Exasperated, Michael pulled out his sword and gave the terrified cat a gentle prod. Jumping and screeching, the cat tore out of her shocked state and ran for cover.

A loud screech caused Adi to jump. Turning to see what the commotion was, she saw a fluffy, white cat take off on a dead run down an alley. What was that all about? Adi wondered. Staring at the ground where the cat had been, a movement caught her eye. Slowly walking toward the green fluttering object, hope welled up within her. Could it be? She couldn't believe her eyes! Fifty dollars? Quickly picking it up, she shoved it in her pocket before anyone could claim it. The tantalizing smell of food captured her attention. With resolve, she marched back into Birches.

"I would like to order the bacon cheeseburger deluxe sandwich, curly fries, and a large cherry soda." Adi looked smuggly at the cashier.

Turning at the sound of her voice, the manager stormed over to Adi. "You can't order food here!"

"Why not, I've got money!" Adi pulled out the bill from her pocket.

"You probably stole it." The manager yanked the bill from her hand, holding it up to the light to check for counterfeit.

"No, I didn't steal it. Now I'm a paying customer, so I shouldn't be denied food."

The manager stared at her with distaste. "Give her the food and get her out of here!" He stormed away as he handed the money to the cashier.

Several minutes later, Adi stood outside with her first real meal in days and change in her pocket besides. Her mood lightened to match the beautiful sunny day despite the chilly breeze. She was about to head to the park, when a woman's voice stopped her.

"Just a minute, young lady!"

Adi whirled around coming face to face with an elderly lady. Her shoulders were stooped as she leaned heavily upon a cane. "I couldn't help overhearing your conversation with that rude manager. I was on my way to drop some clothing off at a thrift store, but if you'd like, you can sift through the bags first and choose what you'd like. I believe you should be able to find some clothes your size." The woman gave a warm smile and shuffled off toward her car.

Cautiously, Adi followed. The genteel woman rummaged through her purse while muttering how one can never find anything in purses. Giving a relieved cry, she triumphantly held up her keys and unlocked the door. Stepping back so Adi could take a look, she waved her hand toward the five bags of clothing. "Go on, don't be shy."

Eagerly Adi grabbed one bag after another quickly sifting through the clothes. Ten minutes later, Adi stood with a bag of clothing in her arms while still clutching her cooling food. "Thank you, so much!" A tear slipped down Adi's face.

"I wish I could do more." The elderly woman sighed

sadly.

"You've done a great deal! Thank you!" Adi reluctantly turned away. Upon reaching the edge of the parking lot, she turned and gave a small smile and a final wave. With lightness in her step, she headed off towards the park to enjoy her meal.

Michael looked over at the woman and watched as she transformed into a warrior. "Good job, Jordan. Did you know this was the first time Adi has said 'thank you'?" Jordan, an angel assigned to Michael's command, grinned, "Her heart must be softening, sir!"

"Yes, it appears that way. I will never understand why Soterians insist on being broken first before they will listen to the truth. It seems to me that they could avoid a lot of pain if they just set aside their pride in the very beginning." Michael gave an exasperated sigh and roll of the eyes.

A loud beating of wings and a rush of air swept over them. Looking up they saw an angry Arman catching up with Adi. Before Michael could move to follow, a brilliant light descended before him. Squinting against the brightness, Michael recognized Gabriel.

"Michael, I have a message for you from Matthew," Gabriel announced.

"What is it?"

"He wishes to speak with Adi at the park. Your orders are to engage the enemy."

Nodding at Jordan, Michael unsheathed his sword

with a flourish, "Then we'd best get going. Arman is already in pursuit of Adi." Without wasting time Michael and Jordan shot up into the air gripping his sword. Light shot out, streaking the sky rallying other warriors in his command to follow. Gabriel watched as King Penuel's dominions streaked across the sky towards the park.

———

Rasha sat at the dingy kitchen table taking stock of his valuable white powder when he sensed within his spirit that King Penuel's dominions were on the move. Without a word to his employees, he yanked the side door open and stood looking up at the light streaked sky. Growling, he marched off vanishing into the air. His Soterian dealers looked at one another in confusion unable to understand what Rasha saw.

Rasha stood in a darkened alley and let out a roar that reverberated against the brick buildings. At once, the sky above the alley turned black with monstrous creatures. One massive being with abs of steel, calves solid as tree trunks, arms that boasted of bulging muscles, and penetrating red eyes glided to a stop in front of Rasha. Bowing respectfully, he questioned, "You summoned, Master?"

"King Penuel's warriors are on the move, did you not see them?" Rasha bellowed.

Keeping his head lowered, Dagon answered, "Yes, sir. We were waiting for your command, sir."

Rasha sent a smashing blow to the side of his subject's horned head sending him sprawling on the ground. "Don't you dare blame your slowness on me, you insolent fool!" he yelled.

Anger and pain ripped through Dagon. He continued to lay there knowing that if he stood before Rasha commanded him to, Rasha would possibly send him to the abyss himself as he had done to others in the past. That was how he got to be the commander of Rasha's Shedim. The previous commander made the mistake of standing too early, and Rasha saw that as a challenge to his authority. He opened the abyss and cast the startled creature in before he could realize what was happening. As humiliating as it was to lay there on the cold damp ground before all his warriors, Dagon thought it was better than being sent to the abyss before his time.

"I am sorry, sir." Dagon attempted to control the tremor in his voice.

Rasha paced, not hearing him. "If Michael is gathering his command, it must mean that Matthew is about to pay Adi a visit, and he's given the order to engage." Chuckling with sick amusement, he rubbed his hands together, "Then engage we will!" Green ooze flowed from his mouth, his red eyes glowing brilliantly as the lust of war burned within.

Finally remembering his commander, he looked disgustedly at the prone Dagon. Giving him a harsh kick to

the side, he shouted, "Get up! Fight the angels!"
Dagon jumped to his feet, unfurling his massive expanse of
wings, "Yes, sir!"

In one accord, the creatures flew into the air with
shrieks that would fill any Soterian with terror if they could
have heard them.

————————

Spotting her favorite bench that overlooked the lake, Adi
smiled with relief. Feeling a contented happiness, she
skipped and twirled her way to the green bench. She sat a
moment savoring the warmth of the sun. Even the chilly
wind seemed a bit warmer and gentler. Her stomach
rumbled reminding her of her now lukewarm hamburger.
She didn't mind, though. How could she? With money in
her pocket, a bag of clothes by her side, and a real meal,
nothing would dampen the joys of this day. After eating,
she would look through her bag and admire the treasures
she had gleaned earlier.

Just as he was about to prompt a dog to snatch the
cheeseburger from Adi's hand, a streak of light pulled
Arman's attention toward the sky. Michael with his
dominion of warriors rushed towards him. In close pursuit
was the Shedim. A fierce rage coursed through Arman as a
loud battle cry roared from his mouth. He shot into the air
whirling his sword around and around his head.
Summoning all his strength, he brought the sword down
onto Michael, slicing his wing. Michael spiraled

downward, unable to right himself. Arman watched with a satisfied smile. Hot pain seared through his chest as Jordan twisted his sword into Arman's spirit, but it was not enough to disable Arman completely. In an effort to deflect Justin's blows, Arman used one expansive wing as a shield while the other beat Jordan back. Arman was well known for the brutal beatings that he could inflict with just his muscled wings.

Others of King Penuel's warriors attempted to form a wall of protection around Adi, but the Shedim were great in number. Their constant attacks prevented the warriors from getting near Adi. Matthew stood hidden in the small cluster of trees watching the battle. Brightly colored leaves of orange and red swirled about his feet. If he was going to talk to Adi, it had to be now while the Shedim were occupied.

Adi was about to take another big bite into her sandwich when she heard a voice behind her, "You'd better slow down or you'll make yourself sick!"

Adi froze, heart thumping as Matthew came into view and sat down next to her on the bench. Self-consciously she pulled her torn overcoat tightly around her in an attempt to hide her filth. In spite of her attempts to clean up, she eventually found it was impossible to do without access to a shower and soap. Overtime, she had become accustomed to the body odor. Now as she sat next to Matthew, she became very aware of how she looked and smelled. Why was it that she always felt unworthy in Matthew's presence? She didn't like it one bit. Grudgingly, she scooted farther away from him.

"What do you want?" She mumbled.

"I heard that you had left Ze'ev and so I wanted to see how you were doing," Matthew stated simply.

Adi finally looked at him, perturbed, "Are you stalking me? How do you know where to find me all the time?"

Matthew chuckled, "I have my ways of knowing where you are. It's my job to protect you."

"Protect me from what?"

"Yourself. From others who wish you harm."

Adi sighed shoving a French fry into her mouth, "I never understand you."

Both sat silently watching the wind create ripples on the surface of the lake. The rustle of trees swaying gently interrupted the peaceful afternoon. A warrior fell with a thump at Matthew's feet. Grasping his abdomen and breathing hard in pain and exertion, he slowly stood to his feet. Giving Matthew a respectful nod, he retreated into the woods for cover, giving his wounds time to heal.

A blackened spirit with two faces and two forked orange tongues dove towards Adi in an attempt to whisper deception into her thoughts. Matthew reached out grabbing the thing by his throat and sent him hurling through the atmosphere. The battle was fierce, but King Penuel's dominion was on the offensive driving the Shedim back.

Adi gave a startled jump when Matthew reached up and batted at something above her head. Assuming that he was saving her from a dangling spider or a pesty bee, she mumbled her thanks.

Matthew turned his full attention towards her. "You haven't answered my question as to how you are doing." Shoving the straw into her mouth, she stared at the ground. "I'm fine," Adi spoke around the straw.

Matthew stared at her with such compassion, "You don't look fine, Adi. You're cold and half-starved." No response.

"Why is it so difficult for you to come to me?" Matthew pleaded.

Tears welled up in Adi's eyes, "Because I feel so dirty and. . .and. . ." She searched for a word then blurted, "UNworthy!"

Matthew pressed his lips together, hope welling up inside, "Adi, look at me." When she refused, he stated in a firmer voice, "Look at me, Adi." When Adi at last looked at him, she was amazed to see love not judgment shining through his deep brown eyes. "I can fix all that for you. If you accept Prince Joshua's proposal, your life will be come new. All the guilt that you carry around will be gone! No longer will you feel unworthy, but instead you'll feel accepted, loved, the daughter of a great King! And Adi, I'll be with you every step of the way showing you and teaching you about how to be a princess!"

By now Adi was sobbing, "Oh, Matthew! If that could only be true!"

Matthew gripped her hand sensing that she was close to accepting it. "It is true, Adi! You only have to believe!"

Adi stared tearfully at Matthew, "Matthew, I..."

Just then terrible wails and shrieks were heard in the unseen world while simultaneously a male Soterian voice was heard, "Adi! There you are. I've been looking for you!" Adi turned, surprised at the mention of her name. Alarmed, Matthew noticed the tide had turned in the battle. More Shedim had accompanied Ze'ev to the park. Noticing the ensuing battle, they rushed ahead to join their compatriots. The King's warriors fought bravely but were being forcefully driven back towards the woods. Angels spiraled downward with torn and battered wings. Matthew was running out of time.

Adi shrank at the sight of Ze'ev walking towards her, looking clean- shaven and as handsome as ever. She remained silent, confused at the conflicting emotion that overwhelmed her. A part of her felt relieved to see someone familiar, but at the same time she drew inward with revulsion and distrust.

Ze'ev frowned at the sight of Matthew who sat there refusing to give up his seat. Ignoring him, Ze'ev purposely slid onto the opposite side of Adi forcing her to slide in the middle. Her beautiful lunch was just getting worse. Ze'ev placed an arm around Adi gently giving her shoulders a squeeze, all the while giving a challenging smile to Matthew. Matthew continued to glare.

"I've been looking for you, Adi," Ze'ev repeated.

Adi craned her neck to make eye contact, "You have?"

"Yes, and then I remembered that this was our favorite spot. My spirit sensed that you would be here on such a beautiful day." Ze'ev said smugly emphasizing the word, our.

Embarrassment flushed Adi's face, "I don't remember us coming here, Ze'ev."

Matthew arched an eyebrow in amusement while Ze'ev fought to hide his frustration. "You poor dear, you look half-starved!" Ze'ev quickly changed the course of the conversation. Sniffing at Adi, he crinkled his nose, "And you smell terrible! When was the last time you showered?" Adi shoved the remaining fries into the paper bag. Before she could respond, Ze'ev's voice continued with false concern, "Adi, dear, why don't you come home with me! I've promised to take care of you, and I will!"

Adi shifted uncomfortably on her seat, fully aware of Matthew's gaze upon her. "I - I- can't."

"But winter is coming, Adi. There's no way you'll survive! I can provide you with shelter, food, clothing, and so much more."

Adi hesitated as she envisioned the restaurants that Ze'ev had taken her to. The wind was growing colder and stronger while the sun disappeared behind darkening clouds.

"Maybe you're..." Adi began.

"Adi, the Prince can provide you the same, but he can provide you with so much more. What Ze'ev offers will never satisfy." Matthew stated quietly.

Ze'ev angrily leaned forward, "Just how is the Prince going to take care of her while he is in prison, Ambassador? From what I hear, he's most likely not even going to survive the seven years, and then where will Adi be?"

Fear for Joshua welled up inside of Adi, "What do you mean the Prince won't survive?"

Upon this announcement, the battle that surrounded them stopped. All went silent. The Shedhim looked at one another in joyful surprise while the King's warriors looked at one another in shocked dismay.

"I hear he's been taking dreadful beatings. They've beaten him with whips that have glass chips tied at the end, just to make it more painful. A person can only survive so long with his skin being peeled away like that." Ze'ev stared boldly into Matthew's eyes, a smile of victory tugging at his lips.

Adi gasped, "Matthew?"

Matthew looked evenly at Ze'ev, "The Prince will survive, Adi, and he will come for you!"

Upon this proclamation, the King's dominion gathered

the last of their strength and cried, "For the glory of King Penuel and Prince Joshua!" Mayhem broke out as the battle began to rage once more.

Ze'ev chuckled, "I doubt that, Ambassador, but, I'll allow you your little game. Adi, if the Prince did survive, what kind of future will you have with him? Most likely, he'll be insane, he'll have lost his throne or may be crippled and you'll spend the rest of your life waiting on him hand and foot."

"You don't know our Prince very well, Ze'ev."
A cold blast of wind hit the trio, causing them to shiver. Ze'ev impatiently grabbed onto Adi's arm, "Come, Adi, it's getting cold and you'll get sick. I'm tired of this conversation."

Adi sat there sickened over the revelation of the inhumane suffering of Prince Joshua on her behalf. Hysteria threatened to overwhelm her; she wanted so badly to get away from both men. She threw off Ze'ev's arm and jumped up from the bench, whirling around to look at both of them. Ze'ev's nonchalant, almost gloating attitude over the Prince's predicament angered Adi, but the guilt she felt around Matthew made her want to hide. She didn't know what to do!

The few remaining warriors positioned themselves between the bench and its occupants. Michael spread his one good wing over Adi while taking the blows from the hideous creatures who wanted to deceive her mind.

"Choose the Prince!" Michael groaned as a bat-like creature swung his sword at Michael's knees. Michael went down, the vultures sinking their claws into him. With the last remainder of his strength, he held tightly to his sword and cried in a loud voice, "Choose the Prince, Adi!"

Adi looked deep within Matthew's pleading eyes. A longing to choose the Prince and to leave with Matthew encompassed her. *The Prince could never love a girl like you! You're worthless!* A very small blob had slipped past the wounded Michael and attached itself to Adi. With a confused cry, Adi shouted, "Leave me alone!" With that she whirled around and began to run.

"Adi, wait!"

Adi stopped, turning to look at who was calling her. It was Matthew. He stood there holding out her bag of clothing that she had forgotten in her haste. "You'll need this," he said quietly, with pain deep within his eyes.

With a sob, she grabbed the bag out of his hand and ran as quickly as she could before she changed her mind. While frantically looking for Arman, Dagon spotted Adi running away. The battle was coming to an end; the last of the King's warriors was retreating to the woods. Michael lay in a heap at the Ambassador's feet. Dagon located Arman kneeling on the ground examining his chest wounds. Flying over to him, he cursed him. "Weren't you ordered to guard the girl?" He demanded.

Arman breathing heavily and grasping his chest,

looked up at Dagon, "Yes," he said tersely.

With a roar, Dagon sent a mighty punch into Arman's goat-like face. "Then why are you here while she is running away? Get moving, NOW!"

Arman struggled to his feet, determined to catch up with the fleeing girl. Dagon walked over to where Michael lay so very still. A twisted smile lit up his hideous features as he sent one last powerful kick into Michael's ribs. A soft moan escaped from Michael. Matthew winced at the scene, but restrained himself from sending the commander to the abyss. The time had not yet come.

Ze'ev stood, "Well, Ambassador, it looks as if neither of us won today. But I assure you, I will win Adi's heart!" Without a look back, Ze'ev walked confidently away. The rest of the Shedhim flew away with Ze'ev.

By now the wind was beginning to blow strongly, sending leaves swirling around Matthew as he bent to examine Michael. "Michael, answer me," he said gently, holding his captain's head. No sound came. Matthew laid his hands on the warrior's torn body. Warmth radiated from his hands spreading healing throughout his limbs. After a moment, Matthew spoke more insistently, "Michael, answer me."

The angel's eyes fluttered opened. "You called, sir?" He asked weakly.

Matthew smiled, "You did real fine, Michael. Now let's sit you up."

Michael, with the help of the Ambassador, slowly sat up, strength pouring into him through Matthew's touch. "Adi? Did she choose?"

"No," Matthew stated simply.

"We lost?"

"No, Michael, we did not lose. She didn't choose Ze'ev either. She's still confused, but on the bright side, we are getting closer to her."

"How do you know?"

"I saw it in her eyes. For the first time, there was a longing there for the Prince. Upon hearing that the Prince was being tortured, she became very upset. Unfortunately, her guilt and pride makes it hard for her to accept the Prince's gift. Don't despair yet, Michael, we are getting closer!"

Looking about at the vacant park, Michael asked, "Where is she now?"

"She ran away. Arman is pursuing her, but he's wounded. He won't bother her until he's healed. Take this time to rest, Michael. There will be more battles ahead."

"With all due respect, sir, I'd like to find Adi. I'll rest when she's in my sights."

Matthew nodded, "Then go."

With a mighty cry, Michael held his sword into the air soaring over the land in search of Adi. Matthew quickly left for the woods to check on the rest of the dominion. They lay scattered on the ground tending their wounds.

Upon seeing the Ambassador's arrival, Jordan staggered up from his crouching position. "Ambassador, sir!" he saluted. Matthew looked at his loyal command struggling to stand in respect.

"No, no, stay where you are." Matthew went from one warrior to the next spreading the warmth of healing throughout their bodies. When their wounds were healed and strength returned to them, Matthew turned to address them, "You did a fine job today! We are getting closer every time I get a chance to talk to Adi. She is softening. Take a few moments to rest. There will be many more battles ahead of us. Listen for the sound of Michael's shout for the next battle. Again, good job!"

With that Matthew turned and disappeared from the woods.

Kristen Zuray

THIRTEEN

At the sound of the motel door opening, Thomas eagerly looked up from the newspaper he was reading. A very tired and cold Matthew shuffled through the door. Upon seeing Matthew's exhausted state, Thomas jumped up and rushed over to the small coffee pot.

"Here, Ambassador, drink this to warm you up!" Thomas offered, handing him a steaming hot cup. "A storm is picking up, isn't it?"

"Yes, it is. The wind has really picked up, and the temperature has dropped." Reaching for the cup, Matthew wrapped his cold hands around it for warmth. "Thank you,

Thomas."

Thomas watched silently as Matthew sipped the
steaming brew. Unable to stand the suspense any longer,
Thomas asked, "Well, were you able to speak with Adi?"

"Yes."

Disappointment filled Thomas, "I see that she isn't
with you, so that must mean she didn't listen."

Matthew sighed, placing his cup down carefully. "She
listened, and she came very close to accepting the proposal,
but then Ze'ev came and distracted her."

Thomas curled his fist up and punched his hand, "So,
she chose him!"

Matthew held his hand up shaking his head, "No, no.
She didn't choose him either. She became so upset by the
news of Joshua that she ran off."

Alarmed, Thomas sat up straighter in his chair, "The
Prince? What news?"

Grief etched Matthew's face causing his shoulders to
slump. Tears rolled down his olive- toned cheeks.
Frightened, Thomas looked away, unable to bear the
emotional pain of the Ambassador. The two sat in silence
as Matthew struggled to find his voice. At last he choked
out, "The Prince..."

———

A fist smashed into Joshua's face sending him crashing
against the long wooden dining table. "I'm tired of you

talking about your kingdom and your father!" A big burly man with decayed teeth spat out. "Just shut your mouth about it!"

A group of ragged prisoners hovered in a circle around the two men, blood lust in their eyes. "Beat him, Bill!" A cheer of support echoed throughout the cinderblock-dining hall.

"Break it up!" An armed guard shouted as he and several other guards shoved their way through the crowd to the two men. "What's going on?" The warden demanded. Bill pointed a shaking finger at the Prince, "He started it by talking about King Penuel and his kingdom of Miskana. I think he's trying to start a rebellion!"

The guard stared in disgust at Joshua, "How so, Bill?"

"He keeps talking about how, if people follow him, he can save them from a coming judgment. He says he'll take them to Miskana with him! Isn't that treason? Sounds like he's trying to overthrow the Soterian government to me!" Bill huffed as if he suddenly became a law-abiding patriot.

The guards all silently stared at the Prince, still leaning heavily against the crude table. All was silent except for the tap, tap, tapping of the beat stick against the warden's hand. Joshua looked up at him silently waiting. The man glared down at him. "I thought we had ourselves an understanding after the last beating. You are not to talk about such things!" He hollered into Joshua's bleeding face.

The Prince remained silent, his gentle stare penetrating through to the innermost being of the guard.

Caught off guard, the warden softened a little, "Why do you continue speaking of such rubbish?"

Not breaking eye contact with the man, Joshua spoke quietly, "My Father sent me to tell anyone who will listen, about him and about Miskana. He sent me to warn people of the coming destruction and of the one who is behind it. I obey my Father's will."

The warden humphed, "I thought you came to marry that thief and druggie girl!"

Joshua ignored the remark, "I've come to lead the way to my Father for anyone who will just believe."

"Treason! This man speaks treason against the Soterian government!" Bill roared, pressing against the guards, fist held high in the air in readiness to strike. "Enough Bill, or I will club you!" The warden warned raising his beat stick in a threatening manner. Bill quieted down and waited for the warden to continue, "Take this Prince and lash him!"

The guards roughly grabbed Joshua half dragging him out of the dining hall and into the arena, known as Golgath, the place of the skull. To keep order in the prison, the prison officials built an arena for public punishment underneath the prison. When a prisoner misbehaved, he was sent down to the arena for a public whipping. This served as a warning for those who were entertaining thoughts of causing trouble. Punishment was meted out according to the crime and according to the whims of the guards. There were many who were dragged into the arena that never came out alive. Because of the brutality of the place, it became known as Golgath, the place of the skull. Upon reaching the dank, stone stairs leading downward to the darkened arena, a guard maliciously gave Joshua a hard shove, "Get down there!"

Losing his balance, the Prince stumbled, crashing down the stairs striking his head against a rock. He lay there as pain and darkness overwhelmed him. Closing his swollen eyes, he envisioned a beautiful woman with soft chestnut hair and soft brown eyes smiling down at him. "Adi!" He whispered. The vision dissolved as pain shot through his arm bringing him back to his senses. Guards had surrounded him, grabbing him, and shouting for him to get up. Unable to do so, the brutal men hoisted him to his feet and pulled him the rest of the way to the whipping post in the middle of the arena. As the jeering prisoners filed in, Joshua was being bound to the whipping post, his back bare of any clothing.

The warden stood near the Prince, raising his arms for silence. A hush fell across the underground stadium. "Let this be a warning to all, there shall be no talk of other governments, other kings! Any of you who were considering following this man into a rebellious uprising, let me assure you, that dream ends here today! Silence!"

Turning to a guard, he commanded, "Thirty-nine lashes with the flagrum!" A gasp of horror and excitement rippled throughout the audience. The flagrum was saved for the most severe punishments due to the lead balls and pieces of bone woven into the ends of the nine leather thongs. Very few survived a beating from this.

A beefy guard stepped up holding the flagrum high above his head. Everyone stood paralyzed with anticipation for the first strike. Joshua closed his eyes. "Father, help me," he whispered.

Crack! A scream of pain as the thongs tore through the outer layers of his skin. In one accord, the crowd counted off - "One!" Another crack! Another agonized cry. The lead balls smacked against Joshua's ribs causing deep bruising. "Two!" The crowd shouted in sick delight.

"Whip him harder! Kill him!" Rasha stood unnoticed near the guard. His lust for blood, especially for the blood of the Prince, caused him to tremble with excitement. A hoard of Shedim stood throughout the crowd chortling, mocking, and cursing the Prince. Joshua saw them all. He saw how the Shedim were manipulating the crowd into a frenzy. His own blood splattered into his eyes as the whip continued, relentlessly peeling away his flesh. "Ten!"

The King's Watchers also stood by, wings folded, swords holstered, tears streaming down their faces, powerless to do anything. The Prince had ordered them not to interfere. The crime had to be paid for, the sentence fulfilled, he had said. Gabriel's stomach twisted with each crack of the whip. "Twenty!"

By now, Joshua's agonizing screams were reduced to deep moans as he floated in and out of consciousness. "Father, forgive them! They don't know, they don't know." He murmured. A vision of Adi being dragged toward a fiery pit screaming in terror ripped through Joshua's consciousness. "Adi, choose me! I will save you!" He cried in his hallucinated state. "Adi! Adi, I love you!" He cried as the thongs tore away the subcutaneous layers of his skin. "Thirty!" The crowd continued its count.

"Father!" Joshua cried in agony.

"Thirty-five!"

"Adi!"

"Thirty-six!"

"Soteria!"

"Thirty-seven!"

"Father, don't leave me!" Pleading, Joshua lifted his bound bloodied hands toward the ceiling.

Thirty-eight!

"Father!"

"Thirty-nine!" The crowd went ballistic with their lust for blood. The Shedim danced with victory at the sight of the Prince's mangled form. Surely, Adi would be theirs now!

Joshua lay face down on the blood-soaked dirt floor, his hands still tied to the post above his head. His skin

hung in strips around him. "Adi, I've done this for you."
He heaved as blackness at last prevailed. The warden
stooped down to feel for a pulse. Satisfied that the prisoner
had not died, he stood silencing the crowd. "This same fate
will be for the next person who dares talk of treason!
Guards lock them in their cells."

As the prisoners were ushered back upstairs, the licter
asked the warden, "What about him?"

The warden looked down upon Joshua's still form,
"Leave him for awhile."

Once the arena was emptied of Soterians and the
Shedim, the Watchers stepped from their hiding places.
Gabriel turned to them, "Watch from a distance. I will
report to King Penuel." With that simple statement,
Gabriel raised his sword and shot into the air towards
Miskana.

———————

Losing his grip on the balcony rail overlooking the city of
Soteria, the King slipped to his knees. His muscled body
shaking in anguish as his son's pain ripped through him.
Father and son had never been separated before. They
were bonded together by the strongest kind of love—a love
that caused the King to feel the torment that his son was
suffering.

Father! Joshua's cries raked through the King's soul.
How desperately he wanted to comfort his son, but he
could not. It was decided long ago, that the Prince would

have to endure this alone for Adi's sake and for the sake of all Soteria. How would it prove their love to the Soterians if they weren't willing to sacrifice everything for them?

A movement caught the King's attention. Quickly drying his eyes, he stood to his feet looking at Gabriel's stricken face.

"Gabriel?"

"I have news about the Prince, sir," Gabriel quietly said.

"I already know. I have felt my son's pain." The King wearily turned toward the skyline of Soteria, his heart longing for Joshua.

Gabriel nervously shifted his feet, ""How much more must he suffer?"

Fighting for composure, the King at last responded, "Much more."

"For how long, sir?" Gabriel cried.

"Until the seven year sentence has been served so that Adi can be fully pardoned."

"That's a high price to pay for just one girl," Gabriel quietly observed.

The King turned to face Gabriel, "One girl? It's not just for one girl, but for all of Soteria, but even if it was just for Adi, it's a price we're willing to pay. She's worth all the suffering because she is precious to us."

Gabriel sighed, not fully understanding, "I hope she'll realize that soon."

Nodding, the King turned back to stare out at the blackened, smoke-filled sky. "Leave me, Gabriel. I wish to be alone."

"Yes, sir." Gabriel quietly stepped into the palace, but not before seeing the broad shoulders once more shaking with muffled sobs.

FOURTEEN

Adi's hair hung in long damp strands around her face. She sat cross-legged, staring into the orange glow of the electric heater. It had been three years since the incident in the park. Since that time, Adi had found a makeshift shelter in an abandoned warehouse. It wasn't a palace, but the small obscure room within the building provided protection from the weather. Thanks to finding some odd jobs here and there, she was able to purchase a few items to make the room a cozy place to come back to. Out of desperation, she had contacted Snake, Rasha's lead drug dealer, who allowed her to do some selling for him. After giving him and Rasha their cut, she was able to have a little left over to buy an occasional meal, but for the most part, it was the garbage cans that provided most of her meals. Life had fallen into a routine of survival. Get up in the mornings and hunt for jobs and food, not much of an existence. There were days when, just as she was about to run to Ze'ev, she would spot money on the ground, enough to sustain her until the next job came her way. Things had to get better, but they didn't. Adi reached into her coat pocket and fingered the now worn card with Matthew's phone number. Even if she had wanted to call him, she couldn't. She had no access to a phone, but she did remember where he was staying. *Was he still there?* She wondered. If only...

Adi sighed, finally crawling into her sleeping bag. "Joshua's probably dead anyway." She murmured. The all too familiar ache settled into her heart. Since the day she had learned that the Prince had been beaten almost to death, she couldn't shake off the guilt that he was doing this for her. Regret at having not accepted his proposal nagged at her. If only...No, it was probably too late now. Even if he wasn't dead, she was sure that he would never want to see her again after all he went through. She would just bring back bad memories for him. And Matthew, Matthew probably hated her. A warm tear slipped down her cheek. If only...

Arman gave a low chuckle as he saw the despair of his words take hold of Adi's mind. He would convince her that the Prince was dead and there was no more hope for her. It had infuriated him that Adi still had not run back to Ze'ev. Whenever he was about to succeed, Michael would lead her to shelter or food or a job which only prolonged the battle. Arman was anxious to get on with other things. He was sick of babysitting this pitiful girl. He should just kill her now and be done with the thing. The taste of blood rose to his mouth. Yes, that's what he would do. Slowly, so as not to attract Michael's attention, he reached out his long claws and grabbed hold of Adi's throat.

Adi, about to slip into sleep, awoke with a start. Frantically grabbing at her throat, she felt a constricting sensation cutting off her air supply. Letting out a cry, she struggled to find the source of the choking. Unable to do so, the realization that she was going to die alone panicked her.

Upon hearing Adi's cry, Michael and Gabriel turned from their conversation, instantly on guard. Unsheething his sword, Michael rushed over to where Adi lay, struggling against Arman's grip. With a mighty cry, Michael swung his sword, cutting into Arman's taloned claws. Shocked, Arman lifted his arm and stared at the empty space where his hand had been. Rage overwhelmed him, "You will pay for this, Michael!"

Adi gasped for air as the constriction around her throat suddenly lessened. Gabriel knelt beside her, gently rubbing her back and speaking gentle words of comfort to her.

Michael dodged the blow from Arman's massive wing, but was unable to escape the second wing's descent upon him. Smack! Michael crashed into the cement wall, stunned. Arman saw his chance and lunged for Adi again. Gabriel unfurled his brilliant irridescent wings shielding Adi from Arman's sword. Before Arman could drive the sword into Gabriel's back, Michael blocked it with his sword. The room filled with brilliant sparks of light as swords clashed against one another.

"Open the abyss, Gabriel!" Michael shouted as he parried Arman's sword.

"I will beat you to pieces, Angel." Arman growled.

Gabriel took his sword and slashed it into the ground, opening an invisible black hole. Arman flew into the air, spreading his wings. Pausing a moment, he sneered at Michael who stood below him poised. Gathering all speed and strength, Arman dove toward the Watcher. Wrapping his massive wings around Michael, he began to crush the warrior. Gabriel gripped his sword tightly, sending a paralyzing light throughout the room. The shock of it caused Arman to drop Michael into a heap upon the floor. Heaving with the exertion of it all, Michael raised his legs and heaved them into Arman's chest, sending him sailing backward and into the bottomless abyss. "Close it up!" Michael gasped.

Gabriel quickly took his sword and made another gash as if zipping something closed. The room suddenly grew silent, the sound of battle over. Michael lay against the wall, catching his breath. Gabriel stood staring at where the abyss was, making sure Arman was forever gone. Quiet sobs grabbed their attention. Michael crawled over to where Adi lay curled up in fright. Gently stroking her hair, Michael whispered, "You're going to be okay."

Looking up at Gabriel, he said, "Go tell the Ambassador what has happened." Michael frowned, feeling Adi's forehead and face.

"What is it?"

"She's sick, very sick. Ask Matthew what he would like to do."

Without another word, Gabriel shot into the air in search of Matthew.

———

Gabriel urgently pounded on the motel room's door. Immediately, the door flew open. Matthew waved him in.

Thomas sat up in bed with a confused and alarmed look on his face, "What's going on?"

"Sir, there was a battle tonight between Michael and Arman."

"Michael and Arman? What has happened to Adi?" Matthew asked alarmed.

"Arman attempted to kill her. Michael interevened. A fight followed and we had to send Arman to the abyss. Adi is very sick, sir. Michael would like to know what to do."

Matthew stood there rubbing his chin in thought. Looking up at Thomas, he quietly ordered, "Thomas get dressed."

Without questioning, Thomas jumped out of bed and rushed into the bathroom to dress. Turning back to Gabriel, he said, "Take Thomas and show him where Adi is. Thomas will take her to the hospital. That will be the best way to get Adi in. If I were to bring her, they'd probably throw us out. I'll visit her in a few days."

"Yes, sir."

"Also, tell Michael to summon the Watchers. Have them ready in case of an attack from Rasha's Shedim. He might retaliate when he hears of what has happened to Arman."

"Yes, sir."

Thomas stepped out of the bathroom, looking expectantly towards Matthew. "I'm ready."

"Go with Gabriel. He'll show you where Adi is. Then take her to the closest hospital."

Thomas nodded. Gabriel transformed himself into a man of average build. Looking at Thomas whose eyes were wide with wonder and asked, "Ready, Thomas?"

"Yes." Thomas followed the man into the darkness of night, happy to finally be apart of something.

It didn't take long for Rasha to find out that Arman had been sent to the abyss. Never fully trusting those in his command, it was his policy to send a discreet little spirit to observe that his commands were being followed. The black wisp of a thing was about to make a hasty exit in search of his master, but stopped short when he heard Michael tell Gabriel to bring instructions from Matthew. The little spy decided that it would be beneficial to himself if he were to come to Rasha with a full story. Hovering just outside the door of the room, he waited and listened. He watched as Michael and Thomas knelt beside Adi discussing which hospital was nearby.

Gabriel rushed into the room, "I've hailed a taxi. It's waiting for us."

Gently, Michael lifted Adi's frail feverish body in his arms. "You'll be safe now, Adi," he whispered protectively. Thomas slipped into the front seat next to the cabbie, "Take us to Soteria General Hospital. Quickly, man!" he said urgently.

As soon the cab peeled away from the curb, the smallest of the Shedim flew with all speed to Rasha. He found his master seated at a kitchen table, the same table that he sat at when Joshua had confronted him. Hatred for Michael coursed through Rasha as he slammed his fist against the table. "He sent Arman into the abyss?" he shouted. Turning to the commander of the Shedim, he forced his voice to remain steady but low, "Dagon, you watch over Adi now and TAKE OUT MICHAEL!" he screamed out the last three words. Without hesitation, Dagon flew off in the direction of the hospital. "Shakti, awaken Ze'ev. Tell him he needs to get to the hospital. I'm sure Matthew will already be there."

Rasha paced back and forth agitated, but soon a plan began to unfold in his evil mind. "Adi, you'll be sorry for the trouble you've caused me. Marrying Ze'ev won't be enough punishment for you..." a low chuckle growing into a loud hysterical laughter escaped from his foaming mouth. The rest of the Shedim who weren't on assignment, cowered in the corners.

———

Ze'ev lay bare-chested on his back, covers off. The palms of his hands facing upward, a peaceful smile playing on his lips. As the theta binaural beats sounded rhythmically through the headphones and into Ze'ev's subconscious, a tingling sensation began to form at the base of his spine. Soon waves of energy moved up and down his spine causing vibrations near his adrenal, thymus, and thyroid glands. A burst of iridescent light exploded into his brain. The colorful light beams joined together shaping themselves into the form of a beautiful woman. She stood there with arms outstretched, her robes shimmering as a prism held against the light. Her wavy blonde hair gently blew enchantingly around her shoulders and ended at her waist,

"Ze'ev!" she called seductively, "Ze'ev, I have a message for you!"

"I'm listening," Ze'ev murmured in his trance-like state.

"I am Shakti the supreme goddess of the universe. I have come to instruct you in how to obtain my favor," her voice whispered eerily. "Adi is in the Soterian General Hospital. Go to her and take care of my child. As a reward, I will give you half of Soteria to rule."

"Yes, my Shakti, I will go." Ze'ev groaned.

"My favor is upon you, Ze'ev." As her voice faded, so did the beams of iridescent light. The buzzing vibrations ceased, and all was still. Ze'ev opened his eyes in wonderment.

"I did it! I awakened the Kundilini!" Feeling exhilarated, he jumped out of bed and began to dress for the hospital.

———

Thomas jumped out of the taxi before it came to a complete stop. Throwing the back door open, he reached in to help slowly ease a semi-conscious Adi out of the cab. Picking her up, he rushed through the sliding emergency room doors

"I need help here!" Thomas called out.

Immediately the receptionist phoned for a gurney to be brought to the front at once. A team of doctors and nurses rushed to the bed, surrounding Adi, while throwing out questions to Thomas. Thomas followed after them answering the questions as best he could. The team whisked Adi through a set of double doors. Thomas was about to follow, but was stopped by a nurse.

"This is as far as you go. Please wait out in the lobby."

Panicked, Thomas balked, "But I have to..."

"Go!" the nurse snapped.

Dejected, Thomas turned and slowly walked back to the waiting area. Michael stood there waiting for him.

"They've taken Adi behind some doors and they won't let me in," he fretted.

"Don't worry, Thomas. She'll be fine."

Looking about, he noticed that Matthew wasn't there. "Where's Matthew? He said he'd be here!"

Michael slapped the despondent man on the back, "He's here. He's with her right now."

"But how..."

"Thomas, no one can see him. Being able to go invisible has its perks, you know."

Michael attempted at some humor to cheer Thomas, but it was lost on him.

Looking perplexed, Thomas stared at Michael, "Michael, do others see you right now?"

"No."

Thomas's eyes widened, "Then it looks as if I'm talking to myself?" he exclaimed.

Michael gave a light-hearted laugh, "Yes, it does, Thomas."

"That's not funny, Michael. Why is it that I can see you in human form and in angel form?"

"Because you are from Miskana, Thomas. Those who reside in Miskana see both worlds."

"Oh." Thomas furrowed his brow and slumped into a seat. "I'm going to talk with the Ambassador. Just wait here for the doctor."

———

Several hours later, the doctor stood before three men who claimed responsibility for the sick woman. Wishing to be on his way home from an exhausting night, the doctor quickly shared the results from the CT scans and blood work. "She's malnourished and underweight. The 104 fever is caused by pneumonia in both lungs."

"Will she die?" Ze'ev asked genuinely concerned, not for her sake but for his. He was afraid that the goddess Shakti would reclaim her promise of wealth if Adi died.

"Don't know. We'll have to just wait and see if she's strong enough to fight off the infection. She's so malnourished that it is highly doubtful that she'll be able to pull through." The doctor paused looking at the three men. The trio was silent. "If there are no questions, I'll be on my way. Another doctor will check on her later tonight."

As soon as the physician left, Ze'ev turned to the two men and gave them a cold, hard stare

"She wouldn't be here if it hadn't been for you," he accused.

Thomas looked nervously at Matthew who now stood in human form. Matthew's eyebrow arched, "I'm trying to save her from who you work for."

Ze'ev gave a nervous laugh, "I don't know what you're talking about. I love her and you best keep away, Ambassador."

A spark of anger flickered in Matthew's eyes, "You love her? Come now, Ze'ev, let's be honest here. What did Rasha promise you - power, wealth, fame if you marry her?"

Ze'ev flared at the accusation. Taking a step toward Matthew, he threatened, "How dare you accuse me of these things! You need to leave here at once or else..."

"Or else what, Ze'ev?" Matthew closed the gap between them and stood towering over the smaller man. Ze'ev was no match for Matthew's strength. Ze'ev faltered, taking several steps back. "Don't pretend to care for Adi when I know the truth! As for leaving, I'm staying right here." To emphasize his point, Matthew crossed to the other side of the bed. He pulled a chair closer to the bed, and sat down, clasping Adi's frail hand in his larger protective one.

Ze'ev glared, sat down in the other chair, and grabbed Adi's other hand. Both men sat in silence, staring at one another. Thomas left muttering about finding another chair.

There were more than just four beings in the room. Dagon and Shakti hovered behind Ze'ev while glaring and taunting Michael and Gabriel, who stood with swords poised ready to defend.

"You're a fool, Ambassador, to think that Adi will ever choose your Prince," Ze'ev snarled.

Growing weary of the taunts of Dagon, Shakti, and Ze'ev, Matthew looked up with all authority and demanded, "In the name of Prince Joshua, I command you to be silent."

Startled, Ze'ev fell back into his chair, unable to speak. Upon hearing the name of Joshua being spoken, Dagon and Shakti trembled, making a hasty retreat into the far corner of the room.

Exchanging amused glances with one another, Michael and Gabriel felt a surge of pride for their King, their Prince, and their Ambassador.

———

The fever burned hot within her body, tormenting her mind. She felt the heat of flames licking at her feet as she teetered once more on the edge of the bottomless cavern.

"No!" she screamed, "Joshua!"

A figure approached the pit. Kneeling down, he placed a cool washcloth on her forehead. *Why are you doing that?* She wanted to shout, but couldn't. Struggling to see the man's face as it leaned toward her, she recognized it as Ze'ev.

"Ze'ev?" Adi's eyes fluttered open. Where was she, in the fiery pit or somewhere else? Her tortured mind couldn't make sense of what was going on. Her eyes closed once more giving into the hallucinations. There before her was a dark arena filled with sand. A tall post was sticking up in the middle. Dread filled her soul, causing her stomach to cramp. Something was wrong or was about to be wrong. Suddenly a screaming crowd appeared all around the stadium. She stood there looking fearfully at the people when a man stepped forward dressed in a flowing black robe holding a gavel.

"You have been found guilty!" the man shouted, pointing at her, "Tie her to the post!"

Crying out in terror, she fought against the men who dragged her to the post. Unable to escape, she knelt whimpering, hands bound.

"Lash her 39 times!" the judge commanded.

"No!" she sobbed.

As the lictor raised the whip above his head, a voice was heard in the crowd, "Wait! Your Honor, I would like to take her place!"

A strong, well-built man stepped from the crowd and rushed over to where Adi was bound. Kneeling down before her, he looked deep into her eyes.

"Don't worry, Adi, I'll take your place." Gently stroking her hair as if she were a child, the man continued to speak gently to her, "I love you, Adi, and I'll do anything for you!"

"Joshua?" relief flooded through her, but quickly left as the same angry men grabbed Joshua. Upon releasing her, they tied Joshua to the pole, ripping his shirt so that his back was exposed. The lictor bore the whip down unmercifully upon the Prince.

"No! You can't do this!" she screamed hysterically.

Another voice broke into the horrific scene. "The fever often causes nightmares, so we need to sedate her."

A cool sensation spread throughout her body as darkness brought relief to her fevered torment.

Matthew slowly released her hand as she began to relax. Ze'ev hovered over her with a damp cloth. The battle raged on. Who would Adi choose even in her dreams?

Several torturous days passed while Adi clung to the last sliver of life. Matthew sat faithfully by her side, while Ze'ev, on the other hand, grew weary of the boredom of waiting. He opted for returning home only to visit her briefly in the evenings. It didn't make a difference whether he was there or not since Adi was unaware of his presence he had reasoned.

Noticing Adi's sleep had changed from restlessness to relaxed; Matthew gently felt her pale cheeks. Thomas looked up, suddenly alert, from where he had been reading.

"What is it? Is she okay?"

Matthew smiled, "Her fever broke. She's going to make it."

Thomas' face brightened, "That's fantastic! Why isn't she waking up?"

Matthew lovingly stroked away Adi's hair from her face. "Her body is exhausted from the fever. She's slipped into a relaxed sleep now."

Thomas placed his book on the table next to her bed and stood stretching out the kinks in his legs and back.

"Sir, you've been in here for days. How about we get some dinner in the cafeteria for a little change of scenery?"

Looking at Thomas' hopeful face, Matthew nodded, "That does sound good, Thomas." Turning to Michael and Gabriel, he instructed, "Keep watch over her. Should she wake up, get me immediately, Gabriel."

"Yes, sir, I will."

Matthew began to walk out of the room when he passed by Dagon and Shakti still hovering in the corner. As an after thought, Matthew turned to Michael, "If these two give you any trouble, deal with them."

Michael bowed his head in acknowledgement while Dagon let out a sulfuric angry hiss.

As soon as Matthew was gone, Dagon edged closer to Shakti, whispering, "Where is that imbecile, Ze'ev? He was your responsibility!"

Shakti, who in its real form, was rather a small creature possessing a lizard like body and a head of a snake, snapped back at Dagon, "Ze'ev's an idiot! Why do I have to keep track of him?"

"Because our Master assigned him to you! Now get over there and tell Ze'ev to come immediately. The girl will wake up soon, and the first person she needs to see is Ze'ev!

Now, go and be quick about it!" Dagon growled low to his subject.

Without another word, Shakti flew with lightning speed through the ceiling and out of the roof of the hospital in search of Ze'ev. Startled at the sudden departure of Shakti, Michael and Gabriel unsheathed their swords in expectation. Dagon chuckled, "Nervous, Michael?"

Without answering, Michael stood resolutely with wings spread in protection, blocking Adi's bed from Dagon's view. Letting out a hysterical laughter, Dagon shot up through the roof and into the night sky. Whipping out his sword, he slashed at the air causing a a thunderous cracking sound. People below looked up at the sky searching for signs of lightning and rain, unaware that the thunder they had heard was a Shedim signaling his force to rally.

Shakti found Ze'ev in his study pouring over his accounting books. The relaxing sounds of rain mingled with the ghostly sounds of a flute, filled the room. Shakti smiled, Ze'ev was ready to receive her.

As the familiar tingling sensation began at the base of his spine, Ze'ev straightened in his chair. Instantly, he closed his eyes and cleared his mind of his work. Shakti was summoning him "Ze'ev!" Shakti whispered into his ear, as she manipulated his mind into seeing a beautiful iridescent woman.

"Yes, Shakti, I am listening." Ze'ev breathed deeply.

"Adi is about to wake up. You must get to the hospital quickly before Matthew gets to her. You need to be the first one she sees. Go now, do not delay!" she ordered.

Before Ze'ev could respond, Shakti disappeared.

Grabbing his coat, Ze'ev ran out the door and headed for the hospital.

FIFTEEN

Adi let out a soft moan drawing the attention of Michael and Gabriel. "She's about to wake up. You had best tell the Ambassador, Gabriel."

Before Gabriel could respond, high screeching screams erupted as the room filled with the Shedim. Pandemonium broke out as creatures slashed at the two Watchers, backing them into a corner away from Adi. Just then Ze'ev rushed into the room throwing his coat off, loosening his tie, and messing his hair, posing as the distraught lover who had been faithfully by Adi's side all through the night.

As Adi's eyes fluttered opened, she stared blankly at the man who was holding her hand.

"Ze'ev?" she weakly whispered.

"Adi, my love! You're awake!" Ze'ev pretended to choke back some tears while kissing her hand.

"Where am I?"

"You're in the hospital. You are a very sick woman, darling." Ze'ev crooned.

Adi lay there quietly struggling to remember. The last thing she remembered was her makeshift room in the abandoned warehouse. Confused, she looked back at Ze'ev,

"How did I get here?"

"I had been searching for you, Adi. My heart is connected to yours, and I knew something was wrong. Thank goodness I found you in time to get you to the hospital!" Ze'ev lied.

"How long have I been asleep?"

"Four days, but the doctor says you're out of danger. With plenty of rest and good food, you should make a full recovery." Noticing the uncertainty and fear in Adi's eyes, Ze'ev leaned over and stroked her hair, "Don't worry about anything, my sweet Adi. I'll take care of you!"

Tears gathered in Adi's fatigued eyes. "Have you been here the whole time?"

Ze've gently smiled, "How could I ever leave the woman I love when she needs me? Yes, I've been here the whole time."

Sleepiness threatened to reclaim her. As her eyelids began to close, a stab of fear jolted them back open, "Ze'ev, you won't leave me will you?"

"Of course not, darling, just close your eyes and sleep. I'll be here watching over you," he soothed.

Relief washed over her allowing her to give into the inviting darkness of sleep.

Ze'ev sat back in his uncomfortable chair, proud of himself for the effective act he had just put on. "Surely, she'll trust me now," he muttered.

Sensing a strong and mighty presence behind him, Ze'ev whirled around in his chair. There stood Matthew in the doorway, his mouth set in a hard line. Behind him, Thomas stood peering over his shoulder in dismay. The two took in the scene before them. Michael and Gabriel were trapped in the corner beating off their attackers, while Ze'ev sat close to Adi's bedside, a triumphant smile on his face. "You're too late, Ambassador! Adi already woke up and has agreed to let me take care of her." Ze'ev laughed at Matthew's frustrated expression. "Give it up, Ambassador. Besides, what would a Prince want with a tramp like her?"

Matthew glared at the mocking man, "Tramp? Watch how you refer to her, Ze'ev. She's the chosen bride to the Prince and the chosen daughter to the King. She's a valuable jewel, something which you are obviously incapable of understanding!"

Ze'ev held his hands up in mock defense, "Ooh, the Ambassador has a temper! Well, it doesn't matter now, she's mine, so MOVE ON!"

Matthew quickly crossed to Adi's bedside peering at her small hands. "Until she wears your ring, Ze'ev, I will continue to pursue her."

Ze'ev glared back, hatred flickering in his eyes.

"Leave!" Matthew commanded. Confused, Ze'ev felt himself turning around and walking out of the room. Along with Ze'ev the horde of Shedim followed after him screeching and screaming hideous obscenities.

As soon as they were alone in the room, Matthew and Thomas rushed over to the now semi-conscious Watchers. Touching their battered heaving forms, Matthew spoke softly to them, his words and touch healing them.

Michael and Gabriel slowly stood to their feet looking ashamed, "Ambassador I am so sorry." Michael stared down at his sandaled feet.

Matthew shook his head. "Michael, Gabriel, do not fear. We will not win every time, that's why it's called a battle." Looking over at the peaceful Adi, Matthew encouraged, "All is not lost. We'll be here when she wakes up again." Taking up his vigil next to Adi, Matthew began to whisper sweet words of love and comfort to the sick girl.

Hours later, Adi awoke her eyes still heavy with fatigue. Noticing a figure by her bed she mumbled groggily, "Ze'ev?"

Matthew leaned forward taking her hand in his, "No, Adi, it's Matthew."

"Matthew?" she asked confused.

"Yes, the Ambassador to Miskana. Remember?"

Adi thought awhile until the memories made sense. "Matthew. I remember." She whispered. "How did you know I was here?"

Matthew smiled, "Adi, I'm never far away. I made a promise to Prince Joshua and to you that I would watch over you."

Frustrated, Adi demanded, "Watch over me? Then why am I here?"

Feeling a pang of hurt at Adi's outburst, Matthew tenderly chided, "Because you chose to stay away from me."

Adi began to protest, but then the truth of what Matthew had said hit her. Feeling embarrassed she asked, "Then why are you here?"

"Because we love you," Matthew said simply.

"We?"

"King Penuel, Prince Joshua, and myself."

Tears gathered in her eyes. "Oh, Matthew, I'm so confused!" she sobbed.

Matthew gently caressed her hand, "I know, Adi. That's why I'm here to help you understand the truth."

"Adi, my love, you're awake!" Ze'ev loudly burst into the room carrying a dozen roses.

"Ze'ev, I thought you weren't going to leave!"

"I wasn't gone long, dearest. I wanted to have these roses here for when you woke up," Ze'ev smiled.

Adi smiled as she breathed in the aroma of the deep red flowers. "No one has ever bought flowers for me!"

"It's their loss," Ze'ev joked as he leaned over and planted a kiss on Adi's cheek.

Adi looked up at him with surprise. Turning to Matthew, Ze'ev said sprightly, "Well, Ambassador, I'm here now. I'll sit with Adi." Even though his tone was light, the expression on his face was cold with hatred.

Matthew slowly stood to his feet. "I'll be back, Adi." Turning to the bewildered Thomas, he announced, "Come, Thomas, we'll let Adi get some rest."

Once out in the hallway and out of earshot, Thomas grabbed Matthew's arm, "I don't understand. Why are we leaving her with HIM?"

"We want it to be her choice, Thomas. How can it be her choice if we force ourselves on her? All we can do is to present the truth when the opportunity comes. We must be patient, Thomas."

"I just don't understand this," Thomas shook his head, feeling frustrated.

"What kind of love would it be if it forces itself upon a person? Would it be real love if the person was forced to return it?"

"No, I guess not."

"Our love is unconditional. We will freely love Adi and all of Soteria even if they don't return our love, but when some do return it, we'll know that it is real and sincere."

"I guess that makes sense. That's the only way to have a perfect relationship - to love without expecting anything in return, and to not force someone to accept you. Adi has to have that chance. If she never got to see Ze'ev's side of things, but only our side, she wouldn't have really had a choice, would she?"

"Now, you're understanding, Thomas." Matthew patted him on the back in approval.

"Let's go get some rest. You must be tired, Thomas."

———

As the days melted into weeks, Adi grew physically stronger but emotionally weaker. She felt like the rope in a tug-of-war game between Matthew and Ze'ev. Just when she began to trust Ze'ev, Matthew would give her a warning causing her to withdraw from Ze'ev; and just when she would decide to accept the Prince's proposal, Ze'ev would say or do something that would contradict Matthew's warning about him. Both men spent hours with her. Ze'ev boasted of all his wealth and power that he was willing to share with her, and Matthew, humbly exalted the Prince and not himself. Both men were complete opposites. Feeling confused, Adi became agitated and withdrawn.

Observing her quiet unsettled attitude, Ze'ev decided to consult Rasha about it. Settled once again on the park bench, Ze'ev turned up his coat collar in an attempt to block out the cold winter breeze. "It's Matthew, Rasha. Can't you get rid of him? He's turning Adi against me."

"How?" the abrupt question was edged with anger.

"I don't know. All I know is that when he spends time with her, she pulls away from me. She always looks at me suspiciously and then gets real moody." Ze'ev grumbled.

"Moody you say?"

"Yes, and she cries a lot."

"I know what will help her. I've got just the thing, but you are not to tell her where you got it from." Rasha often disguised as a businessman when out in public, quickly searched in his briefcase for the drug. Upon finding it, he handed the bottle to Ze'ev.

Cautiously, Ze'ev reached out examining the bottle. "Okay. What is it?"

"Phloxine. It's a drug that raises serotonin levels to help with depression, which is Adi's problem."

"What if she won't take it?"

Rasha's eyes narrowed as he glared at Ze'ev, "Make her." Rasha stood indicating that the matter was settled and walked away.

———

After some persuasive pleading on Ze'ev's part Adi agreed to take the pills. Anything would be better than to continue feeling confused, guilty, and overwhelmed.

The night before Adi was going to be discharged, Matthew stopped by to make another appeal. He had spent tireless hours telling Adi all about King Penuel, the Prince, Miskana, and the future demise of Soteria. On more than one occasion, Adi appeared as if she would accept the Prince's proposal, but was always interrupted by a doctor or Ze'ev causing the moment to pass. Matthew knew that tonight would be her last night at the hospital before she would go home with Ze'ev.

As Matthew walked into the hospital room, he found Adi sitting up in bed blankly staring at the wall. When she turned to meet his gaze, her eyes were dull and empty. Alarmed at the change in her, Matthew scanned her room for any signs of what may have caused this. Then he saw it, a brown pill bottle on the table by her bedside. Picking it up, he read the label Phloxine.

"Adi, you're not taking this are you?" He demanded.

Adi slowly nodded. "Ze'ev said that it would make me feel better. He said I was depressed."

Sighing with frustration, Matthew sat down in the chair next to her. "Adi, you are not depressed! You've been through some tough times and you've been sick. It's natural and completely normal to feel weak, fatigued, and even emotional. There's nothing wrong with you, Adi!"

Adi shrugged, "I don't care. For the first time, I feel free from guilt and fear. Come to think of it, I don't feel anything at all. How can that be bad?"

Matthew sighed, "These pills numb you, Adi. You lose your sense of guilt and responsibility. I know this doesn't sound like a bad thing, but you've got to realize that there is a good form of guilt and a bad form. The good guilt makes you realize your need for King Penuel who will lead you away from harm. False guilt comes from the inability to live up to false expectations. Unfortunately, many Soterians can't distinguish between the two and they turn to pills which numbs both kinds of guilt. Can't you see how dangerous that is? True guilt is a moral compass that points to King Penuel and life! It's a GOOD thing!"

Adi glared at Matthew, "And next you're going to tell me that fear is a good thing, too?"

"Well, when danger looms before you, fear helps you run from it. You should be afraid of the coming destruction of Soteria. You should be afraid of what will happen to you if you don't accept the Prince's proposal. He won't be able to protect you, Adi!" he pleaded. Seeing that his words weren't processing in her mind, he leaned back sighing, "So, if you stop to think about it, then, yes, fear can be a good thing to help you turn from danger and seek safety. Don't squelch that fear, Adi!"

Adi sadly looked down at the blanket that was twisted up in her hand.

An urgency filled Matthew's voice as he desperately tried to reach her with truth.

"Adi, look at me." Adi slowly lifted her eyes and stared into Matthew's deep, chocolate eyes. They were filled with concern. Matthew continued, "Joshua promises to replace that fear and give you complete peace if you accept him. With Joshua, you will be safe from harm!"

Adi numbly looked away, "I have peace now."

"No, Adi, this is not true peace. These pills create a facade, a false peace that will push you further into danger," Matthew firmly stated.

Stubbornly, Adi shook her head, "If you don't like these pills, why don't you just get rid of them yourself so I can't take them?"

A pained look crossed over Matthew's chiseled face. "Adi, you've got to believe me when I say that I want to take these pills and throw them as far away as I can, but I can't. It has to be your choice, Adi."

"Well, then, I choose to take the pills, and I'll be going home with Ze'ev tomorrow." Adi once more stared vacantly at the wall, blocking Matthew's presence from her mind.

Despondently, Matthew slowly stood to his feet and quietly shuffled out the door.

————

Deep in the recesses of the Soterian men's prison, a tormented cry was heard from a brutally beaten Prince, "Adi!"

King Penuel stood at the balcony staring at the distant city, tears streaming down his cheeks, "Adi! Why won't you let me be your father?"

"So that's it? She chose Ze'ev over the Prince?" Thomas blurted in a panicked voice.

He had been quietly listening to Matthew recount the details of his conversation with Adi, but then couldn't contain himself any longer.

"We haven't lost yet, Thomas. Just because she is going home with Ze'ev doesn't mean that she will accept his proposal. It isn't until she officially marries him that we've lost," Matthew tried to encourage.

Thomas protested, "She's all but married him now!"

"We must remain hopeful, Thomas. We must not quit!"

Thomas sat silently for a few moments contemplating strategies to win Adi over. An idea came to him causing him to sit up straighter, "I've got it! What if we told Adi what happened to the Prince. Surely she would choose the Prince when she hears of the whipping that he took on her behalf!"

Matthew looked down at Thomas' hopeful face, compassion for his faithful protégé filled his being. "She already knows," he said quietly.

Thomas' mouth opened with shock, "Then how can she possibly turn her back on him?"

"Soterian's search for security is for this present life. They have a hard time seeing beyond tomorrow. In Adi's case, Ze'ev is with her now in the present, and she's taking that security. Unfortunately, she won't believe that it is the Prince who will be with her now and in the future, not Ze'ev."

"I don't think I'll ever fully understand Soterians," Thomas mumbled.

"Remember, it's easier for you to understand what is at stake because you've seen both kingdoms, and you personally know the King and the Prince." Matthew patted Thomas on the back, "We'd better get some rest. We've got our work cut out for us."

Kristen Zuray

SIXTEEN

A year had past since Adi moved back in with Ze'ev.
Matthew had not "bumped" into her during the year like he
had done in the past. She did occasionally have very brief
encounters with Thomas, but Ze'ev usually diverted her
away from him. Even though she didn't see Matthew, he
had been there with her. Every day Matthew faithfully
stood nearby whispering into her thoughts and tugging at
her soul, but she felt disconnected from the world mentally
and emotionally. In spite of the medication, the peace that
she assumed she had found still alluded her, instead she
felt lifeless. As hard as she tried to conform to Ze'ev's

expectations, she just couldn't. In the beginning he had
tried to reach out to her by taking her to plays, dinners,
and introducing her to high society life, but she just
couldn't get enthusiastic about it. Ze'ev began to grow
impatient and abrupt with her. Afraid that Ze'ev might
throw her out, she decided to find a job in hopes to give her
life purpose. Amazingly, Ze'ev listened and supported her
plan.

Adi was once again on the streets looking for a job, but
this time was different. She had a home to go to, lavish
clothes, and a reputation for being Ze'ev's girl. She was
feeling hopeful as she headed to a little flower shop that
was just opening. That morning as she and Ze'ev sat in
their robes having coffee while perusing the morning
paper, she noticed a help wanted ad for a start up flower
shop. Something about it pulled at her heart. Once her life
had been filled with things that were ugly, but now she
wanted to fill it with things of beauty. As soon as she saw
the ad, she wanted to get down there immediately before
anyone else.

Michael and Matthew followed along beside her
careful to keep themselves invisible. Dagon cautiously
followed behind, mystified as to what the Ambassador and
the Watcher were up to.

As Adi walked through the shop's door, an elderly man
with white hair that stuck up in tufts around his head

looked up peering at her over his glasses. "What can I do you for you, young lady?"

"I'm here to inquire about the job that was in the paper."

"Oh, yes, yes." Shuffling around the counter, the man stuck his hand out in greeting. "My name is Jordan." Waving his hand around at the half-stocked shelves and the unopened boxes of merchandise, he chuckled, "As you can see, I am in need of help stocking the shelves and organizing this place before it opens. I'm not as young as I once was!"

Adi smiled, "I'd be glad to help!"

He looked quizzically at her stylish clothes and jewelry. "You don't look like you need a job. May I ask why you want one?"

Adi shrugged, "Oh, I've been in a slump and my boyfriend thought I needed something to distract me."

The old man cleared his throat, "Well, investing yourself into others will give purpose to your life. You can start tomorrow morning!"

A spark flickered in Adi's eyes, the first sign of life all year. "Thank you, Mr. Jordan!"

After Adi, Dagon, and Michael had left the store, Matthew turned to the shopkeeper with a mischievous smile, "I like your disguise, Jordan, I think it becomes you!"

The Watcher smiled in return, "Thank you, Ambassador! Your plan worked!"

Matthew gave a little laugh, "It definitely did. When she saw that ad, she convinced Ze'ev that she had to get down here before anyone else did!"

Jordan grinned, "Little does she know that she was the only one to have that ad in her paper!"

Turning serious, Matthew instructed his warrior, "The first priority is to convince her to get off those pills. We've got to get Adi feeling again. Think you can do it, Jordan?"

"Yes, sir. I will, sir."

"Good." Matthew quickly turned to catch up with Adi and Michael. The plan had been successful.

———

Months passed as Adi fell into a routine with her work. She found it pleasant enough especially working with Jordan. He was easy to talk to and had a way of getting her to open up without fear of judgment. Somehow he had managed to pull her life's story out of her except for the part with Joshua and Matthew. In spite of the friendship and the easy workload, Adi still felt empty. Forcing a smile was so difficult. Ze'ev became angry with her and threatened that if she didn't participate in the meditation with him, she would be back out on the streets again. Out of fear, she dutifully complied. A mixture of feelings swirled through her mind as she thought about the meditations. On one side, she enjoyed the relaxing music and did gain a sense of empowerment, but on the other hand, she felt twinges of fear that something wasn't right. Not wanting to make Ze'ev angry, she remained silent about her misgivings, until now with Jordan.

"Adi, you've been telling me about your life these past months. It's obvious someone is looking out for you," Jordan probed.

Curious, Adi asked, "Why do you say that?"

"Well, you were sentenced to jail but were set free. Somehow you survived on the streets for three years, and when you were sick, someone found you in the abandoned warehouse. It sounds to me that someone cares about you."

An image of the Prince looking deep into her eyes and pledging his love to her entered her mind. Squirming uncomfortably in her chair, Adi shrugged, "Ze'ev says it's fate or our destiny. He says that my thoughts were always negative and so I attracted those bad events into my life. He says that I'm in control of my destiny and that I make my life positive by thinking positively."

Jordan carefully snipped a thorn off a rose, "Hmm. Interesting, but if you were attracting the negative, then why were you freed from going to prison? How did that elderly lady just happen to be there when you needed clothes and a warm jacket before the weather turned cold? How did you find money on the streets for food? And how did anyone find you when you were sick? All of these positive events don't seem to mesh with your boyfriend's philosophy."

Feeling a bit perplexed, Adi sighed, "Well, I'm still learning. Ze'ev has helped me get in touch with my inner spirit guide."

"Spirit guide?"

"Yes, Ze'ev says that we are all divine, and we have to learn how to connect with our spirit guide to teach us how to tap into our divinity."

Jordan furrowed his brows in concern, "Interesting."

"My spirit guide's name is Shakti. She's so beautiful and she's teaching me how to be beautiful as well. She says that I must first believe that I am beautiful, worthy, and powerful before I can become those things."

Laying down the clippers, Jordan peered through his glasses at her. "So, is it working?"

Sighing Adi admitted, "I don't know. I just don't seem to feel anything anymore. It's like I really don't exist."

Jordan nodded in confirmation, "Yes, I can see that in your eyes. They're empty." Covering her small hand with his aged one, he pointed gently to the rose, "Look at that rose, Adi. It's beautiful isn't it? Smell its aroma."

Confused at the change in conversation, Adi leaned forward to smell the rose. "The aroma is strong but sweet."

"Does the rose have any thorns or blemishes?"

Adi shook her head.

"Did the rose remove the thorns all on its own?"

"No." Adi looked at him mystified as to what his point was.

"The rose could not pull the thorns off itself nor could it protect itself from bugs or disease. I had to tenderly care for it, protect it from the cold, and spray it with pesticide to keep it healthy. I had to feed it the proper food so it could stay nourished. Now that the flower has blossomed, I've trimmed off the thorns so that it could be beautiful. You are the rose, Adi. Someone has watched over you, fed you, clothed you, protected you, and wishes to turn you into a flower of beauty! You can not do that yourself, only the Gardener can!"

"Gardener?"

"King Penuel, Adi."

Shock coursed through Adi at the name of King Penuel. "You believe in King Penuel?" She asked incredulously.

"Yes, I do. I know the Prince as well, and I know they love each one of us. That includes you, Adi."

"No!" She shouted panicked.

"Adi, why do you resist him? It will do you no good to keep running from the truth!" Jordan pleaded.

Dagon sidled up to Adi and began whispering into her thoughts, "He's lying. The King would never love worthless scum like you."

Letting out an anguished cry, Adi ran from the flower shop. When Dagon reached the door, he turned to the old man and to Michael, "When will you two ever learn that we will win?" With a laugh he flew into the sky, keeping watch over the fleeing girl.

Transforming himself back into a warrior, Jordan stared dismally in the direction that Adi fled. "I failed."

Michael turned placing a comforting hand on the warrior's shoulder, "You did not fail, Jordan. You planted another seed of doubt in her mind, and that's all we can do."

"What will the Ambassador say?"

Michael smiled reassuringly, "He'll tell you just what I've told you."

Jordan sighed, "I guess that's the end of the flower shop."

"I wouldn't close just yet, my friend. When things begin to make sense to her, she'll come back."

———

Stopping at the street corner to catch her breath, Adi looked behind her to make sure she hadn't been followed. "You're overreacting. How is an old man going to follow you?" Adi mumbled to herself. She was shocked by the mixture of fear and longing that overwhelmed her at the mention of King Penuel. If what Jordan had said was true about King Penuel taking care of her, then why was she running from him instead of to him? Why was she so scared?

Dagon sensed her hesitation and jumped on the opportunity. *Adi, you must prove that you are worthy to be the King's daughter first. He'll never accept you as you are now.* Dagon whispered. Noticing a palm reading sign in the window across the street, he prodded Adi, *Stop torturing yourself with deciding over Ze'ev or the Prince. Go over there and discover your future so that you may find peace.*

Adi stared at the sign that seemed to offer resolution to her inner conflict. What harm can it do me? With resolve, she crossed the street and opened the door. The sweet and heavy fragrance of incense greeted her making her want to gag. Looking about the darkened room lit only by candles, Adi felt apprehensive. As she was about to make a quick exit, a beautiful woman with long blonde hair and porcelain skin came from behind a beaded curtain. Adi's eyes grew wide with shock. The woman looked just like her spirit guide, Shakti!

"I've been expecting you!" The woman smiled warmly, her brilliant blue eyes penetrating through Adi. "Please, have a seat!" She waved her hand towards the small table and chairs, the only pieces of furniture in the room.

Mesmerized by the woman's gentle voice and beauty, Adi silently obeyed.

"My guess is that you are facing a difficult decision. You feel that you are stuck in a rut with no way out, and you are here to find answers to what decision you must make."

Adi's face paled, "Yes, how did you know that?"

The woman gracefully shrugged her slim shoulders, "It's my job to know about the people that walk through my doors." Grabbing the set of tarot cards, she began shuffling, all the while not breaking eye contact with Adi. Once satisfied that the cards were mixed, she placed the deck in front of Adi and said simply, "Cut the deck."

With a trembling hand, Adi cut the deck then looked expectantly at the fortuneteller.

"I'm going to use the three card reading." As she began to pull off the top cards from the deck, she explained, "The card to your left represents the past, the card in the middle - the present, and the card to the right-the future." Pausing long enough only to see if Adi understood, she continued, "I will turn the middle card over since it represents the present. This is considered to be the power card."

Adi sat intently watching the fortuneteller as she slowly and reverently flipped the middle card over. Leaning in for a closer look, she saw an angel dressed in blue with its wings outspread looking down upon a man and a woman standing in a garden. Below the picture were the words, "The Lovers."

Adi curiously looked at the woman waiting for an explanation. "This is telling me that you are struggling between two paths. I assume that's why you're here to help you decide which path to take. This also represents harmony and that a union will be made."

Excitement coursed through Adi, "With whom?"

The woman smiled. "Let's look at the card representing the future, I'm sure that will give you the answer you are looking for." Adi eagerly nodded.

"I will turn over the card to the right, the card representing the future." This card appeared upright to Adi. A brilliant sun gleamed its rays touching the sky and earth while a small child rode bareback on a white horse through a field of sunflowers. The name of this card was simple – "The Sun." "This represents your future should you make the right decision in the present. You are promised good health, wealth, and approval from those around you, children, and abundant energy. You will be filled with joy and contentment."

Gasping, Adi's thoughts turned towards Ze'ev. This prediction matched all that Ze'ev had promised her if she were to marry him. Eager to receive confirmation, Adi pointed to the last remaining card. "And this is the card to the past, right?" Without a word, the woman turned the card over. Noticing that the card was upside down, Adi leaned forward to get a clearer look at the picture. A woman, wearing a white gown with a blue robe draped over her shoulders was sitting on a throne which was adorned with what appeared to look like sunflowers. A black pillar and a white pillar were on either side of her while a crescent shaped moon lay at her feet. At the bottom of the picture, Adi made out the words "The High-priestess." Feeling perplexed, Adi looked at the woman inquisitively, "What does it mean?"

"When the picture appears upside down to you, it means that it is in the reverse position. Usually it has a negative meaning. The past can help us understand what is holding us back from moving forward. This card suggests that you are experiencing a lack of personal harmony. You are having a hard time accepting who you are, and you continually ignore the facts about who you are."

Heat rose into Adi's face as she snapped, "I know who I am. I'm a thief, a prostitute, and scum. I get it!"

The woman continued to speak in a soothing tone, "No, Adi, you are divine, and that's what you won't accept!"

Stunned at her response, Adi sat back in the chair. "I don't understand this at all."

"This is trying to teach you that you perceive yourself one way, and because you won't accept the truth of your divinity, then you feel that you don't deserve happiness. Because you are being held back by the perceptions of the past, you run from the present, and miss out on the future."

Pausing, the woman cocked her head as if listening to someone. Giving a slight nod, she turned her piercing blue eyes back to Adi. "This is unusual, but I feel compelled to flip the card that is on the top of the deck." The picture of another woman clothed in white and a blue robe with a golden crown sat on a throne decorated with cherubs. In her hands she held what appeared to be a golden urn.

"This is the Queen of Cups. She encourages you to be queen of your life. You have the ability to create your destiny." Looking straight into Adi's eyes she became urgent, "Adi, you need to let go of the past and accept the man that will bring you into your golden future. You have the power to make it happen."

Adi sat in stunned silence. As the full impact of the meanings hit her, excitement coursed through her. At last, she would be able to make her decision and find the peace she longed for.

"Placing the sign to have your future read was a smart plan, Shakti. It worked." Dagon rarely gave his approval to anything, but this time he was more than happy to finally have something good to report back to Rasha.

"Yes, it was. I'm glad you recognized the sign." Laughing with glee, Shakti transformed herself back into her original hideous state. "It was like taking candy from a baby!"

Kristen Zuray

SEVENTEEN

Through swollen eyes, the emaciated man silently watched the rain splatter against the ground from his cell window. Muscle spasms shook the twisted frail body causing him to grip the bars for support. Memories of the last four and half years flooded through his exhausted mind. If anyone were to see this being, they would never recognize him to be the handsome Prince that valiantly offered to take Adi's place in prison. A jagged scar ran around his scalp where the prisoners had shoved a crown of thorns deep into his skin mocking his Princely heritage. His shaggy beard boasted of red oozing sores where Bill had pulled out clumps of hair in a fit of rage. Although he had not died from the whipping as many had expected him to, he lived a tortuous life of physical pain and constant infections.

In spite of the beatings and torture, Joshua still reached out with love and compassion towards his fellow inmates and guards. Feelings about the Prince were divided. As the years went by, most inmates grew increasingly agitated and hostile while others were swayed by Joshua's message of love. They met when they could in secret to learn all they could from the Prince. Strangely enough, the guards silently watched from a distance. Why should they interfere when it seemed as if Joshua's presence had calmed some of the toughest prisoners? They reasoned among themselves.

As painful as the physical and emotional abuse was, the worse yet were the visits from Rasha. Appearing during the times of isolation when the pain and the gnawing hunger were at their worst, Rasha would tempt Joshua to give up by promising him freedom. He would even allow Joshua to rule over Soteria if Joshua just agreed to worship him. During one of his beatings from another prisoner, Rasha appeared in an attempt to persuade him to summon his Watchers to defend him. Through it all, Joshua remained resolute to his father's plan. He would carry on for the sake of Adi, for the sake of Soteria.

Now as the disfigured Prince stood once more in solitary confinement watching the rain, he felt a familiar chill run through his body. Rasha was here. Without turning from the window, Joshua asked with a hoarse voice, "Why are you here, Rasha? Come to torment me again?"

An evil chuckle came from the shadowed corner. "I've come with news that would interest you."

Turning, Joshua stared at the monster that stepped from the shadows. "What news could you possibly have that would interest me?"

"Oh, I don't know, maybe news about a certain girl." Rasha toyed with the Prince relishing the alarm that now showed on the Prince's scarred face.

"Stop toying with me, Rasha. Out with it! Now!" The Prince commanded. All he wanted to do was to send Rasha to the abyss, but he knew the time was not right, and so he took a deep agonizing breath to restrain himself.

Holding his hands up in mock defense, Rasha stated, "Okay, okay. Adi has accepted Ze'ev's proposal of marriage. They are engaged!" Evil laughter erupted from the creature.

Shock coursed through Joshua's spirit preventing him from responding. "What makes it even more beautiful to me is that Adi actually begged Ze'ev to marry her! Once Shakti showed her that Ze'ev was the man that would fulfill all her dreams, she went running back to him begging him to accept her!" Rasha doubled over with cruel hysterical laughter.

The worst kind of pain ripped through Joshua's heart and soul, crumpling him to his knees. "Adi what have you done?" Joshua cried out in agony. "Does my sacrifice mean nothing?"

Rasha's taunting overpowered the Prince's cries. Finding renewed strength, Joshua slowly stood to his feet. With tears streaming down his face, he looked squarely at Rasha, "This isn't over. Her engagement to Ze'ev isn't binding until they marry. You will never win, Rasha!"

"Doesn't look that way to me, Prince." Rasha sneered.

Anger flashed through Joshua, "Leave me!" He ordered.

Rasha gave a mocking bow, "As you wish, Prince." With that Rasha vanished into the air leaving Joshua alone with tortuous scenes of Adi's future should she follow through with the marriage. Once more Joshua dropped to his knees, burying his face into the cold cement floor. Great sobs heaved through his body as he envisioned Adi blindly running down a path that led her right into the flaming abyss. Worse yet, he saw the future in which he would have to send her into the inferno. She stood before him so clearly. Her warm brown eyes stared up at him in petrified terror as the reality of her poor choice sank in. She had rejected him and now she would have to pay the punishment herself. Filled with the anguish of the moment, Joshua pleaded,

"Adi, why didn't you listen? I warned you that if you didn't choose me, someday I would be before you not as your groom but as your judge. Why didn't you trust in my love? I gave you my life, my love, what more could I have done to spare you from this judgment?" He wept in agony. Unable to peer into her terrified eyes any longer, he turned away from her. "Be gone!" He said with finality. Adi's terrified screams filled his ears.

A pounding on the cell door and a guard's shout to shut up startled Joshua back to the present. Realizing that it was he who was screaming in such terror, he quieted down to a soft moan. "Oh, Adi, you're running out of time." Rocking back and forth, he whispered over and over, "I love you, Adi."

———————

Hearts beating in one accord with the Prince, King Penuel and Matthew heard and felt Joshua's pain at the same time. Both fell on their knees and wept for the woman they all loved.

———————

Even though it was mid day, the sky grew ominously dark over Soteria. With a sense of foreboding, Adi moved restlessly about in her room. Sighing, she wrapped a warm blanket over her and curled up on the love seat. Once more she lifted her left hand to stare at the diamond ring Ze'ev had given to her. It was a beautiful one-karat emerald cut diamond surrounded by smaller diamonds. Ze'ev wanted to make sure that no one would miss the fact that she was taken, he had proudly explained. Staring at the glittering diamonds, she wondered for the hundredth time why she couldn't feel more excited. Marrying the most sought after bachelor was a dream true. Shouldn't she be happier?

Growing sleepy, Adi closed her eyes and drifted off to sleep. In the darkness she could make out a faint cry. Slowly feeling her way toward the sound, the darkness opened up into a damp cold room that held an unstable cot with a stained mattress. Shock resonanted within her as she realized that she was standing in a prison cell. The weeping that she had heard increasingly grew louder drawing her attention away from the bars on the windows. Turning around, she saw a man kneeling on the cold floor with his face pressed against the cement sobbing in desperation. The loneliness and pain of this man pulled at her heart. Unable to bear watching him cry, she moved toward him, kneeling next to him. "It will be okay," she whispered.

Upon hearing her voice, the man tearfully looked up. Without condemnation, the man pleaded, "Adi, what have you done? Does my sacrifice mean nothing to you?"

Adi recoiled in shock as she recognized the voice of the Prince. Scrambling to her feet, she desperately searched for a way to escape back into the darkness. Tears streamed

down her face as she hit the walls frantically. All the while
the Prince kept whispering over and over, "I love you, Adi!"

"No!" She screamed jolting awake. She lay there a
long time quietly sobbing. If only... A flash of anger
coursed through her, *He's dead and no use crying over
something that is lost.* She thought.

With resolve, Adi marched over to her nightstand
pulling open the drawer. Reaching in, she pulled out her
bottle of antidepressant and read the possible side affects.
Vivid dreams it said. *I need to get off these pills and enjoy
being with the one who is alive!* Quickly she threw them in
the trash. Fearful that Ze'ev would find out, she retrieved
the bottle and flushed the pills down the toilet. *There's no
need for Ze'ev to know. Once I'm happy again, he won't
care.* She reassured herself.

Kristen Zuray

EIGHTEEN

Warm rays of sunlight cast a glow on the secret meeting taking place on the usual park bench. Ze'ev squinted against the light as he turned to face Rasha in annoyance, "I don't want to marry Adi. She's so boring and moody. She never wants to do anything!"

"I'm paying you handsomely for marrying her, am I not?" Rasha barked.

"Yes, and that's not the point. I just don't see how I can keep being so nice to her when she drives me insane!"

Rasha chuckled, "Don't worry, Ze'ev. You only have two years left with her."

Puzzled, Ze'ev craned his neck to take a better look at Rasha, "Two years?"

Giving a satisfied sigh, Rasha crossed his beefy arms over his rotund belly. "Tell her that you'll marry her April 20th two years from now. That is the date the Prince will be released from prison. Can you imagine the shock he will feel, when he discovers that Adi just got married?" Rasha clapped his hands in delight.

Ze'ev, feeling a little less enthusiastic, grumbled, "But what about me? I don't want to be married to her."

"You won't have to be. Just after the wedding ceremony, I'll make sure she disappears forever."

"What are you going to do to her?"

"I'm going to send her to a place that not even the Prince is allowed to go. And the best part is, I'm not really sending her there, it's where she has chosen to go! If she doesn't accept the Prince's proposal, then she has sealed her fate forever." Again, Rasha clapped his hands with delightful anticipation.

Confused, Ze'ev just shrugged. What did it matter to him just as long as he made out okay.

Rasha stood to leave, pausing to give a word of warning, "Keep her on the anti-depressants. We don't want her to think for herself again after we've come so far. You will be paid well for doing so."

Ze'ev hesitated, wondering if he should bring up the subject, but he figured he deserved to know, so he plowed ahead, "Rasha, you had promised that I would be able to rule Soteria if I married Adi. When does that happen?"

Rasha smiled, "Now. I will make sure that your engagement will be widely publicized. You and Adi will be seen as a magical couple, a couple that offers true love to young starry-eyed girls and hope to broken marriages. By the end of these two years, you will be widely known and people will want you as their next leader. When they hear of your bride's tragic death on your wedding day even those who oppose you will be moved with pity to vote you in. We will meet this weekend at your home with a group who are tired of the political parties Soteria has now. Our dream is to bring someone into power who can unite both sides and usher in the next stage of evolution - the New Age! We believe that you are the man for that job, Ze'ev!"

Glowing at the confidence that Rasha displayed in him, Ze'ev grinned, "I'll be ready!"

Late Saturday evening, a group of men quietly met in Ze'ev's office. Looking about suspiciously, Rasha gruffly asked, "Where's Adi?"

"She went to bed hours ago." Ze'ev replied as he looked over the group of men. Lounging in a smooth leather winged chair, sat Adi's doctor. Dr. Lawrence was the prominent physician for the upper class and spokesperson for all things medical. To his left, sitting in another leather chair was the president and CEO of the largest pharmaceutical company. John Tyler kept his company on the cutting edge of technology by hiring the best scientists and by planting secret agents among other companies. Several lawsuits were brought against him for stealing formulas, but nothing could be proven, most likely due to the help of Aiden Bristol. Ze'ev had met Aiden the night of the gala almost five years ago. At the time, Aiden had been a successful lawyer that was quickly moving up. Now he was a judge presiding in the Supreme Court of Soteria. Ze'ev tried to cover the chuckle that threatened to escape. The irony of it all, seeing a man that was supposed to uphold the law, and yet here he sat plotting to overthrow the Soterian government. Ze'ev's eyes traveled to the distinguished gentleman who stood pouring himself a drink from the mini bar. Of course, every secret group had to have a banker/politician. William Bennet, the man accused of murdering his wife, looked up from the drink he was pouring to stare at the person who just walked into the office. Surprised by the intrusion, Ze'ev turned to see who it was. Lorretta Van Hilt, the famous actress! What was she doing here? Sensing the unspoken question of the group, Rasha announced, "Many of you don't know that Loretta is not just an actress. She is the one who strongly influences the ideologies that the entertainment industry pushes. We need her on our side."

Casually taking a sip of his vodka, Bennet asked, "So what's the plan to get Ze'ev into office, Rasha?"

"The plan is simple, mind control. He who controls the mind, controls everything!" Rasha grinned at the simplicity of his statement.

Confused, Bennett pressed, "Mind control makes sense, but how do you plan on accomplishing that?"

Rasha laughed with glee, "It's almost already done, and most of you aren't even aware of it!"

Feeling annoyed, Bennett snapped, "Enlighten us then."

Lorretta interrupted, purring like a cat, "Allow me. It is said that the eyes are the windows to the soul. The entertainment industry at first showed them what they wanted- values and family, but through the years, we integrated the New Age philosophies without the audience even knowing it. Little by little, we introduced violence, vulgarity, immorality, and self-worship. Because entertainment provided an escape to their mundane lives and gave them pleasure, they were willing to overlook the offense. It didn't take long before they craved more and more. The more violent and sexual the better. Over time, they have become desensitized and have forsaken their principles. In place of morality, they have accepted the New Age idea that there is no absolute truth. They create their own truth because there really is no right or wrong. They will believe only in themselves."

Rasha gave Loretta a pat on the back, "I say Lorretta has done a fine job." Looking over to Dr. Lawrence, Rasha asked, "How are your patients doing, Dr. Lawrence?"

Clearing his throat, the doctor straightened in his chair. "Quite well. I have found that many patients who have compromised their morality and depend only upon themselves to battle guilt, loneliness, and sadness. They describe it as a void that cannot be filled. In their search to be released from this illness they come to me. Naturally, I recommend they take Phloxine to help their 'depression'." He chuckled at the inside joke. "Their senses are dulled, making them easily influenced."

"Wait a minute. Are you saying depression isn't real?" Ze'ev asked suspiciously.

"No, I'm not saying that at all. Depression is real and there are some that truly need the medication, but I have many patients that struggle with normal sadness brought on by a tragic event in their lives, or as stated before, are searching to escape guilt or lonely feelings. They come to me thinking they are clinically depressed and ask for the prescription."

"Mr. Tyler is doing a great job in finding "medicinal" ways to sabotage the mind!" Rasha laughed as John Tyler smiled deviously. "Speaking of drugs," Rasha continued, "Crystal meth and heroin use is spreading quickly among the teens and young adults of Soteria. They are so desperate to be accepted among their peers that they'll try anything. Little do they realize that with one try, they can become addicted. They have been deceived into destroying their own minds!" An evil chuckle went around the group.

Another voice sounded in the room, "And I am trying to pass laws that prohibit free speech. If anyone speaks against the new morality or even of King Penuel, they will be considered closed minded, intolerant, and a bully. Anyone who speaks or even dares to think differently from society will be considered a threat. No one would dare go against the New World Order!" Aiden looked smug as he lit his cigar.

Not to be out done, William Bennett chimed in, "I think we need to plan an economic disaster. When a person's way of life is threatened, they will agree to anything. Order out of chaos will be how we get Ze'ev into power. If he can bring stability to the economy, people will follow him."

Excitement coursed through Ze'ev as he began to understand the deceptive plan that had already been in place for years. The lust for power and wealth burned within him causing him to wish that he didn't have to wait the two years to marry Adi.

———

A few weeks passed since the meeting with Rasha, and Ze'ev's patience with Adi wore thin. If he thought living with her when she was detached from everything was difficult, he was wrong. Never knowing what mood Adi would be in from one moment to the next was irritating. One second she was happy and wanting to get out and the next she would be crying before they could even get out the door. She had spent several days in bed complaining of having the flu and dizziness. To him, life was miserable. He was used to being a free man coming and going when he chose. Now he felt suffocated and trapped. As he walked into the kitchen to fix his morning coffee, he saw that Adi was already there fixing breakfast.

Eyeing her cautiously, he gruffly asked, "How are you feeling this morning?"

Adi looked up at him and smiled brightly, "Much better. I'm sorry, Ze'ev, for being so difficult lately. But to show you that I'm feeling better I made you some breakfast and coffee!"

Just as she turned to hand him his plate of steaming scrambled eggs and toast, the room tilted and swayed. Losing her balance, she fell dropping the plate of food. Eggs splattered everywhere.

Kneeling down to face a now sobbing Adi, Ze'ev squinted in agitation, "Adi, have you been taking your pills?"

Closing her eyes against the spinning, she cried, "Why do you ask me that right now?"

Growing impatient, Ze'ev snapped, "Because these dizzy spells, mood swings, and even the flu symptoms are all signs of discontinuation symptoms."

"What?"

Grabbing her wrists, Ze'ev roughly pulled her to her feet. "Get your pills, Adi, I want to see your pills!"

Weak from the dizziness and frightened by Ze'ev's reaction, Adi stammered, "I-I don't have them. I flushed them down the toilet."

Gripping her shoulders tightly, he yelled in frustration, "You fool, don't you know that you need those? You're no good without them!"

Tears streamed down Adi's face, "But I did it for you, Ze'ev! I wanted to be happy again for you!"

Pushing her away, he snapped, "For me? If you were thinking of me you would have stayed on them. You are so selfish, Adi." Grabbing his keys from off the counter he headed toward the door.

"Where are you going?" Adi cried in alarm.

"Away from you." Ze'ev hollered as he slammed the door.

Adi spent the rest of the day nursing an excruciating headache. Seeing an opportunity, Michael stood close by whispering doubts into her thoughts. "Why does Ze'ev want you on the pills so badly?" "Do you want to spend the rest of your life with a man that you are afraid of?"

Hours later, Adi heard the front door shut firmly. The sound of Ze'ev's footsteps in the hallway caused Adi to sit up in bed. Clutching the blankets closer to her, she fearfully stared at her bedroom door with apprehension. Ze'ev had been gone all day. Hoping that his getting out of the house would put him in a better mood, Adi debated on whether or not she should venture out to meet him. Before she could decide, the door opened and Ze'ev walked in brusquely. His eyes were cold and unfriendly as he threw a small bag onto her bed. Adi tried to hide the shiver that swept through her.

"Here are the pills. I've counted them out and each day I will count them and there had better be one missing." With that, he turned and left.

Adi's stomach knotted with misgiving as she stared down at the brown bottle. *How dare he order me about as if I were an imbecile!* Warning bells were going off in her mind, something was not right. *Fine. I'll play his little game and in the end he'll come to understand that I was right!* She decided.

The next morning, Adi showered and dressed. Reaching for the bottle, she spilled a pill out and threw it in the toilet. Michael breathed a sigh of relief. Gathering her courage, she put a smile on her face and yanked the door open. Finding Ze'ev already at the table drinking his coffee and sifting through his emails, she quietly approached placing the bottle of pills on the table. Without a word, Ze'ev spilled out the contents and counted. Satisfied that one was missing, he finally said, "Good. When you start feeling better, you'll thank me for being so rough on you. You'll see."

Time will tell who's right. Adi thought angrily. The game continued, Ze'ev counting the pills and Adi throwing them out. As the discontinuation symptoms subsided,

Ze'ev claimed the credit for Adi getting better while Adi quietly applauded herself for making a good decision. She was excited that she could feel again even though some of her emotions were of sadness and guilt, but she took this as a step closer to feeling joy and happiness. Even Ze'ev's attitude had changed from impatience to tolerance. Realizing that her moodiness had hurt their relationship, Adi worked hard at regaining what was lost. Whatever Ze'ev wanted her to do, she did. If meditation and talking to her spirit guide brought her closer to Ze'ev, then she did it. If attending the many social functions helped Ze'ev get into a better position in society, then she encouraged him to attend. To the outside world, they were a couple in love. Their romance was the most talked about in the social circles and in the tabloids. She was Cinderella and Ze'ev the Prince that saved her from the brutality of her stepfather. At times, she could almost believe that the stories were really true. She loved the times when Ze'ev would shower her with jewels and clothing for the next event and how he would show her affection in public. But in between events, Adi felt unsure of how things really were between them. Ze'ev would slip out quite frequently for secret meetings with someone. When he would return, he would be gruff and withdrawn. Several times, Adi caught him staring at her with cold hard eyes. The insecurity of it all caused Adi to try even harder to please Ze'ev. After a year and a half of reaching out to him, Ze'ev surprised her one day by inviting her out to lunch.

Sitting across from him, Adi took in his strong masculine form. He was dressed in a dark blue suit with a white shirt unbuttoned at the collar. His neatly combed black hair and clean-shaven face made him the most attractive man in Soteria. A longing for his approval welled up inside of her, *I wonder if he really loves me.* She thought.

Placing his menu aside, Ze'ev reached across holding onto Adi's hands. "Adi, we've been engaged now for over a year. I think it's time we discuss a wedding date!"

Joy and relief flooded over her, "Really?"

"Of course, I've only held off because I knew you were struggling with your health. I didn't want to pressure you, but now that you're better we should discuss it!"

Tears gathered in her eyes, "Oh, Ze'ev, I thought that maybe you didn't want to marry me after all!"

"Not marry you? Why would I not want to marry the most beautiful girl in Soteria?" Ze'ev feigned surprise.

Blushing, Adi smiled happily at him, "When would you like to get married?"

"In six months."

Adi looked at him in surprise. "You've already thought about this?"

Ze'ev shrugged looking sheepish, "Of course I have. There's a lot to do since this will be the biggest event in Soteria by far. What do you say?"

"I say, yes!" Adi grinned excitedly.

———

Frustrated, Matthew tossed the paper onto the motel bed and stared at Gabriel, the bearer of the news. Thomas looked up from where he sat searching the internet.

"What's wrong, sir?"

Letting out a great sigh, Matthew responded, "Adi and Ze'ev have set a date for their wedding. It's all over the papers that Gabriel brought. They are to be married the same day the Prince is released from prison."

Thomas shook his head sadly, "Well, I guess... Wait a minute, you said Prince Joshua will be released on the same day?"

Matthew nodded. "But, but, why doesn't she just wait to see what the Prince has to say?"

"This is clearly Rasha's plan. It serves two purposes, one - it distracts people's attention from the Prince's release. Word leaked out about the beating and so most Soterian's think he's dead. Rasha wants it to remain that way so people won't see that the Prince fulfilled his promise of pardon. Secondly, what better way to inflict more pain upon an enemy than by stealing away his love on the same day he could have had her."

"That is just sick." Thomas shook his head in disgust. "I guess Adi got what she wanted - love, fame, and fortune!"

Shaking his head despondently, Matthew replied, "No, Thomas, she did not get what she wanted. She only thinks that she did. Her fame and fortune won't last. Once the wedding is over she won't even be a memory to anyone. As for love, she never found it. Her "love" will betray her."

Thomas remained silent for a moment absorbing what the Ambassador had predicted. Breaking the silence, he solemnly asked, "You know what's going to happen to her, don't you?"

"Rasha and Ze'ev are plotting to have her killed after the wedding ceremony. While partiers think that the happy couple has retreated to their honeymoon suite, Rasha will be sending Adi to the fiery abyss where the Prince cannot go. She'll be lost to him forever."

Thomas gasped in horror. "Sir, we must warn her!"

"What do think we've been doing, Thomas?" Matthew snapped. "She won't believe us! Very soon, Adi will realize that her unbelief has sent her to the place of her worst nightmares." Turning his attention to Gabriel, Matthew commanded, "Tell Michael to double the forces and have the Watchers ready at a moment's notice. If they need to engage, now is the time. They are not to hold back. Also, instruct Michael to persuade Adi to visit Jordan in the flower shop."

"Yes, sir. Will that be all, sir?"

Matthew nodded in deep thought waving away Gabriel. Gabriel shot into the air in search for Michael.

Kristen Zuray

NINETEEN

When Ze'ev first mentioned that they would have to wait six months before getting married, Adi felt that it would be a long wait, but she was wrong. The months were speeding by quickly as the demands of public appearances increased, especially after Ze'ev announced his intent to run for President of Soteria. It didn't come as too much of a surprise to her. Since the time they had announced their engagement, his popularity increased to the point of being well known in all of Soteria. She had been apart of the conversations in which people prodded Ze'ev to run. Even though her relationship with Ze'ev wasn't where she wanted it to be, she still felt a thrill of excitement seeing Ze'ev's promises to her coming true.

Three months passed in a whirlwind of activities leaving Adi exhausted. Shuffling towards her desk, she picked up her daily planner to see who she was meeting with that day. Squinting from the hangover from the night before, she rubbed her head as she strained to make out her handwriting. *Florists.* Sighing, Adi knew she would have another long day a head of her to decide on which florist to choose for her wedding. It seemed as if her wedding had turned political. Ze'ev's "secret" advisor told him that she had to choose the vendors that were willing to trade favors. If the business agreed to offer financial and political support to Ze'ev, they would choose them to be apart of the wedding, ensuring that their sales would increase.

Tugging a brush through her hair, Adi sighed with disappointment. She was living the life of her dreams: popularity, wealth, prestige, and love. Why did she feel so empty? She had begun to hate these quiet times when she stood face to face with her doubts. Questions constantly plagued her - who was Ze'ev meeting? Why was there a growing darkness in his eyes? Something was not right. Sighing, Adi threw the brush down muttering under her breath, "You're imagining things, Adi". Leaning into the mirror she continued to talk to herself, "You need to give yourself a day off, girl!"

Upon arriving at the wedding coordinator's office, Adi was ushered into the conference room. Hours dragged by as the coordinator and Adi interviewed each florist. Growing weary, Adi sat back staring at the coordinator, "How many more?"

Looking at her calendar, she responded, "One left. We can cancel if you'd like."

Sighing, Adi leaned forward stretching her back and shoulder muscles, "No, let's just finish it."

Upon hearing Adi's request, the woman rushed out to call the last florist in. At the sound of movement, Adi looked up locking eyes with the newcomer. Straightening up with surprise, she squeaked out, "Mr. Jordan?"

The older man grinned. "Do you think that I would miss out on the opportunity to help my young friend? I've been following your wedding plans in the paper. I have several ideas on how to do the arrangements!"

In spite of her embarrassment over how she had last left him, she couldn't help but warm up to him. Waving a hand to the empty chair next to her, she invited, "Sure, Mr. Jordan! You always were very creative!"

As she sat there listening to his excited descriptions of how he envisioned the floral arrangements, she couldn't help but notice the feelings of peace and security that she felt when she was with him. When he was finished, Adi stood smiling, "Well, Mr. Jordan, you're hired."

Looking pleased, the stooped man took her extended hand that she had extended to him and shook it gratefully. "Come by the shop tomorrow, and we'll go over the details!" Without waiting for a reply, he shuffled out the door.

Feeling pleased with herself, Adi turned to stare in the disapproving face of the coordinator. "Adi, Ze'ev will not approve of this choice. He's a poor florist who will not be a benefit to the campaign."

Raising her chin slightly, Adi stared back stubbornly, "True, but he's my friend, and I want to help him. Not everything has to be about the campaign."

Snapping her black leather notepad shut, the coordinator repeated, "Ze'ev will not like it, but I'll just let him deal with you."

Heat crept up Adi's neck. "Deal with me? Why should he DEAL with me? This is MY wedding!"

Shrugging, the woman looked coldly back at Adi, "If you say so. I have other clients waiting for me now." Quickly she left the room, leaving Adi standing there angry and confused. What was going on? It seemed as if there was more to this wedding that everyone else knew but her. Memories of Rasha standing over her with his beefy fist raised in the air ready to strike caused her to shudder. *What did the coordinator mean - deal with her as if she were a prisoner?* The thought struck her - a prisoner? *Is that what I really am - a prisoner to society's*

expectations? A prisoner to Ze'ev? Am I really free?
Shaking off the fear, Adi made a quick decision to visit the flower shop before going home.

———

"Jordan, Adi has decided to visit the florist shop now. She's on her way." Gabriel announced to the startled Watcher. "Help encourage her to talk about her doubts and inform her that the Prince will be released from prison the same day as her wedding."

"Yes, sir."

"Get there before she does. Now go." Gabriel commanded.

Jordan flew like lightning, arriving in plenty of time to unlock the shop and gather some roses to work with. Adi found him sitting perched on his stool, glasses pushed to the end of his nose, gently cutting thorns off the perfect red rose he held. "You're the rose, Adi." Memories came flooding back to their last conversation about the Gardener taking extreme care of the rose.

Looking up at the sound of her approach, Jordan smiled in surprise, "Adi! If you had come tomorrow, I would have had a centerpiece to show you for your approval."

Dismissing his concern with a wave of her hand, Adi smiled, "Don't worry, Mr. Jordan. It was good to see you again today. Your visit made me realize that I missed our talks." Sensing her uneasiness, Jordan remained silent allowing her time to sort out her thoughts. Finding the courage to continue, Adi quietly apologized, "I'm sorry for the way I ran out the last time I was here."

Jordan raised an eyebrow at her, "You're forgiven, Adi. I'm so glad that you came back." Seeing Adi's face brighten, Jordan asked, "So, how are the wedding plans coming?"

"Exhausting." It wasn't long before Adi began chattering about all that had happened, is happening, and is about to happen. Listening silently, Jordan continued working on sculpting and trimming. When Adi came to the end of her story, Jordan quietly questioned, "Sounds like maybe you're having some doubts? Maybe Ze'ev is not who he really is?"

Adi moved about uncomfortably. "It's just cold feet. I hear that all brides go through this. I'm sure everything will work out fine, he's just under a lot of pressure."

Seizing the opportunity of Adi's insecurity, Jordan inquired, "Did you know that Prince Joshua is to be released the day of your wedding? He will have fulfilled his promise to you."

Gasping, Adi cried out, "But Joshua is dead! They killed him!"

"Do you really think that he would go through such great lengths knowing that he would never make good on his promise?"

Seeing that his words were making an impact, he held up his now completed project. "What do you think?"

Looking at the painted glass jar filled with water and glitter, she crinkled her nose, "What is it?"

"What is it?" The old man chuckled, "Haven't you seen a snow globe before?"

"Yes, but most globes have a scene in it, and this one is just a painted jar!" She laughed.

"Oh, I guess I am showing you the wrong side." Turning it around, Adi took a deep breath in. The scene was so familiar. A beautiful waterfall cascading down a mountain into a blue pool of water. At the base, stood a bride and groom embracing. Where had she seen that scene before?

"It's beautiful!" She gasped.

Handing the globe to her, he sheepishly said, "Call it an early wedding gift."

With appreciation, Adi threw her arms around his neck, savoring the comfort she felt. Jordan gently held her. After a few moments, she pushed back, "I have to go. Ze'ev will be worried."

After Adi left, Matthew stepped from the shadows. Acknowledging the Ambassador's presence, Jordan bowed. "Sir, she didn't recognize the scene in the snow globe!"

A look of excitement was on Matthew's face. Hearing Adi put a voice to her doubts about Ze'ev and her lack of defensiveness showed great progress. "Don't worry,

Jordan, she will remember the dream that she had, and
when she does, she'll be surprised to see who her groom
really is!"

————

Adi walked into her bedroom placing her purse down on
her bed. Just as she was about to give into the temptation
to run a hot bath for her tense muscles, she heard Ze'ev's
voice call her name.

"Adi?" Ze'ev angrily hollered.

Slowly, Adi walked down the hallway towards the
kitchen. "What is it, Ze'ev? Is everything okay?"

"Where have you been?" he demanded.

"I've been with the wedding coordinator picking out a
florist!"

"Ah, yes, the florist!" Ze'ev sneered sarcastically.
"What were you thinking in picking that old man?"

Confused by his anger, Adi shouted back, "Mr. Jordan
is my friend!"

"I don't care if he's your friend, he won't support us in
the election, Adi!"

"Does everything have to be about you, Ze'ev?"

Losing control, Ze'ev slapped her cheek, "How dare
you? After all I've done for you, can't you give a little back
to me?"

Touching her stinging face, Adi stared in shock as
Ze'ev continued on his tirade, "You have no clue how hard I
am working to ensure a good future for us! We need to

have people with money and influence helping us to push us to the top! I've explained this to you before!"

"But I don't see how Mr. Jordan will ruin that?"

"Are you stupid? He's from the other side of town and he's not to be trusted." He growled at her.

Summoning up courage, Adi plowed on, "But he's my friend!"

Sticking a finger in Adi's pale face, Ze'ev shouted, "He's not your friend! You are to never see him again! Do you understand?"

Adi pushed him away, "You have no right to talk to me like that! I'm not your prisoner. You don't own me!"

Ze'ev slapped her again. "You're mine, Adi. I'll talk to you anyway I want to."

Refusing to be intimidated, Adi threatened, "I'm not yours yet, Ze'ev! Maybe I'll call the wedding off and marry the Prince when he gets out of prison!"

Ze'ev stared at her in surprise and then began to laugh, "Marry the Prince?" He mocked. Grabbing her by the nape of her neck, he shoved her forward to his office, "The Prince is dead! They killed him! Would you like the gory details? No? Maybe some pictures will convince you!" Pushing her hard against his desk, he let go and reached for a manila envelope. Pulling the contents out, he waved the pictures in her face. "Here is your Prince, Adi!"

Adi stared in horror at the graphic pictures of Prince Joshua being beaten and his still, bloodied form lying in the sand. "NO!" she screamed in terror.

"Oh, yes, Adi! The Prince is dead, and he didn't fulfill the sentence. Do you know what that means, Adi?" Ze'ev sneered.

Not waiting for a response, he continued, "You'll have to go to prison and serve out the seven years or you marry me! Looks like I'm your only hope now, Adi!" Bursting into laughter, Ze'ev left the room.

Adi stood there paralyzed with fear. She had never seen this side of Ze'ev before. She had only sensed this darker side lurking below the surface, but she just assumed she was being paranoid. Now the real Ze'ev was beginning to show and the truth of him nauseated her. The pictures proving Joshua's death robbed all hope from her. Either way she looked at it, she was a prisoner. "No!" Running from the office, she fled to her room locking the door behind her.

Michael stood silently in the shadows watching the ugly scene unfold. For every harsh word and every slap on Adi's face, he flinched and clenched his sword. Every part of his being wanted to protect her from the abuse, but he remained still, knowing that it was in her better interest to see the truth about Ze'ev. Surprised that Michael did nothing, Dagon chortled, "What's the matter, Watcher, lose your nerve? Or have you finally realized that she's not worth it?"

Michael stared angrily at Dagon, but kept silent.

————

When all the tears were shed and Adi could cry no more, she reached for the snow globe that Jordan had given to her. Staring into it she wished that she could just disappear inside and live in that magical world with whoever the mystery man was. She now realized that the groom inside with love in his eyes was not Ze'ev. Poking through her clouded thoughts, a memory of a dream surfaced. Once more she saw the cascading waterfall tumbling over jagged rocks and into a blue pool of water. As the mist floated upwards, the water molecules twisted themselves into the formation of a bridal veil. Hearing her name being called, she turned to see a man running toward her with arms outstretched. Immediately, she recognized the deep brown eyes and compassionate smile. The groom in her dream and in the snow globe was Prince Joshua!

Kristen Zuray

TWENTY

It was a week before the wedding and Adi just wished it were over. After the realization that Ze'ev didn't really love her, all the joy had vanished from the wedding preparations. Life had fallen into a routine of pretending to be a happily engaged couple to the public and separating upon their return home. So often Adi had thought of locating Matthew, but then decided it was too late for her since the Prince was dead. In an attempt to deal with the situation, she tried to find happiness in the fact that she was no longer bound to Rasha and no longer starving on the streets. Other than love, all her other dreams had come true. Sighing, she broke away from her musings and looked out at the warm sun streaming through her window. It was going to be a beautiful day and she was going to enjoy it at her favorite park. Every bride needed a break from the stress of planning a wedding!

"Ambassador, Adi is headed to the park, ALONE." Gabriel announced placing special emphasis on the word *alone*.

"Ze'ev's not with her?" Matthew inquired.

"No, only Dagon follows. It seems as if the Shedim believe they have already won." Gabriel smiled.

Matthew's eyes lit up with hope. "Gabriel, summon as many Watchers as you can, but do it so as not to attract attention from the Shedim. I am going to talk to Adi one last time and there must be no interruptions. Have some of the Watchers throw Shakti into the abyss before he can alert Ze'ev, and put a guard around Ze'ev. He must not interrupt my meeting with Adi!"

"Yes, sir!" Gabriel responded with energy. It wasn't long before Gabriel found Jordan and a small band of Watchers entrenched near the flower shop. A few moments passed as the group huddled in a tight circle formulating a plan. As soon as Gabriel left, Jordan discreetly transformed once more into the elderly florist. Hailing a cab, he headed off towards Ze'ev's home. One by one the other Watchers followed suit. Some remained in their natural state casually flying towards the target while others blended into the bustle of the busy streets and sidewalks. Arriving undetected, they gathered in the shadows across the street from the house.

"Gabriel, where's Michael?" Jordan asked half expecting to meet up with the commander.

"He's protecting Adi at the park." Gabriel explained as he stared intently at the quiet house. "I don't see any Shedim. That's very odd. Either Ze'ev isn't home or they've really grown lazy."

"Or maybe they found out we were coming and have planned an ambush," Jordan whispered.

Gabriel nodded thoughtfully. "Watchers, be on guard and if you have to engage, do so in a way that will not attract other Shedim. In other words, no bolts of light! The Ambassador wants you to get rid of Shakti. Understood?"

The band of Watchers all nodded their heads in understanding. Stepping out of the shadows, Jordan waved the rest to follow slowly and cautiously. Making it across the street undetected, they entered into the house. All was quiet except for a faint chanting music that seemed to float on the air. Stealthily, they crept towards the sound. Upon reaching the door from which the music was coming, Jordan motioned for swords to be drawn. Pushing the door open a little, he was able to see Ze'ev sitting peacefully, legs crossed, palms upward. Shakti hovered above instructing him while two other Shedim loafed nearby. Turning to the waiting Watchers, Jordan signaled the number of Shedim.

Taking a deep breath, Jordan yelled, "For the glory of King Penuel and Prince Joshua!"
The band of Watchers burst into the room startling the Shedim. Before they could react, the angels thrust them quickly into the abyss. Shakti quivered before Jordan's sword. "You can't throw me in before the time!"

"Your deceiving days are over, Shakti!" Swinging with all his might, Jordan sent Shakti tumbling and screaming into the fires.

"Shakti?" An alarmed voice broke through the fading screams. Jordan looked at Ze'ev who sat blinking in confusion.

Ze'ev had been sitting completely mesmerized by Shakti's words when he felt a disturbance of energy enter the room. He had seen Shakti's look of alarm before disappearing completely. Not understanding what had happened, Ze'ev jerked awake and called out to her.

Jordan looked at the band of warriors with approval. "That went well. Now if the rest of the plan can go as smoothly, the Ambassador will have a chance to speak with Adi. We are to stay here and guard Ze'ev."

Gabriel found Matthew once again hidden in the grove of trees tenderly watching Adi. "Sir, Shakti has been taken care of and Ze'ev is under guard. There have been no other signs of the Shedim."

"Gabriel, help Michael with Dagon. Keep him away from Adi so he can't whisper deception into her thoughts."

Matthew gingerly stepped away from the shelter of the trees and walked nonchalantly towards Adi. When he drew near he remarked, "I hear you're getting married at the end of this week, Adi."

Adi sat up straighter on the bench in surprise. Dagon hissed at the Ambassador. With quick movements of their swords, Michael and Gabriel backed Dagon away from Adi. Realizing that he was outnumbered and there was no help in sight, all Dagon could do was to comply.

Nervously, Adi cleared her throat, and replied, "Yes, I am. I haven't seen you in a long time, Matthew. Where have you been?"

Matthew smiled sadly, "I've been here, Adi, waiting for you."

Adi furrowed her brows in confusion, "Waiting for me? Why didn't you go back to Miskana once you heard that I chose Ze'ev? There's nothing left for you here, especially with the Prince being dead."

Matthew frowned. "Joshua isn't dead, Adi."

Anger coursed through her. What kind of sick joke was this? "Of course he's dead! I heard about the beating. I saw the pictures of his mangled body lying in the sand. There's no way anyone could ever survive that! Besides, Ze'ev told me that he was dead."

Shaking his head Matthew looked at her, "Of course Ze'ev would tell you that. Don't you see? If you believe that Joshua is dead, then you would have to marry Ze'ev. What other alternative would you have?"

Adi sat there stunned at the preposterous idea. "Nothing makes sense anymore." Adi's voice trembled in defeat. "Why would Ze'ev marry me if he doesn't love me?" She asked, more to herself than to Matthew.

Not wanting to push too hard, Matthew gently prodded, "He's been promised great wealth and power if he marries you."

Confused, Adi stared at Matthew, "Promised? By whom? And why me, why would I matter?"

"Ze'ev works for a wicked man, Adi. This man is an enemy of the King and the Prince. What better way to hurt the Prince than to take away the woman he loves?"

Adi gasped. "But the Prince is dead!"

Matthew edged closer to her, leaning down to look her in the eyes, "No, Adi, the Prince is not dead. He is alive and will be released in just four days! He will come looking for you!"

Giving an unsure laugh, Adi retorted, "That's not possible, Matthew. I saw the pictures. The only way I would believe otherwise is if I saw him alive for myself."

Matthew gently squeezed her hand, "I understand that it is difficult to believe in something that you cannot see, but have faith, Adi. Belief is what will save you!"

Adi pulled away, "You're not making sense, Matthew. If what you say is true, that Ze'ev is marrying me to hurt the Prince, then he has no need to go through with the marriage since Joshua is dead. He must have some kind of love for me in order for him to go through with it."

Matthew quickly jumped on her thought, "Or the reason why he is continuing with the wedding is because the Prince is alive! That ought to be proof enough right there, Adi."

Standing up in frustration, Adi inquired angrily, "Oh, why do you confuse me so?"

Jumping up, Matthew towered over her, "And why do you refuse to accept the truth, Adi? If you go through with this, Joshua nor I will be able to help you. You'll have brought the consequences upon yourself."

Fear squeezed her heart, leaving her breathless. With a sob, she turned and fled.

"Adi!" Matthew called after her, "Find out who Ze'ev is meeting with!"

Turning to Michael and Gabriel, Matthew quietly said, "Let Dagon go." With a stoop in his shoulders, Matthew walked slowly back to the grove of trees.

———

Rasha growled in a low threatening tone to the commander of the Shedim. "You allowed the Ambassador to talk with Adi?"

"No, sir. I was in a vicious fight against Michael and Gabriel!" Dagon lied. "There was no back up, sir!"

Rasha shoved Dagon hard against the brick wall. "Don't give me excuses! And you sent Shakti to the abyss!"

Dagon cowered against the wall, "I had nothing to do with Shakti!" Immediately Dagon regretted his words as Rasha began to beat him in a fit of rage.

When Rasha saw that Dagon was sprawled before him nearly lifeless, he took a step back and addressed the rest of the Shedim that had gathered around. "We have four days until the wedding. You all had better be on guard. If I lose Adi, I will send all of you to the abyss after I beat you!" Rasha glared at each Shedim. "Now go!" He screamed.

———

The next three days passed in fearful torture for Adi. It seemed as if all of Soteria was bracing itself for an event other than her wedding. The sky seemed to grow darker with each passing day as an eery stillness settled over the city. Peering out her window at the foreboding dark sky

with its flashes of bright lightning, Adi shuddered. Odd.
Lightning with no thunder.

Shedim gathered from all over Soteria while more and
more Watchers flew in from Miskana. Mild clashes
between the King's warriors and Rasha's horde erupted
over the skies of the city causing Soterians to hunker down
with anticipation of a coming storm.

Adi turned at the sound of the front door shutting
softly. Quickly walking over to her bedroom door, she
quietly opened it a crack. Upon hearing deep muffled
voices, Adi slowly slipped out into the hallway. Creeping
toward the retreating tones, she craned her neck to see
Ze'ev follow someone into his office. Once the door was
shut, Adi tiptoed across the kitchen and to the office door.
Placing her ear against the door, she held her breath
listening.

"So, tomorrow is the big day, Ze'ev!" Rasha chortled.

Ze'ev gave a short nervous laugh, "Finally. Is
everything ready?"

Rasha clapped Ze'ev on the back, "Don't worry.
Everything is in order. Adi will be well taken care of."

"Good. Now what about everything else, when will that
happen?"

Laughing, Rasha replied, "Patience, Ze'ev. It won't be
long now until Soteria is ready for the New Age. My drugs
whether street drugs or pharmaceutical drugs are working
quite well. Between the drugs, the distorted media, and

political unrest, soon all of Soteria will be thrown into chaos, too afraid to think for themselves. Rasha chuckled with amusement, "They are so used to giving into their desires, that their appetite for more is never satisfied. The economic collapse will be brought about by their own greed, and they will welcome anyone who can give them back their pleasures."

Ze'ev almost giggled with amusement, "How clever to use them against themselves!"

"Hmm. That's why I am the master deceiver!" Rasha proudly proclaimed giving a slight arrogant bow.

"What will happen to those who oppose the New Age?" Ze'ev asked growing serious.

Hatred gleamed in the brute's dark eyes. Ze'ev could almost see a hint of green oozing from the corners of his mouth. "They will die."

Ze'ev sucked in his breath not in shock or fear, but with eager anticipation. Excitement coursed through him. The plan was coming together. Soon he will rule over all of Soteria and it would all start with tomorrow.

Sensing that the conversation had come to an end, Adi quickly slipped back down the hall and into her bedroom. Jumping into bed, Adi thought it best that she pretended to be asleep just in case Ze'ev checked in on her. Adi's thoughts tumbled over one another in terror. Ze'ev is planning on overthrowing the government? Who was that man with him? Why did his voice sound familiar? Adi lay there clutching her blankets. Memories of past conversations with Ze'ev about the New Age came back to her in a rush. He had warned her that if she didn't get on board, something bad would happen to her. Now she understood, she would die along with the others who would oppose him. *How do I get out of this?* She silently cried.

Another memory flooded back to her. The beautiful fortuneteller had predicted that she would become powerful and wealthy - a goddess, she had said. Adi's survival instinct kicked in. In order to survive this coming change she would have to marry Ze'ev and support him in this endeavor. *Didn't the man promise Ze'ev that she would be taken care of?* Feeling a small relief, Adi fell into a fitful sleep.

———

The next morning, Adi awoke with a start. This was her wedding day! Instead of feeling joy, fear created by last night's conversation pierced through her heart. Crawling out of bed, she slowly crossed over to the window. Disappointment filled her as she looked at the darkening sky. Even though it was morning, the sky looked as if it were early evening. With despair, Adi turned to begin the preparations for the ceremony.

In his bedroom, Ze'ev paced back and forth with nervous anticipation. Today he would at last be free from Adi and this would mark the beginning of his rise to power!

Rasha was unbearable to be near. On high alert, Rasha kept a close eye on the Soterian's Prison for Men. Joshua was not going to come near Adi!

King Penuel stood with back rigid, tightly gripping the balcony rail. His deep brown eyes never wavered from Soteria. He was overjoyed at the prospect of his son's release, but agonized over the final decision Adi had to make. He would not rest until the day was over.

With a mixture of excitement and concern, Matthew looked over at the tense face of Thomas, "Let's get to the courthouse."

Both men left the safety of what had been their humble home for the past seven years.

With a loud clang, the cell door opened as a large burly guard stepped into the smelly small space. "You're to come with me," he ordered the prisoner.

Joshua humbly followed the officer down the row of cells. Angry voices shouted out from behind locked doors

as the Prince past by. Nearing the end of the row, a hand
shot out through the bars.

"Prince Joshua, remember me!" a fellow prisoner
pleaded.

Turning to the emaciated man, Joshua tenderly
vowed, "I promise. You will be with me in Miskana." The
hand retreated and a soft sob was heard, "Thank you."

Ushered into an armored truck, Joshua was whisked
away to the court house.

———

A small Shedim flew undetected toward the judge's car and
slashed the tires. His orders were to delay the judge.

———

Adi sat in front of the mirror applying her make up.
Looking down, she noticed her snow globe. A tear slipped
down her cheek as she remembered Joshua and his
declaration of love.

———

Angrily, Judge Wilson hit her car. "I'm going to get
whoever did this!" she muttered through clenched teeth.
The realization that she was going to be late for court made
her even angrier. Storming back inside her townhome, she
called for a cab. Before she could even set the phone down,
a car horn honked impatiently outside. Perturbed, the
judge marched to her door. Throwing the door open she
stared wide- eyed at the cab. Quickly, she rushed down the
steps jumping into the car.

"Where would you like to go?" Jordan turned around giving her a big smile.

"To the courthouse, immediately," She said brusquely.

TWENTY ONE

Joshua sat quietly looking about the courthouse. Seven years ago, the room was filled with bystanders and reporters. It was chaos, but now the courtroom was virtually empty with the exception of the bailiff, guards, and lawyers. It seemed as if everyone had forgotten about him. That is, all except for Matthew, Thomas, and Rasha who now sat in the back row seat invisible to the Soterians. With his muscular arms crossed, Rasha sat clenching and unclenching his fists. Green ooze dripped from his mouth as his eyes glared with red-hot hatred for the Prince. Calmly, the Prince returned his gaze.

A guard lightly punched the Prince's arm distracting him. "Weren't you the one that was going to marry that Adi girl?"

Joshua silently nodded.

The guard looked sympathetically at Joshua, "Rotten luck. You did all this for her and she gets married to another man."

"She's not married yet," Joshua stated as a quiet challenge to Rasha.

The guard looked at his watch. "Oh, she will be in about an hour. Guess you won't make it in time to see her."

———————

A sharp rap on the door startled Adi out of her reverie. "Adi, are you almost ready? The limo will be here in thirty minutes to pick you up."

Trying to sound cheerful, Adi called back lightly, "Okay, sweetie. Don't come in, it's bad luck to see the bride before the wedding!"

Ze'ev gave a short laugh, "Fine. I'll see you at the Plaza when you walk down the aisle."

Looking at her clock, Adi knew it was time to get her bridal gown on.

———————

Despite the lack of Soterians in the courtroom, the place was crowded with the Shedim and the King's Warriors. With swords brandished and glowing brilliant, the Watchers stood forming a barricade three rows deep between the Shedim and the Prince. Knowing full well that if they were unable to kill the Prince in these past seven years, there was no hope to defeat him now. They were reduced to doing nothing more than hissing and cursing at him.

Judge Wilson rushed in and sat down, not waiting for the bailiff to announce her. Pounding on the gavel, she commanded in a rushed tone, "Prisoner, please rise."

Joshua rose slowly to his feet. The Judge stared at the man before her. He bore very little resemblance to the strong strapping man that had stood before her seven years earlier. Pity filled her as she looked into his soulful eyes. "Prince Joshua, by some miracle you have served out the seven year sentence on behalf of Adi. The requirements of the law have been fulfilled. Adi will receive a full pardon contingent upon the acceptance of your proposal. You are thereby released." The judge once more pounded her gavel in confirmation of her decision.

Turning to face the Shedim and Rasha, the Prince proclaimed in triumph, "It is finished!" Much to the astonishment of the judge, a brilliant light swirled around and around the Prince enveloping him. A surge of energy burst forth with such force that the windows of the courtroom blew out. Fragmented glass flew everywhere. The judge and the guards dove to the floor in fear. People passing the courthouse screamed and cowered at the loud explosion of glass.

When the light softened to a mild glow, Joshua stood, completely healed of his wounds. Only a few scars on his hands, feet, and head remained. Upon hearing that declaration, the Shedim let out a frenzied scream, drawing their swords. With a roar, Rasha shot into the sky flying furiously toward the Plaza. Adi was going to marry Ze'ev if it was the last thing he did.

"For the glory of King Penuel and Prince Joshua!" Jordan raised his sword high into the air. A brilliant light burst from his sword, illuminating the courthouse and the skies above. Upon seeing the ball of light, Watchers from all over Soteria joined in the battle cry, "For the glory of King Penuel and Prince Joshua!"

The strong healthy form of Joshua turned to Matthew and Thomas, "Let's find Adi," he stated with resolve.

———

Adi froze in the doorway of Ze'ev's house, her bridal gown billowing around her. Reporters and cameramen shouted questions and snapped pictures of this historic event. As she was about to step into the limo, a loud blast of thunder and an electrifying bolt of light streaked across the dark sky and rocked the car. Terrified, Adi covered her ears and sank to her knees as the ground began to shake. What was going on? It was black as night out there. Screaming, reporters and cameramen alike scrambled in several directions seeking shelter.

"Hey, lady, let's get out of here!" The limo driver called frantically.

Michael fought to get near the bride, "The Prince has been released. He's coming for you," he shouted as he crumpled into the mass of Shedim who beat and pummeled him.

Adi slipped into the limo unaware of the pleadings of the faithful Watcher who had been by her side for the past seven years. As the limo sped towards the Plaza, Adi stared out the window watching the bolts of lightning dance across the sky. Was Joshua somehow connected to this? But he was dead! Doubts nagged at Adi.

———

Upon hearing the cry of battle, Matthew turned to Thomas commanding him, "Meet Adi at the Plaza. You must be there when she steps out of the limo. Tell her that the Prince has just been released and is searching for her."

Without a word, Thomas rushed out to do as he was told.

———

The limo pulled up to the Plaza. People were frantically running about in a confused state. No one seemed to notice the bride stepping out of the car, all except for one person.

Quickly, Thomas stepped up to Adi. "Adi, do you remember me?"

Annoyed, Adi briefly glanced at the lean man with a baby face. "Should I?" She snapped.

"I am with the Ambassador. I mean, Matthew."

Recognition flickered in her eyes, but she denied knowing him. Not to be deterred, Thomas continued, "I wanted to let you know that Prince Joshua is not dead, he is alive! He has just been released from the court house and is on his way to find you."

Picking up the hem of her dress, Adi pushed past Thomas. Running into the lobby, Adi was greeted by an agitated Ze'ev. Grabbing a hold of her arm, he asked forcefully, "Where have you been?" Before Adi could respond, Ze'ev rushed on, "We need to get these people calm NOW!"

"And how do you propose that WE do that?" Adi snapped.

"By getting this ceremony started now! No storm is going to stop this wedding!" Turning from her, Ze'ev called in a loud voice gaining everyone's attention. "If you could take your seats, we intend to start the ceremony right now while we still have electricity!" He gave a chuckle hoping that a little humor would settle the guests. His attempts worked. In a few short minutes everyone was calmly seated remembering why they were there in the first place. Ze'ev looked back toward Adi, gave a curt nod, and rushed up the aisle. As the door closed behind him, Adi wondered at the fear she had seen in his eyes. Pushing the concern aside, she took a deep breath in an attempt to regain her composure. At the sound of the music, Adi threw open the doors before she could change her mind. All eyes turned toward her. Nausea threatened to overcome Adi. Squaring her shoulders and setting her eyes upon Ze'ev, Adi took a small step down the aisle.

Rasha stood in a shadowed corner watching with delight as Adi made her way slowly down the aisle. Frantically, a tattered Michael looked about for a way to distract her. A movement in the shadows caught his eye. Rasha! Quickly, Michael shot through the sky summoning for Jordan. In a split second, Jordan was there, concern etched on his face as he stared at his commander's condition. "Jordan, you need to cause a distraction," Michael heaved in pain.

Adi was half way down the aisle. Her legs were shaking so badly that she thought she might collapse before getting to the front. The closer she came toward Ze'ev, the more sinister he became. A look of triumph was spread across his face. Just as she was about to take another step, someone called out her name.

"Adi, don't do it! The Prince is....." Frantically looking about for the one who called out to her, she saw guards grabbing at an old man. Horrified she watched as they roughly dragged Mr. Jordan out. Another movement caught her eye, a short bulky man with strong beefy arms stood in the shadows watching her. Even though she couldn't see him clearly, there was no mistaking her stepfather! Adi trembled with fear. The voice! It was Rasha who was talking with Ze'ev the night before! All of Matthew's warnings about her demise came rushing back to her. If Rasha and Ze'ev were working together then that could only mean that they plan to kill her, not take care of her! And if Rasha was Joshua's enemy and was bent on her marrying Ze'ev that would also mean Joshua must be alive!

Michael hovered near the door watching Adi as she continued to stand there. "Come on, Adi," he whipsered.

Alarm spread across Ze'ev's face. Quickly, he stepped off the stage and rushed towards her. With a small cry Adi whirled around and ran back down the aisle.

"Stop her!" Rasha shrieked at his Shedim.

Ze'ev reached out, grabbing at her sleeve. Sticking his foot out, Michael tripped Ze'ev. Still hanging onto Adi's sleeve, Ze'ev fell, ripping her dress. Adi kept running, feeling as if someone was pulling and pushing at her. Several Watchers including Michael attempted to form a wall of protection around Adi, but the fierce onslaught by the Shedim scattered the Watchers. "Run out of the city, Adi!" Michael yelled before turning to fight off a horned attacker.

Adi ran as hard as she could, sensing that Ze'ev was not far behind. Raindrops pelted her face. Before she knew it, a deluge of rain was coming down. Heavy footsteps sounded behind her. Quickly, she ducked into an alley hoping that it would provide her some cover from her pursuer. Unable to see clearly from the rain, Ze'ev ran past Adi, but Dagon found her. Flying low, he reached out his sharp talons and tore through her dress and skin. Screaming in pain as something sharp cut into her, Adi jumped from her hiding place. Hearing Adi's scream, Ze'ev quickly turned and ran toward the direction of the noise.

Michael and Jordan swooped in for the attack. Just as Dagon reached again for Adi, Michael slashed his sword across Dagon's wings, causing him to lose his balance. He fluttered momentarily before righting himself. "So this is it, Michael. You will lose."

"Jordan, follow Adi!" Michael ordered swinging his sword with all his might. His sword crashed into Dagon's sword sending sparks flying. There they hovered, neither one giving in. Exhausted from the recent beating, Michael began to lose his grip. Seizing the opportunity, Dagon heaved Michael's sword upward and then, just as quickly, brought his sword down onto Michael's hand sending the sword spiraling into the atmosphere. "Now what are you going to do, angel?" Dagon hissed with glee. Glancing behind him, Michael saw Adi fleeing down a concealed mud road. Realizing that Dagon no longer cared about chasing after Adi, Michael flew off in the opposite direction of Adi luring Dagon into pursuit.

Pain seared across Adi's back weakening her, but she pressed on with determination. Finally reaching the outskirts of town, she found an obscure dirt road. Running toward it, she tripped on her dress, falling into a mud puddle. Completely exhausted and in pain, Adi knew she could go no farther. Footsteps sounded behind her, and then, above the ringing in her ears, she could hear Ze'ev calling her name.

As the rain slowed and the mist parted, she saw the forms of two men walking toward her. Joshua? Matthew? Her tired eyes strained to see. "That was a foolish thing to do, Adi. You should never have run away from me!" Ze'ev was standing before her looking livid.

Rasha stood towering over her, his face twisted with cruelty. "Get up!"

Fear held Adi down. With hatred, Rasha reached down pulling her up violently. Adi screamed out in pain. Not letting her go, he shouted, "You will marry Ze'ev, you imbecile!"

Gathering up courage, Adi shouted back, "No!"

Slapping her soundly across the face, Rasha screamed, "You are mine, Adi! Don't defy me!"

Not caring anymore what happened to her, Adi weakly cried, "Joshua, I believe! I accept!"

A blast of light burst forth sending Ze'ev sprawling in the mud.   Joshua suddenly stood beside Adi and Rasha. Holding onto Rasha's wrist in a vise like grip, Joshua commanded in a low threatening tone, "Get your hands off my bride. She is no longer bound to you, for I have redeemed her!" Joshua's grip on Rasha's hand tightened as Rasha wrestled to maintain his hold on Adi, but the pain was unbearable. With a cry of rage, Rasha released his hold on her arm causing Adi to fall backwards into the mud. A welcoming darkness settled over her stunned mind.

———

Michael descended to the ground as his wounds sapped him of strength. Dagon followed suit. Now the two stood, eyeing one another in a quiet challenge.

"Michael!" Both Watcher and Shedim looked up. Jordan threw down a sword to Michael and flew away. Catching the sword, Michael smiled coyly at Dagon.

"In your condition, you will be no match for me. Pity. I've been looking forward to a fair fight with you." Shrugging non-chalantly, Dagon raised his sword and lunged toward Michael. The weight of Dagon's body pushed Michael against a boulder. Unable to move, Michael waited for the deathblow. As Dagon raised his sword, a brilliant white light burst through the impenetrable gray.

A voice cried in triumph through the mist, "She is no longer bound to you for I have redeemed her!"

A loud shriek of pain mixed with defeat, echoed throughout the valley. That was the voice of the Prince! Dagon looked up just in time to see Rasha fly away leaving a trail of green against the blue sky. A horde of Shedim screamed in terror over him as one by one Watchers were flicking them into the abyss as if they were nothing but pesky flies.

A surge of power washed over Michael bringing healing to his tattered body. "No match, Dagon? I believe you just lost," Dagon's face blanched. With insurmountable strength, Michael shoved Dagon away, bringing his sword down on the creature. The abyss opened up, gratefully accepting another evil resident.

TWENTY TWO

"Adi, Adi, can you hear me?" A gentle voice called out to her in her unconscious state. Slowly the veil parted in her mind. Moaning, she opened her eyes, squinting against the sun.

Someone was cradling her. "Adi?"

Looking toward the voice, Adi stared into the warm chocolate brown eyes. "Matthew?"

The voice chuckled, "Not quite."

Struggling against the pain, Adi sat up and looked at the man before her. Tears gathered in her eyes, "Joshua?"

"Yes, my love, it's me!"

Sobbing, she threw her arms around his neck, "I'm so sorry! I was so wrong!"

Holding her close, he gently caressed her back, bringing healing to her wounds. "You are forgiven. I always have and always will love you with an eternal love, my precious Adi! Will you marry me?"

"Oh, yes!" Adi cried gripping Joshua even tighter. At once, all her guilt and fear disappeared and in its place was joy, peace, and love. Truth had set her free!

Matthew stood nearby, tears of joy and relief rolled down his face. Thomas stared in wonder at the transformation of Adi, for when she stood up out of the mud, her dress had changed from filthiness to clean and pure. She positively glowed as she embraced the Prince.

Michael raised his sword up high and yelled, "To the glory of King Penuel, and Prince Joshua and to his new bride, Adi!" The heavens echoed with the warriors' shouts of joy for Adi had come home.

King Penuel stared at the one lighted spot in Soteria. Tears ran down his rugged face.

"Gabriel, tell the cooks to prepare a banquet. There will be feasting tonight, my son is coming home and I have a new daughter!"

Smiling radiantly, Gabriel enthusiastically responded, "Yes, sir!"

———————

Rasha furiously paced back and forth before a quivering Ze'ev. "You have failed!" He bellowed in rage.

"It doesn't matter if Adi marries the Prince. We can still go through with our plan!" Cried Ze'ev in fear.

"I don't work with failures. You are of no use to me now, Ze'ev. I need someone whom I can depend on to usher in the New Age!" Rasha reached down and squeezed Ze'ev's head. Screaming in pain, Ze'ev's eyes bulged, popping blood vessels. Rasha crushed the man's skull as if he were crushing a can. Ze'ev slumped to the floor, lifeless.

Rasha stared off in the distance, hatred burning in his eyes. "I'm not finished with you yet, Joshua! Nor with your precious bride!" A slow cruel smile spread across his face, "Let's see how she will fare when I usher in the New Age!" Laughter bubbled up inside. Throwing his head back, he cackled with pleasure as a new plan began to form.

Kristen Zuray

The *Redemption*  of You

Many years ago, a student in my Sunday school class asked me what the Marriage Supper of the Lamb was. I didn't really understand it myself so I began to research it. As I studied it, a beautiful love story began to unfold. It was a story of love, sacrifice, and redemption made by God the Father, His Son Jesus Christ, and the Holy Spirit for all mankind.

In order to understand the beauty of this love story, we must understand the ancient Jewish wedding custom and how it relates to us. So as you read pretend that you are a Jewish bride! But before we can become a bride, there first has to be a match...

The Match

In the ancient Jewish wedding custom, the father of the potential groom is the one that first initiates the match between his son and the intended girl. All throughout the Bible, we can clearly see how God the Father follows these ancient wedding customs to draw us to him. I John 4:19 says, *We love him, because He FIRST loved us.* In this verse, we see that God the Father has initiated the match between his Son, Jesus, and mankind. He loved us FIRST and desired to redeem us from this sin cursed world.

The Match Maker

Once the groom's father has chosen a bride for his son, he sends a matchmaker to approach the bride's family. Of course, the matchmaker is going to speak highly of groom to persuade the bride to accept the proposal. Following this tradition, God sends his Holy Spirit to draw us to his Son. The Holy Spirit testifies to us of God's Son. Jesus describes this in John 15:26, *But when the Comforter is come, whom I will send unto you from the Father, even the Spirit of truth, which proceedeth from the Father, he shall testify of me.*

Bride's Consent

When the Match Maker has testified on behalf of the
groom and his father, the bride and her family now have a
choice to make. She can either accept the offer or reject it.
We, too have the same choice, to accept God's Son, Jesus
Christ, or to reject Him. We accept Christ's proposal by
repenting of our sins and believing in Jesus' death and
resurrection. Acts 2:21 says, ..*whosoever calls on the name
of The Lord will be saved.*

The Bride Price

There two stipulations for the bride price. First, the price
was required by law. Secondly, it had to be paid by the
groom's father. Before the birth of Jesus, the Israelites
had to perform animal sacrifices in order to receive
forgiveness. This was the law. The law also stated that the
animals had to be pure without spots or blemishes.
Hebrews 9:22 explains that, *According to the law almost
everything is purified with blood, and without the
shedding of blood there is no forgiveness.* Jesus Christ,
who had no sin, came to fulfill the law by shedding his
blood so that we might have eternal life. The requirement
of the law had been fulfilled.

To be a real bride price, the groom's father had to pay for it. God the Father paid the debt through his son. *For God so loved the world, that **He gave** his One and only Son, so that everyone who believes in Him will not perish but have eternal life.* John 3:16. I Corinthians 6:20 states, *For you are bought with a price...* This shows the greatness of God's love for us. We are valuable. You are valuable!

Love Gifts from the Groom

Up to this point, the groom's father has gone to great lengths to unite his son with his chosen bride. What does the groom do in this ancient tradition? The groom is expected to give gifts to his future bride. As our groom, Jesus gives to us many gifts. To name a few, He gives us eternal life. Jesus promised in John 10:28, *And I give unto them eternal life; and they will never perish- ever, No one will snatch them out of my hand.* He also gives us peace in John 14:27, *Peace I leave with you. My peace I give to you...* Thirdly, he gives us answers to prayer, *If you ask Me anything in my name, I will do it.* (John 14:14). Jesus Christ definitely knows how to shower us with beautiful gifts!

The Dowry

After the groom and his father have showered the bride with gifts, it is time for the bride's father to give her his gifts. Often his gifts would be things to help her set up her new home or help with a good financial start to their new life. Once we have repented and put our faith in Jesus, we are now apart of God's family. God the Father now acts as the bride's father. He will provide the gifts that will help us in our new way of life. What are those gifts? He once more provides the Holy Spirit who will teach us and direct us in how we should live, Galatians 4:6, *And because you are sons, God has sent the Spirit of His Son into our hearts...* God, our Father, also provides us with spiritual gifts that help us serve in the church. A list of these gifts can be found in I Corinthians 12. God does not leave us alone to figure things out, instead, He provides us a dowry to help us in our new life as the sons and daughters of God!

Have you noticed that in all the gift giving, the bride has never had to give a gift? She does not have to earn these gifts, they are given freely to her! We do not have to earn God's grace. It is freely given!

Marriage Contract

The beautiful gifts have been given and both parties are ready to sign the marriage contract. This Jewish contract explains the bride price, the rights of the bride, and the promises of the groom. What represents the marriage contract between mankind, God the Father and Jesus? The New Testament! In the New Testament, we can read about the Bride Price - God's payment by his son to fulfill the law. We can also read the rights of the bride - eternal life, children and heirs of God, answered prayer, courage, victory over sin and sorrow, and forgiveness! From the N.T., we can find the promises of the groom - salvation, no more death or crying, to never leave us, that he will return, and many many more promises! If you want to know what you can expect from God and Jesus just read the new marriage contract, the New Testament!

And for this cause he is the mediator of the new testament, that by means of death, for the redemption of the transgressions that were under the first testament, they which are called might receive the promise of eternal inheritance. Hebrews 9:15 (KJV)

Engagement

The Marriage Contract has been written up and signed. After the signing, they seal it with a cup of wine. The couple is officially engaged now! We see this picture in what the church calls Communion. In Matthew 26:27-28, we see Jesus encouraging his disciples with these words, *Then he took a cup, and after giving thanks, he gave it to them and said, Drink from it, all of you. For this is my blood that establishes the covenant; it is shed for many for the forgiveness of sins.* Communion is a time of reflection on the price Jesus paid for our redemption; we are sealing our commitment to him.

Groom's Job During Engagement Period

After the engagement has become official, the bride and groom part ways for a time to fulfill their duties. The groom returns to his father's house and builds a room called a huppa for his bride. So it is with Jesus. After his resurrection he returned to heaven with a promise to prepare a place in heaven for those who put their trust in him. We see this promise in John 14:1-3 *Your heart must not be troubled. Believe in God; believe also in Me. In My Father's house are many dwelling places; if not, I would have told you. I am going away to prepare a place for you. If I go away and prepare a place for you, I will come back and receive you to Myself, so that where I am you may be also.* (John 14:1-3)

Bride's Job - Purification

In this ancient culture, once the bride has sealed the engagement with the wine, she now purifies herself in what is called a mikveh. This signifies to the community that her status has changed. She is now setting herself apart. The mikveh is much like the baptismal tanks found in churches. Through his example, Jesus instructed for those who have placed their trust in him, to be baptized. This is to signify to the world and to the family of believers that there is a change in status, they now belong to Christ. *Therefore we were buried with Him by baptism into death, in order that, just as Christ was raised from the dead by the glory of the Father, so we too may walk in a new way of life.* (Romans 6:4)

Waiting Period

While the groom is away preparing a place for his bride, the bride is keeping herself busy with wedding preparations and gathering essentials for her new home. Just as the Jewish bride is focused on her preparations, so must the Christian be focused on being a faithful witness to others and developing a relationship with Christ. *Therefore, since we also have such a large cloud of witnesses surrounding us, let us lay aside every weight and the sin that so easily ensnares us. Let us run with endurance the race that lies before us.* (Hebrews 12:1)

While the Jewish bride and the Christian are preparing, they both are to watch diligently for their groom's return. Unlike today when brides set a date for the wedding, the Jewish bride didn't have that luxury. Not knowing exactly when her bridegroom would come, she always had to be ready and watchful. Usually the groom and his groomsmen would come at night to escort the bride back to the huppa. Much like the Jewish bride, Christians don't know the day of Christ's return either. Because of that, Jesus admonishes Christians to be watchful. *Therefore be alert, since you don't know what day your Lord is coming.* (Matthew 24:42)

The Wedding

Once the huppa is completed, the father of the groom let's his son know when he can return for his bride. Following this pattern, Jesus, too waits for His Father's permission to return for all those who have believed in his name. Matthew 24:36 says *Now concerning that day and hour no one knows — neither the angels in heaven, nor the Son — except the Father only. Therefore be alert, since you don't know what day   your Lord is coming.* (Matthew 24:36, 42)

Most often, it is at night when the groom returned for his bride. A groomsman would go ahead to announce the groom's soon arrival. Usually this was done with trumpets. So it is, before Jesus returns, a shout will be heard and a trumpet blast will sound from heaven just before all believers will be caught up in the air to meet Jesus. This is what is known as the rapture. *For you yourselves know very well that the Day of the Lord will come just like a thief in the night.* (1 Thessalonians 5:2) *For the Lord Himself will descend from heaven with a shout, with the archangel's voice, and with the trumpet of God, and the dead in Christ will rise first. Then we who are still alive will be caught up together with them in the clouds to meet the Lord in the air and so we will always be with the Lord.* (1 Thessalonians 4:16, 17)

The Marriage

In today's culture, we often have the wedding ceremony followed by the reception. Afterwards, the couple escapes to their honeymoon. But for the Jewish culture, it was reversed, the honeymoon first and then the celebration feast. The groom would escort the bride back to his huppa and there they would stay hidden for seven days.

Once the rapture occurs, the believers of Christ will spend seven years in heaven receiving awards for the good things that they have done on earth. Revelation 19 likens this time of celebrating to a wedding, *Then I heard something like the voice of a vast multitude, like the sound of cascading waters, and like the rumbling of loud thunder, saying: Hallelujah, because our Lord God, the Almighty, has begun to reign! Let us be glad, rejoice, and give Him glory, because the marriage of the Lamb has come, and His wife has prepared herself. She was given fine linen to wear, bright and pure. For the fine linen represents the righteous acts of the saints.* (Revelation 19:6-9). Even though these seven years will be amazing for the believer, those who are left on earth will be experiencing great atrocities and terror. This period is known as the tribulation in which the rest of mankind has to make their final choice to accept Christ's invitation or to reject it for all eternity.

The Presentation

When the seven days are over, the bride and groom are presented to the community as husband and wife. At that time, the feasting and celebrating begins! At the end of the seven -year tribulation, Christ returns to earth along with his bride, those who believe in His name. Revelation 19 describes this event, *Then he said to me, Write: Those invited to the marriage feast of the Lamb are fortunate!"* *He also said to me, "These words of God are true." Then I saw heaven opened, and there was a white horse. Its rider is called Faithful and True, and He judges and makes war in righteousness. His eyes were like a fiery flame, and many crowns were on His head. He had a name written that no one knows except Himself. He wore a robe stained with blood, and His name is the Word of God. The armies that were in heaven followed Him on white horses, wearing pure white linen. A sharp sword came from His mouth, so that He might strike the nations with it. He will shepherd them with an iron scepter. He will also trample the winepress of the fierce anger of God, the Almighty. And He has a name written on His robe and on His thigh: KING OF KINGS AND Lord OF LORDS.* (Revelation 19:6-9, 11-16)

Marriage Feast

Just as the happy Jewish couple celebrated their marriage
with a feast, so does Jesus celebrate his final return with
the church at the Marriage Supper of the Lamb. Then he
said to me, *Write: Those invited to the marriage feast of
the Lamb are fortunate!" He also said to me, "These words
of God are true.* This marks the beginning of the
millennium, the 1,000 year reign of Christ! Towards the
end of the 1,000 years there will be one last uprising from
those who still have not yet trusted Christ. This is the last
time mankind will be allowed to choose. Those who reject
Him will spend eternity in the lake of fire. Revelation 21:8
describes this, *But the cowards, unbelievers, vile,
murderers, sexually immoral, sorcerers, idolaters, and all
liars — their share will be in the lake that burns with fire
and sulfur, which is the second death."* Those who have
trusted in Him, will now enter into eternity, and will live
happily ever after. Revelation 21:3-7 shares God's final
commitment to his bride, *Then I heard a loud voice from
the throne: Look! God's dwelling is with humanity, and
He will live with them. They will be His people, and God
Himself will be with them and be their God. He will wipe
away every tear from their eyes. Death will no longer
exist; grief, crying, and pain will exist no longer, because
the previous things have passed away. Then the One
seated on the throne said, "Look! I am making everything*

*new." He also said, "Write, because these words are
faithful and true." And He said to me, "It is done! I am
the Alpha and the Omega, the Beginning and the End. I
will give water as a gift to the thirsty from the spring of
life. The victor will inherit these things, and I will be
his God, and he will be My son.*

There you have the amazing love story of all time! God the
Father, Jesus Christ his Son, and The Holy Spirit have
followed this ancient Jewish wedding custom so that we
would understand the unconditional love they have for us.
We are of great value to them! We are jewels!

Have you accepted Christ's proposal? I encourage you,
don't leave here today without accepting Him. He loves
you! If you would like to talk more about this important
decision, please contact me at www.kristenzuray.com.

*All Scripture references are taken from the Holman
Christian Standard Bible.*

ABOUT THE AUTHOR

Kristen Zuray has served faithfully in church ministry for seventeen years. Currently, she serves on the board for The Trail Ministry reaching homeless and drug addicted youth. She is an author of four books and speaks at conferences, retreats, and various church events. She and her husband reside in Seattle, WA with their four children.

If you would like to schedule Kristen for a speaking engagement, go to **www.kristenzuray.com**.

OTHER BOOKS BY KRISTEN

Gift Book
- Standing at the Wall

Women's Bible Study
- Journey to Surrender

Self Help
- Walking on Water

Kristen Zuray